FOREST OF CORPSES

P.A. BROWN

mlrpress

www.mlrpress.com

MLR Press Authors

Featuring a roll call of some of the best writers of gay erotica and mysteries today!

M. Jules Aedin	David Juhren
Maura Anderson	Samantha Kane
Victor J. Banis	Kiernan Kelly
Jeanne Barrack	J.L. Langley
Laura Baumbach	Josh Lanyon
Alex Beecroft	Clare London
Sarah Black	William Maltese
Ally Blue	Gary Martine
J.P. Bowie	Z.A. Maxfield
Michael Breyette	Patric Michael
P..A. Brown	AKM Miles
Brenda Bryce	Jet Mykles
Jade Buchanan	Willa Okati
James Buchanan	L. Picaro
Charlie Cochrane	Neil Plakcy
Kirby Crow	Jordan Castillo Price
Dick D.	Luisa Prieto
Ethan Day	Rick R. Reed
Jason Edding	A.M. Riley
Angela Fiddler	George Seaton
Dakota Flint	Jardonn Smith
S.J. Frost	Caro Soles
Kimberly Gardner	JoAnne Soper-Cook
Roland Graeme	Richard Stevenson
Storm Grant	Clare Thompson
Amber Green	Lex Valentine
LB Gregg	Stevie Woods
Drewey Wayne Gunn	

Check out titles, both available and forthcoming, at
www.mlrpress.com

Forest of Corpses

P.A. Brown

mlrpress

www.mlrpress.com

Published by
MLR Press, LLC
3052 Gaines Waterport Rd.
Albion, NY 14411

Visit ManLoveRomance Press, LLC on the Internet:
www.mlrpress.com

Cover Art by Deana C. Jamroz
Editing by Kris Jacen

ISBN# 978-1-60820-163-1

Issued 2010

ACKNOWLEDGMENTS

Carol Percer for reading the very raw draft of this book and offering invaluable help on its growth and to Ann Hoyt for telling me about mountain quail chicks and screaming rabbits.

To my editor Kris Jacen, Deana for her great cover art, J.P. Bowie, and Laura Baumbach for taking me under her wing as one of her authors. AJ Morgan, Corky McGraw, and Nix Winter for their invaluable insights into the world of pleasure and pain and bondage.

To GaywritersandReaders and all their support and good times, and CrimeSceneWriters for getting the police and forensic stuff right.

To all my wonderful American friends

Nobody died today.

That's a good day in my books, but I knew it wouldn't last.

Westside had a major hard on for Eastside. War was brewing. Fideo and his WS crew shot up the East Beach, then a week later, on Memorial Day, did the same at a market on Anacapa Street. That time their aim had improved. They dropped two Eastside bangers and a ten-year-old boy out buying milk for his grandmother. Both OGs made it. The kid didn't. Chalk it up to collateral damage from the drug war.

We canvassed the market and caught a couple of witnesses who saw the whole thing. So we nailed Fideo along with two members of his posse, and tossed their *cholo* butts in jail. Fideo lawyered up with a good uptown legal beagle, but still sat in lockup, no bail. Then another drive-by took out witness one. Suddenly our only remaining witness "made a mistake." The paperwork wasn't dry before the scrotes were back in the hood and the witness was in hiding. Fideo rode with his *ese* through his hood, crowing how he beat 5-0. His street creds firmly embellished by his latest exploits, he was back, and he was stronger.

And took up his business of dealing drugs, death and taxes without losing a night's sleep.

Miguel, my new partner, snapped his frustration. "How can we stop these people if no one will testify against them?"

I shrugged. "It bites, I agree. But look at it from their side. Hard to testify from a pine box."

"God will take care of them."

"Right." I rolled my eyes, making sure he couldn't see the gesture. "I'm sure Mr. Gillespie's family feel the same way." Gillespie had been witness number one, a businessman leaving a wife and two young kids behind. He told me when I interviewed him the first time he had to talk. That it wasn't right that these men could terrorize a neighborhood and get away with it. What kind of example did that set for his kids? Well, I guess his kids learned a valuable lesson there. But probably not the one their old man wanted to give. We had gone to Gillespie's funeral yesterday, per department regulations. Not surprising, no one from Westside showed or sent their condolences. Not that there was much we could have done if they had. As usual, we had no proof that put any Westside banger anywhere near the vicinity of Gillespie's untimely death. What we had were two bullets from a 9 mil that couldn't be tied to any other crimes. A clean gun for a clean hit.

There was a time when my frustration level would have surpassed Miguel's. Those days are long gone. First thing you learn on the job, leave it at the station. Taking it home with you is the surest way to give yourself high blood pressure and a date with your own duty weapon, or your cardiologist.

There was a time I used to share my world with dead people. The homicides I couldn't solve would follow me home and make me hold them in my memory. The more brutal they were, the more they clung to me, needing closure I couldn't give them.

Then Jason burst into my life, unasked and unlooked for. I hooked him up and tossed his ass in jail for the murder of a man it turned out he'd never met. A lot of people would have flipped me the bird for what I did, but Jason wasn't like that. There wasn't a vengeful bone in his perfect body. Instead, once he was released from jail, we'd gone out to dinner, ended up back at my place with my dick up his ass, and my heart in his hands. I realized then I never wanted to let this guy go. It took me months to be able to admit my feelings to myself, let alone to Jason. Then, I damn near fucked what we had up permanently when my petty jealousy turned me into a dangerous fool. It probably would have served me right if Jay had told me to fuck off when I got up the nerve to follow him to Los Angeles. He didn't, and here we are, two months later, sharing a bed and a bath, and hopefully, a future.

Sometimes my dead people still come around to stalk my dreams, but now there's an anchor to hold onto when I wake up in a cold sweat, with my heart pounding and my mouth dry with unspoken fear; there to whisper soothing words, not press me for explanations I was loathe to give anyone. Even for Jason I didn't show weakness.

He gave me back my life. So why can't I give him the one thing he wants? Because I'm a fucking coward who's afraid of losing control again? Afraid? Fuck that. Alexander Spider isn't afraid of anything. Or anyone.

The morning after Gillespie's funeral I got up before Jason. Dressing after my shower, I stood over our bed, studying him while I buttoned my shirt. Sometime during the night he had kicked his covers off, exposing his delicious butt, and all I had to do was reach out and stroke the peach soft skin. I knew my touch would instantly wake him up, and I had no trouble imagining those sleepy eyes falling on me and that slow, sexy smile he only gave to me. We'd both been too tired last night to do anything but fall into bed. There was nothing sleepy about my body now. My dick pressed painfully against my briefs and I shifted, trying to ease the sudden constriction.

I knew he didn't have any classes until ten, so unlike me, he didn't have to get up at this God-forsaken hour. For one hot minute I almost gave in, ready to tumble him over onto his stomach and spread his legs, no questions, no words. It would take me two seconds to pull my cock out, another two to be inside him. It would be rough, but rough didn't bother Jason. Neither did the bareback sex we now indulged in since our last tests had given us both clean slates. Just the thought of my naked dick inside him made my balls ache and tighten. I knew he'd submit to me willingly, hell, eagerly, but a part of me always held back. When I was tempted to let go, like I knew he wanted, all I could do was see him hanging from my straps, barely conscious as I punished him for a sin he never committed. I had done us both harm that night. I was still paying for it.

I let my hand fall to my side, then with a muttered curse, spun around and left the room, carefully shutting the door behind me. Tonight, I'd make sure I wasn't too tired when we went to bed.

Then I'd do it right. Something we'd both remember in a good way.

As usual, I beat Miguel in on Monday morning. I guess Bible study kept him up at night. I barely glanced at my newly assigned, wet-behind-the-ears partner when he arrived, and still managed to think black thoughts. Though I kept telling myself my former partner, now boss, Nancy Pickard hadn't deliberately assigned Miguel Dominguez, savior of sinners and sodomites alike, to me for some do-him-good-reason or, God forbid, do-me-good reason. She would never be so cruel. So far I'd kept him at arm's length, and he seemed content to read his Bible to himself during coffee breaks. But ever since we had been assigned as a team, there had been a growing furrow between his eyes that deepened every day. His brown eyes had a decidedly hornet-mad look, as though he wondered just what that brown stuff was he had landed in, and how much longer he'd have to put up with it. I'll give him one thing, he was too professional to voice his feelings aloud. Which is about the only thing that made me think this partnership might work. I didn't want to get into a pissing contest with the guy, but I was the boss here, and he'd better not challenge that.

I pulled a nine-day-old blue crime book out from under a stack of files folders and unfiled reports, and opened it to the first page. I tapped my booted foot on the scuffed linoleum floor while I studied the chrono report, which included the transcript of the original 9-1-1 call. The call that had brought out the first uniformed cops early one morning nine days ago, and marked the beginning of our, so far fruitless investigation, that had come in at oh-four-fifteen. An hysterical woman, later ID'd as Rebecca Long, had called from Milpas Market, reporting shots fired.

I flipped through the CR, the one I put together from the reports I had collected from everyone involved in the case, from the first responder who had answered the original 9-1-1 call, to the second one that had come in last night.

First officers on the scene after that first call, a rookie and his training officer, had discovered a cooling corpse in the back stall of an East Beach rest stop, where the homeless often hung out during the day. It was the first call Miguel and I had gone on together. Our third homicide to date. It was our first unsolved. The other two were down as closed, but with no convictions in sight, not very satisfactory. Not exactly an auspicious beginning.

I flipped the page. A booking photo of the old, dead black man, from a previous arrest for vagrancy, stared up at me, showing serious signs of the chronic alcohol abuse and malnutrition that marked him even then as one of the multitude of Santa Barbara's homeless. So what had possessed someone to put a pair of slugs into a man who had nothing and whose biggest offense was probably his hygiene – or lack of it? I'd probably never know what was behind this senseless killing. But I'd be happy tossing the mutt who was responsible into Pelican Bay for the duration of his miserable life.

Of course I had to find the guy first. And the problem with crimes that had no obvious motive, was there were also no obvious suspects.

I dragged a yellow legal pad over and dug a Bic out of the chipped coffee mug I used as a pen caddy. Chewing on the already battered end, and tapping my restless foot on the floor, I read through report after report, studying the crime scene photos and scene sketches, notes I had jotted, notes from Miguel and everyone we had interviewed. Finally I scanned the twenty-page autopsy report, trying to niggle out the one overlooked detail that would give me the lead I needed to clear this case. It wasn't there. Or maybe my mind couldn't focus.

Against my wishes, it kept going back to this morning's missed opportunity. I had met Jason seven months ago. After a rocky beginning, we had become lovers and, I thought, friends. Then a couple of months ago we'd taken the next step and moved in together, something I hadn't done with anyone in over five years. Something I gather Jason had never done. We were still feeling our way around that. Still in the honeymoon phase, I guess you could say. I only had to remember this morning to bring that home. I couldn't remember a time or a person who had made me feel the way Jason did. Sometimes that made me nervous. I had one failed marriage behind me. I wasn't sure I was ready for another one, even with someone as perfect as Jason Zachary. I also knew there was no way I was ready to send him away. By this time I sported a low grade, painful erection as I thought about the sounds he made with my prick down his throat, or pumping up his ass. I shifted in my chair, trying to give space to my swelling dick. I tried to concentrate on the words and images in front of me, using the tip of the pen to guide my wandering eyes over the pages of the murder book, and the excruciatingly detailed coroner's report. Hard to believe more detail could go into a man's death than he'd ever earned in his life.

My efforts to forget Jason weren't working. They rarely did.

I squinted and stared harder, as though I could force some meaning to come from the combination of words in front of me. A shadow fell between me and the nearest light source. Even before I looked up, I knew who it was.

I glared over my glasses at Lieutenant Nancy Pickard, my boss and ex-partner.

"You ever consider getting reading glasses there, Detective? Or maybe bifocals?"

"I don't need no fucking bifocals," I snapped, since the same thought had been going through my head. But that would mean admitting I was getting old, and I wasn't ready to go there. I was barely thirty-three—hardly old, right? "Did you want something, Lieutenant?"

"What are you looking at?" She leaned over to study the pages of the murder book. I leaned away from her, my arms crossed over my chest. "Which one is this?" she asked.

"The Isaac Simpson case."

"The homeless guy in the john?"

"That's the one."

"Any new thoughts on it?"

I braced my booted feet on the floor and unfolded my arms

to lean toward her. "No." I tapped my chewed up pen on the page we were both staring at, the one that detailed the autopsy report for the hapless Simpson. "This might give us something." I pointed to the recording of the 9-1-1 call. "Not sure what it is yet." I filled her in on the circumstances of the call.

"Let's hear it."

I signaled Miguel to come around and join us. Once he was standing behind Nancy, I punched the on button. A scratchy smoker's voice barely identifiable as female came out of the speakers. The voice was low and indistinct. I'd have to send it down to the lab to see what they could do with the quality. But for now all three of us strained to make out the mumbled words.

"They're the devil, Momo. He didn't have to die. It wasn't right. He promises he stop them." The voice went off muttering and mumbling into incoherence. Then, "Stop them." A wail like a thousand cats being tortured made me wince and pull back. Nancy did the same. Only Miguel didn't react. His eyes narrowed when they met mine.

"Who is Momo?" he asked.

"The victim?" I said. "Isaac Simpson? Her invisible playmate?"

"Any idea who the caller was?" Nancy asked.

I shook my head. "Call came from a payphone near Milpas Market. Maybe another witness? I was going to head out there this morning." I threw another look at Miguel, who watched me without blinking. He nodded once, then spun around and returned to his desk. "You and me," I said across our desk.

Nancy looked pleased. "See that I get a report ASAP."

Since I doubted anyone higher up was breathing down her neck on this DB, this had to be personal. Face it, Mr. Isaac Simpson would barely register on any one radar in city hall. I knew for a fact none of the local news media had gone beyond a mention of the homicide on their back pages. Simpson, one of the homeless nobodies, came and went in the city's awareness.

"Will do," I said, more determined, like Nancy, to find the

man's killer. I don't like it when people die in my city. I like it less when no one seems to notice, or care, about their passing.

"Well, I hate to be the one to say it, but don't get locked too tight into this one. How many others are you working on?"

I glanced over at Miguel, who I knew was still watching us and listening in on our little *tête-à-tête*, like any good partner would. So I directed my next question at him. "How many we on now, Miguel? Total."

"Eleven, including that one. Most ag-assaults, four rapes, one attempted rape. A failed drive-by. Only three homicides – our two drive-bys and this one."

"You wish it was more?"

"No!" He looked furious as though my question disgusted him. It was the strongest emotion I'd seen from him since we'd been partnered. He threw his hands up as if pushing me away. "How can you say that?"

"Just wondering." I threw Nancy a look and found her frowning at me. Okay, baiting my new partner wasn't cool. "I'm going to keep looking at this one for now. It is our only active homicide."

"Just don't neglect your other cases, okay?"

"We wouldn't dream of it, would we?" I directed that to Miguel.

"No, we won't, sir. We'll take care of all our cases, Lieutenant."

Nancy looked amused. "Carry on, then."

She returned to her office and shut the door. Nancy practiced an open door policy most of the time, but when it was time do the political dance with her bosses, she kept the rest of us out of the loop. For which I was very thankful. That was her game. Not mine. I threw a shrewd glance at Miguel, who watched me with that hawk-like gaze of his that looked a lot like the one I used. I wasn't too sure about the loyalties of my newest partner.

In fact, I was beginning to suspect he was a very political animal, with about as much loyalty as one, which was going to make an interesting partnership in the weeks and months ahead. How much could I trust the guy?

Nancy came out of her office. She bent down and spoke briefly to Miguel, who nodded and picked up his phone. She came around to my desk, looking pensive. She leaned toward me, her feet planted wide. Her look was grim. Had she figured out what I was thinking? Sometimes I swore my newest boss was a mind reader. Not a pleasant thought.

She jerked her head at her office. "Can we talk?"

I followed her in and watched pensively as she shut the door.

"Something up, Lieutenant?"

"You could say that," she said, then fell silent. She stared at the stack of papers on her desk beside the phone that could connect her to every division and half of the city's emergency services, if the need arose.

I waited, standing at parade rest. Watched her scribble a signature on a form and shove the paper into her out basket. I waited some more. Finally I glanced at my watch. It was nearly four-thirty.

Even though I swore she wasn't looking at me, she saw where my eyes went. She instantly straightened. "Got a hot date, Spiderman?"

"Jesus, didn't I ask you not to call me that?"

She fiddled with the papers on her desk, shuffling them in some order that didn't mean anything to me, but must have been important to her. She put them back down decisively. "And don't I usually ignore you?"

I knew Jason would be getting home from UCSB soon, and would be getting supper on in anticipation of my arrival. He might be getting something else on too, like the skin-tight leather pants I had recently purchased for his last birthday, along with some other gear, so maybe I was going home to a hot date. Not that I'd ever tell her that. There are definitely some things your boss should not know.

"What I've got is an empty stomach," I said to fill the silence and keep her talking. "And I have a yen to fill it."

"Gotcha. I just got off the phone with the University. They're looking for a guest lecturer to give a series on crime scene processing for their first year criminal justice students. They asked me to see if any of my men might be interested."

"And you thought of me? Why?"

"Since Robertson retired, you're my most experienced detective. There's Paige, but he's more of a gang expert. These people want an all around investigative pro. I agreed to find someone. Plus, I thought it would be good PR for us."

It never hurt to have someone in the public sector look positively on our little corner of the world. I could see where her devious mind was going. But did I want to follow it?

"Me, teach?" I thought about it and frowned. "Me?"

"You're personable, behind that stone wall you put up to keep us all out. And you're professional. Both good qualities. Besides," she grinned, relaxing into the Nancy I had partnered with for so many years before her promotion, "Don't you want to influence the next crop of LEOs?"

"Uh..."

"Good. I'll let them know you'll meet with their department head tomorrow to plan out your curriculum. I'm sure she has some ideas she wants to run by you."

"Oh does she? Lucky me." I knew it was a done deal and sighed. I guess I was going to be a teacher. "God help us all."

I was thoughtful on my way home. It wasn't something I would have sought out, but now that it was in my lap, so to speak, I was intrigued by the idea of teaching.

By the time I pulled into the drive behind Jason's Honda, there was a bounce in my step. Jason was in the kitchen, putting the finishing touches on chicken mole, grilled potatoes and asparagus. My boy had gotten a lot more adventuresome in the kitchen of late. I patted the soft mound of my belly and knew

I was going to have to do something about that. Maybe start spending more time at the station gym, or join Jason on his numerous walks through the back hills above our place.

I came up behind him, took a moment to admire his trim ass encased in hot black leather, remembering what it had looked like this morning, and slipped my hand between his legs. I grabbed his balls at the same time as I pressed my lips on his neck. He smelled of herbs and apple and tasted just as good. A pulse jumped like a skittering mouse under my lips, and I licked him.

He jumped and spun around, holding a potholder in one hand, his face suffused with a flush.

"Alex! I didn't hear you."

"Good." I hauled him against my chest and went in for another taste. My own pulse thundered as our tongues tangled in a deeply satisfying kiss. We were both breathing hard when I broke away. "So, when are you going to feed me, boy?"

"Twenty minutes."

I swatted his butt. "Good. Time enough for a shower."

Dinner was excellent, as I'd come to expect. Jason had selected a fine Syrah for our dinner wine. We both had one glass. I no longer overindulged; a promise I had made to myself and Jason in the aftermath of that violent explosion fueled by jealousy and alcohol. It was hard enough controlling the jealousy, I didn't dare add booze to the mix anymore. Jason always followed my lead in everything we did.

I spent most of the meal with a swollen dick pressed against my thigh. The remainder of the evening we lounged on the leather sofa in front of the TV, watching Lauren Bacall films. Jason nestled, half asleep under my arm, his hand firmly planted between my legs as Bacall and Bogart found their way in a hostile world.

Over a Mexicali beer I ordered him to get, I told him about my offer.

"You're going to be a teacher?"

"Tweed jacket, corn cob pipe and all."

He grinned up at me from the shelter of my arms. "Sexy professor."

"You think?"

"I know." He outlined the shape of my swelling dick though my jeans. "When do you start?"

"I go talk to someone tomorrow. I guess I'll find out then."

"I think you'd be a good teacher." He withdrew his hand and sat up. Then he dropped his first bombshell of the evening. "I'd like us to take a vacation. I'd say we both have lots to celebrate."

I had visions of Vegas or Hawaii. Sun, sand, a little gambling, hot sex. We'd never gone anywhere together. Then he dropped his second bombshell.

"I'd like to go camping. Hiking in the Rafael Wilderness area."

Hiking? Wilderness? That sounded ominous. The wildest thing I'd ever done was at the police softball game years ago between the Santa Barbara PD and the fire guys, where a few of us smuggled in flasks of whiskey, sneaking them behind the outfield bleachers, where we traded war stories between innings.

He seemed to sense my unease. I could see the eagerness on his face, the need to convince me. He really wanted this. Was I going to give it to him? "You're always telling me you want to get more active. It's great exercise."

"Yes, I suppose it is."

"Trust me. It'll be fun."

Anyone else said that and I'd scoff. I knew better than to trust anyone. But this was Jason. He looked so damned earnest. I considered what it would mean to agree. I still had doubt, so I said, "Well, I might consider it."

"At least try it for a week." His eyes were fixed on me. He only dropped his gaze when I frowned. He chewed on his lower lip.

"A week, huh? How about a weekend?"

"Weekend's not long enough to do any real hiking. We need a

week at least. What can it hurt?"

At least he hadn't suggested an ocean cruise, knowing how I felt about water. I frowned. Idly, my free hand traced the outline of his ear under his shaggy hair. "Let me think about it."

He knew better than to argue with me.

"Sure," he said. His soft, sexy eyes lasered into mine. "Bed?"

We didn't make it that far. We rarely did.

JASON

I slipped into the lecture hall, taking a seat in the back row. I don't think he saw me. He was too busy explaining the image he had just put up on the screen. He had donned his uniform for his lecture, maybe to remind everyone of who he was. He stood on the floor of the lecture hall, feet planted wide, his shoulders thrown back. He had the authority to back up his stance. I stared at the winking metal cuffs tucked into his back pocket, and the sidearm on the Sam Browne belt he never wore as a detective. I knew he'd won several marksman trophies with his Beretta.

I was amused by the ripple of disgust that flashed through the roomful of eager young students. Not that I didn't feel a twinge myself. The image on the screen was a corpse – don't ask me what sex, I couldn't have told you – in an advanced state of decay. A mass of what might have been hair fanned out over pebbly ground around a moldering skull.

A seven-year veteran of the Santa Barbara Police, Alex was teaching the first month of his visiting lecture at UCSB. I guess if the course proved a hit, they'd bring him back next year for a full semester. If he wanted to do it, of course. I couldn't help but notice a large segment of the female student body was more interested in their professor than his lecture. Not that I could blame them. He was a hot guy. Buff and lean hipped, with a deceptively boyish face behind metal frame glasses. I forced my gaze off of him and back to the large screen. Oblivious to the numerous lecherous eyes watching him, he kept on talking. "These pictures were all taken at the Body Farm, a research facility at the University of Tennessee where forensic students study the effects of the environment on human corpses. This sort of research has been vital in our goal of being able to better estimate things like time of death. Establishing that is critical in determining who might have committed a crime. Or clearing a suspect. Remember in crime scene investigation, it's motive, opportunity, means, and, I always like to add, method. Find out those four things and you will find your killer. Of course, that's where the fun starts. Sometimes you know who did the crime, but you can't prove it in a court of law. If you're going to pursue a career in law enforcement you need to consider that reality. Learn to deal with it, or find a new line of work."

A new image appeared. Same body, different angle. This one showed a mass of white maggots spilling out of dark flesh. I could only imagine the smell. "The level and type of insect activity can tell an experienced forensic entomologist a wealth of information." The next slide showed another mass of writhing maggots and beetles. In this one, I could see rib bones through the rotting flesh. I was just thankful they were still images and not video.

Then a third image appeared. Different body, dusky brown skin. It looked like a leg to me.

Alex faced the roomful of eager faces. His gaze swept over them without expression. "Can anyone tell me the difference between this image and the previous two?"

Students exchanged glances. I saw a few uneasy shrugs, then a young Asian man put his hand up. "It's not as decayed?"

"Good guess, but no. Anyone else?" Alex pointed at a woman on the right side of the hall.

"He's black – African American."

"How do you know it's a he?"

The woman blushed, her pale skin growing pink. "There's a lot of hair on it. Women usually shave..."

"Good observation, but no, that's not it either. Any more guesses? Then perhaps this will give you more to work on."

Another image, this one of the whole body. The girl was right on one thing, it was a guy. But this photo was not taken outside. It was inside and the man was on a bed that looked suspiciously like a hospital bed. Alex confirmed it.

"This is a patient in an east coast hospital. He's undergoing maggot debridement therapy." A murmur went up. He ignored it and went on as though he was talking about what to order for dinner. "Maggots only consume necrotic tissue and since the Civil War have been used to clean out wounds. It was only stopped when antibiotics came into vogue. The practice is being resumed today under controlled conditions, and is proving to be successful."

My own stomach turned and I almost groaned along with a few others. I got over it by looking at Alex instead. His calmness and visible strength made me straighten and look back. I could take it if he could. A lot of the students around me were visibly fighting to keep their lunches down. A few more looked positively green. I swear, if one person threw up I was going to lose it. That was when he looked up and saw me.

"Does it...does it hurt?" The girl who had spoken earlier sounded like she was in pain.

Alex looked away from me and shook his head. "Not at all. It might not be pretty, but it works." He flipped to the next image. This one was of a new maggot-infested corpse. "It's not something you'd ever need to deal with unless you go into medicine, but I've always found it interesting that insects have more uses than most of us suspect. Most people view them as utterly gross and undesirable." For one brief second his face lightened. "Remember things are not always what they seem. Remember that, and you will go far and save yourself a lot of heartache."

This time, he showed a new image. A corpse almost devoid of any skin except for a few leathery patches, one of which showed a tattoo of, appropriately enough, a skull. The gut of the body was literally crawling with shiny, dark-shelled beetles. Alex ignored the screen. Instead his gaze came back to me. Locked on, and drilled into me. I shivered and felt heat flood my face. But I couldn't look away until he released me.

Nothing crossed his face. He remained impassive as always. There was a brief moment of tension in his shoulders, then he smoothly answered another girl's question before moving on to the next slide. His voice was strong and sure. I never realized what a good public speaker he was. But then we didn't spend a whole lot of time talking, did we?

He finished up his lecture with an admonition that there was an essay due on Monday, which drew a slew of groans, then he dismissed the class. I was half way to my feet when his voice boomed out, freezing everyone in their tracks.

"Mr. Zachary. My office, please."

Wide eyes looked around to see who was being summoned. Once everyone realized it wasn't them, they hurried to make their exit before he could change his mind, leaving me alone in the suddenly cavernous lecture hall. The last of their echoing footsteps faded until there was nothing but the sound of my breathing and the tick of the clock on the wall behind me.

"Now, Mr. Zachary."

I stood and looked down at him. But instead of giving me the illusion of superiority, I felt overwhelmed by him. He threw his papers into the cowhide briefcase I had given him just a month ago, clicked it shut, and climbed the stairs to my level, one step at a time, but still he moved quicker than I had expected, and in an instant he was beside me. Without a word he kept going, passed me, leaving me to hurry after him. His boots thudded and squeaked on the tile floors. I couldn't help but watch the swing of his hips under the weight of his uniform jacket and his gun. I was all too aware of his scent. Something dark and masculine that set my nerves singing, and my cock thickening in my suddenly too tight jeans. I looked at his ass, remembering what lay under there. I had thoughts that were not appropriate for this place.

I stammered to fill the silence between us. "I know you told me not to come until next week. But I had to. Don't you see? I had to see you. I didn't think to ask you if I could come by right now," I added. "I was done for the day and thought it would be a good time to catch you before you left..."

His office was at the end of the corridor, behind a series of ominously closed doors. It was late in the day and I knew most of the other professors would be gone for the weekend. We were alone in the building. His footsteps echoed. The only other sound was our breathing, mine growing raspy, his still level and almost silent.

He didn't speak as he unlocked the last door, letting us both in, and locking up behind us. The air was redolent of furniture polish, and the scent of age that only old buildings have. The only window was the one in the door, and it was frosted glass, letting little light in. The stained wooden floor underfoot creaked as he led me across the narrow room toward a large wooden desk that took up most of the space. The desk held nothing but a Dell laptop, a blotter, a gooseneck lamp, a landline phone and a pile of folders, no doubt student papers. Even in the dim light, I had no trouble seeing the glitter of his gray eyes behind his glasses. I opened my mouth to speak but he silenced me with a look.

The phone on his desk rang. He scooped it up without taking his eyes off me and barked into the handset, "Spider here." He listened a moment then snapped, "I'll call you back. Monday." He broke the connection and shut the phone off. Then his glacial eyes focused on me.

I felt goose bumps crowd my arms. "Maybe I was wrong. I shouldn't have come—"

"Shut up." He pushed me back against the massive oak desk. "It's too late to change your mind," he said. "But you knew that when you showed up today, didn't you? You're the one who came here."

He spun me around and shoved me down, over the desk, leaning down to whisper in my ear, "You knew this was going to happen, yet you came anyway. Why is that, do you think?"

"I had to." One hand on my back forced me face first down onto the bare desk. I struggled futilely when I felt the cold snick of metal around my wrists. He spun me around to face him. The heat from his too close body overwhelmed me. His intoxicating smell filled my nostrils. "We can't do this," I tried one more time. "Someone will come in. We'll get in trouble." It was only his twelfth day as a teacher and knowing he was in the same building had preyed on my mind. I couldn't stay away. That's what he did to me. And he knew it, too.

"No one's going to come in. Now, not another word." Then he made speaking impossible by overwhelming me with his touch. His mouth on my throat, fingers pressing my jaw closed, sliding down to grab my rock hard dick through my jeans. I lunged up in need. His hands tightened on my shoulders and he held me in place without any effort. "Give it up, Jason. This is what you really wanted, isn't it? You're a tease, and you know what happens to men who tease, don't you? You pay for it." One hand went to the fly of my jeans. We could both feel the heat from my groin. "Just like this."

He shoved my jeans down my legs, exposing my shivering thighs to the cool air of the office. He left my jock on; it barely covered my swelling cock. He guided me back around and bent me over the desk. "Sir!" I squeaked when his hand slid between my ass cheeks, probing the puckered flesh behind my balls. Oh God. Yes!

His mouth pressed against the skin below my ear. "We both know what you are, don't we?" His tongue stroked my ear, sending shivering ripples of desire down my spine to lodge in the base of my cock. Then he bit me. Hard. "You're mine. You always will be. That's why we're going on this vacation you want. To prove that you're mine anywhere we go." He stroked the spot he had bitten, using his rough tongue. "You can never escape me."

I grunted, thrusting my hips forward, scraping my swollen flesh against the smooth surface of the desk, wanting more than the touch of wood. I closed my eyes and let the sensations swamp me. His touch was sure and all too knowing.

He bit me again, the pain a jolt of raw lust. He shoved two fingers into my ass, his thumb probing the soft skin behind my balls.

I wanted to beg him to stop. I wanted to beg him to bury himself inside me. I wanted—

I whimpered when I heard the whisper of his zipper, the rough play of his fingers going deeper, stroking my prostate.

A light burst behind my closed eyes. I tried to straighten and turn around. I wanted to see his face. I wanted his cock down my throat or up my ass; I couldn't decide which I needed more. He jerked on the metal pinning my hands to my back. A burst of pain shot through my shoulders and I cried out, a muffled groan that he responded to with whispered words demanding my silence, "Hush, boy. Stop fighting. This is going to happen. Enjoy it. I know I will," he whispered hoarsely.

His fingers traced a pattern down my trembling skin, slipping under my jock and shoving it aside. He cradled my swollen cock in one hand, his thumb slowly circling the head, spreading the wetness of my precum, tugging at my balls before wrapping his fingers around my prick and stroking me. I fucked his fist, feeling my balls crawl up as my orgasm approached. But before I could let go, he pulled his hand away and stepped back, leaving me shaking with need. I humped the air, silently begging him to come back.

His breath stuttered on my shoulder, then his lips and tongue sampled my skin, sliding over the Chinese tattoo on my neck. "Fate," he murmured. I shivered when he slipped the buttons of my shirt open, exposing my chest to his touch. He stroked the skin below my pecs, over my bird of paradise tattoo. I sucked in my breath when he roughly stroked my pierced nipples. "Beautiful. You are so beautiful."

Then he wrenched the shirt off my shoulders, further binding my arms. It took him about two seconds to drag my jeans off, turning them inside out as he hauled them over my Nikes, forcing my legs apart with his knee.

He grabbed my hips in both hands and planted his mouth over my collarbone. I could feel my pulse under his lips. Then I could feel his thick cock between my ass cheeks. He nudged at my hole and I moaned my need, thrusting back against him, silently pleading with him to take me. But still, he held back. He wouldn't let himself go, like I knew he wanted to. I could feel his desire, but I could also feel his fear. The fear that he would lose it again, like he had those terrible months before.

"I've got you," he growled and slid his cock up my ass. I arched across the desk. He kissed my shoulder and plowed into me with long, smooth strokes that drove deep into my gut. His hand wrapped around my cock again, this time his strokes were hard and unforgiving. His other hand swept over my chest, pinching my nipple; his cock pulsed deep inside me. His fingers left bruises on my hips as he kept pumping into me, gasping and groaning, his heart hammering in his chest. His breath gusted hot on my damp skin. After moments of sheer torture, he brought me to a screaming climax. If I wasn't too breathless to shout, the whole campus would have known what we were doing.

He kept pumping into me, his thrusts brutal. He moaned against my throat, then with a yell, emptied himself into me.

"Oh fuck, baby," he whispered, pulling out of me with a soft kiss on my shoulder.

He released the cuffs and spun me around to face him. He pulled my shirt back up, leaving it undone, exposing my heaving chest. Grabbing a handful of Kleenexes from a box on the desk he wiped my stomach and flaccid cock clean of spunk. Then he cleaned the desk and tossed the dirty Kleenex into the trash. His hands came up and cupped my face. His thumbs traced my lips. His eyes, gray and sated, looked down at me from behind his glasses.

"So," his voice still shaking, "how was your day?"

I tried to keep from laughing. "Pretty so-so." I traced the outline of his hip and leered. "At least until my professor took advantage of me. I've never been fucked by one of my teachers before. If I'd known it would be this good, I'd have gone back to school years ago." I rubbed my wrists and looked at him slyly. "Tell me you really didn't want me to come to your class today."

He raised an eyebrow. "I'm not your professor, Jason. That would be so wrong." He nuzzled my throat, nipping my skin, his tongue licking and tasting the salt from my flesh. His grin was lazy when our eyes met again. "I could get into serious shit doing something like that." His look grew stern. "And you'd better not fuck anyone else around here."

"Wouldn't think of it, Detective Alex. So, how is it, trying to inspire all these wannabe cops?" Of course, it had really been his idea to meet following his lecture. His orders, really. Even down to pretending I was disobeying him. He knew the building would be empty of staff this time of day. We could indulge in "our play" as he called it. I had been all too happy to comply with his orders. "Or should that be professor?"

He stuffed his cock back in his pants, smoothed his uniform and shoved his handcuffs back in his pocket. With a shrug of his shoulders he straightened his belt and the Beretta and other gear it held. Shortly after we moved in together he had insisted I go out with him to a public firing range where he taught me how to shoot. I wasn't going to win any ribbons, not like him, but at least I would no longer shoot my foot off either. I ran my fingers over his thick, military-short hair. The nap of it bristled under my questing fingers. His body was so perfect, every inch of him. I could never get tired of exploring it. I curled my finger around his ear lobe, feeling the incredibly soft flesh there. "I'm surprised you didn't wear your hat. Isn't that part of the look?"

He grimaced. "Those things give me a headache. You think it was too much?"

"It was just about perfect. You made all the schoolgirls wet and half the boys hard. I heard that kid's question. You get a lot like that?"

"Sometimes they ask inappropriate questions. If it reflects an ingrained attitude, I'm sure the psych tests will pick up on it before they get into the Academy. If they don't drop out before they even reach that point." He smiled crookedly. "Don't you think it's time we went home?"

"Sure," I said. "Got plans for the weekend, professor?"

He pulled me into his embrace. "Nothing that doesn't involve you. If you like we can go into town for dinner."

"Yes, please."

"Holdren's sound good to you?" he asked.

That's where our first date had started. It had ended up with his dick up my ass, but then most of our dinners out ended up that way.

"Yes, Sir," I said. "Always."

I straightened, pulled my jeans back up and would have headed toward the door, but he stopped me with a touch.

"Sir?"

"I have something for you. With this trip coming up, it might be even more useful."

"Sir?"

He opened his briefcase and pulled out a small package, which he handed me without fanfare.

I opened it and stared down at the black iPhone. Frowning, I met his steady gaze. "I have a cell."

"But this one is better. I can find you anywhere with this. It's got full GPS, a digital compass and just about all the bells and whistles."

Finally it dawned on me what he had done. "You Lojacked me."

"Every minute of every day. How many times do I have to tell you your ass is mine?"

"You Lojacked my ass?" Then I grinned. I should have been pissed, but the idea was flattering – and very arousing.

"Lojacked and owned. Come on." He grabbed my arm and steered me toward the door. "Let's go eat. We can talk more at home."

"You can test out my new device." I walked my fingers up his chest, then raised my eyes to stare at his mouth. Studying the light reddish stubble of five o'clock shadow on his cheeks and chin. "You can find me and when you do, you can take advantage of me. Then maybe we can try out that new butt plug."

"You bet I will." His grip tightened on my arm. "After you do your homework."

I made a face, which he ignored. Then I brightened again.

"Are we really going on vacation?"

"Only if you get all As."

"Oh I will, professor. Trust me, I will."

"Good, then there's no problem, is there?"

Funny, he still didn't sound convinced. I leaned against his broad chest and smiled. I knew my Alex would only do this because he wanted to, not because I asked. But it was nice of him to let me think he was doing it for my own good.

He took my chin in his hand and tilted my head up. His intense gaze probed mine and I found myself a little breathless. He held my eyes prisoner, then with his thumb, brushed my open mouth.

"Come on," he whispered. "Let's get out of here."

"Yes, Sir."

The next day, I dropped Jason off at the University on my way into town. We'd meet up later in the day. Again, I beat both Miguel and Nancy in. While I waited for them, I listened to the 911 tape again. My first stop this morning would be another visit to the pay phone where the call had originated. The first two times we had swung by had yielded nothing. It remained a long shot, but maybe somebody had seen something and sooner or later we'd find them. And persuade them to talk.

The market employee we had talked to told us the manager would be in this morning, so we were heading back. Meanwhile, I needed to catch Nancy and put in my vacation request. I rarely took holidays, had never seen a need. But then I'd never had anyone I wanted to go away with.

I spent the wait time fielding phone calls and going over old case books.

Miguel came in right on Nancy's heels. I opted to tackle Nancy first. I caught her as she was booting up her PC, ready to check her overnight messages in her Inbox. She looked up at my knock.

"Yes, Detective?"

"Dominguez and I are heading back to the market to talk to the manager. Maybe he saw something no one else did."

"We can hope, right?" She saw me hesitate and cocked her head. For the first time I noticed her hair was silvering. Had it always been there, or had she stopped coloring it? Whatever the reason, it gave her a distinguished look. Maybe that was the point. "Something else?" she prompted.

"I'd like to put in for some vacation time."

She stared at me for several heartbeats. "Vacation?"

"Yeah, you know, days off. Ten days to be exact."

"Since when do you take vacations?"

"Jay wants us to go camping." I knew what was coming next. She didn't disappoint.

She crowed with laughter. "Camping? You?"

"Yes." I ground my teeth. "Me."

"My God, what that man does to you. Alexander Spider, mister-I-don't-care-about-anybody. A domesticated Spiderman. I never thought I'd see the day."

"Are you going to go on, or are you going to approve my holidays?"

"Sure. Consider them yours. Send me the forms with the dates, I'll okay them. Give my best to Jason, will you? Haven't seen the guy since, well, you know..."

I frowned. I didn't like remembering the circumstances she was referring to. Jason had nearly died at the hands of a grieving father who had carried his revenge too far. I had also nearly lost him to another set of unfortunate events that were entirely my fault. We managed to get past those days, but they still hung over me like an uneasy cloud. Maybe a vacation was just what we needed to get all the way past that, and back to what we had before I screwed things up.

I returned to find Miguel on the phone listening intently to whoever was on the other end. He met my gaze and his eyes hardened. He sat straighter, leaning back in his chair, lips crimped in a thin line. The boy was going to have to learn to park his personal issues at the door when he came to work. Either that, or ask for a transfer. Miguel hung up with a snap of his wrist then twisted his arm around to study the face of his watch.

"That was trace. They got results of the material collected at the crime scene. Fabric threads pulled off the vic's clothes and corpus were a red and gray polyester blend."

I frowned. It was an easy thing to dehumanize the victims. Never a good path to go down. I knew. It was something I struggled with all the time. "The *victim* has a name, Detective Dominguez. Isaac Simpson."

He flushed, eyes flashing at the rebuke. "There's more, sir. The trace technician also pulled some animal hairs off the vic – off Mr. Simpson – and determined they're dog hairs. Unknown breed, but something with long hair, like a collie, only white. We want them tested for breed, we have to send them out to CFSI."

And wait a year for the results if we were lucky. CFSI, L.A. County's newest forensic lab serviced the LAPD and LASD, which would be higher on their priority list than a Santa Barbara mystery dog.

"Collie?" I tried to remember what a collie dog looked like. "Ah, Lassie. Anyone in the area have a dog? Do collies come in white?"

"No, but Shih Tzus do, or Samoyeds."

I looked at him and he grudgingly admitted, "The kids want a dog. They like those two. And poodles." He grimaced, and this time it wasn't because of me.

"So let's go ask someone if there are any long-haired white dogs in the area."

"I was just going back to canvas it."

"Then let's go do it."

I drove, leaving Miguel to fill out reports. I don't let other people drive me around. We found the manager of the Milpas market stocking beer in his cooler when we entered the empty store at nine minutes past nine. He stared at the badges we flashed, taking his time, studying each one like he was looking for something to explain why we were in his store. From the broken red veins on his thick nose I figured him for someone who drank his own product.

Wiping his hands on the front of his gabardine pants held up by a worn belt, he kept piling cans into the cooler. A massive belly protruded over the too-tight belt.

"Mr. Hardy?" I asked. He nodded. I badged him again. That brought on a frown.

"Ayuh," he said with a heavy New England accent. "Help

you?"

"Yes, you can." Miguel was in his face. "Are you familiar with the homicide that occurred near here nine days ago?" When all he got was a blank look for his troubles, he added, "The indigent man. On the beach."

"Ah, that one," Hardy said. "Ayuh."

"Did Mr. Simpson ever come in here?"

"Simpson?"

"The dead man."

"The colored one? Not in my store. I called the police on that one. Bad smelling man, drive away payin' customers."

I had to wonder if it was only his smell that made Hardy so hostile. I looked toward the open door. The phone our 911 caller had used was barely visible, situated as it was between the parking lot and the stretch of sand bordering the washroom where Simpson had died. I knew if I stepped outside I would be able to see the beach. Children's voices rode on the salty air along with the cries of the gulls Jason loved so much. I couldn't hear them without thinking of him.

"You ever see anyone around here with a dog?" Miguel asked.

"Dog? Lots of dogs 'round here," Hardy said. "Too damn many. Dirty, mangy things. Leavin' messes all over the place."

I didn't know whether he meant the dogs or their owners. "Any long-haired white ones?" I asked.

Hardy looked over my shoulder. I knew the minute he remembered. A light went off behind his eyes. His mouth wrinkled up in distaste.

"Who is she, sir?"

"Ayuh, that one. Crazy woman. She'd come in here to get their hootch."

"Their? Whose hootch? Simpson's? She bought alcohol for both of them?" Was that why she knew him? "Or were there others, too?"

"Nayuh, just her and that man." He made a face and shook his head.

"Who is she, Mr. Hardy?"

"Momo."

"That's her name?"

"Don't know her name. That's all anyone calls her."

"Momo?" Miguel and I traded glances. For the first time there was no hostility in his eyes. "How often does she come around?"

"Who knows with that one. Spends all day talkin' to herself and that dog."

"Why do you let her in here then, sir?" Miguel asked softly.

"Her cash as good as anyone's," Hardy said, with New England pragmatism.

"Was she black too, Mr. Hardy?" I asked.

"Ayuh. Big and black indeed. Midnight black."

So her color didn't make her unwelcome. I guess pragmatism overcomes bigotry.

"Do you know where we can find her?" Miguel asked.

He waved out beyond the doors of his market. "She's out there most days. Hard to miss, her and that dog. Tried to bring it in here, once. I straightened her up on that, pretty quick."

We thanked the man and stepped outside. Moving from the cool of the icy air-conditioned market to the midday heat of the beach was a hot slap in my face. A cloudless sky overhead beat down on our bare heads as we crossed the nearly empty parking lot toward the restroom where Simpson had been found by Rebecca Long and maybe, just maybe, this Momo had seen something.

The crime scene tape was long gone. I crossed the threshold into the rank coolness of the cinder block structure that stank of urine and brine. A trio of ragged, overdressed men looked up, startled at our entrance. Before either of us could ask what they were doing there, they fled, leaving a reek of booze, human stink and a pile of dirty blankets in their wake. I debated pursuing them, but decided to let them go for the time being. We could round them up later if we needed to ask questions. They weren't going very far; they'd left their property behind.

Skirting the blankets, we moved through the rest of the washroom, peering into toilet stalls. I had studied the crime scene photos before we'd come out here to refresh my memory. I stood over one urinal looking down at the stained and cracked cement floor. No way to tell if one of those stains was Simpson's life blood, or just the dirt of ages.

Miguel saw me looking. Shook his head. "Evil men."

"Yes." What else could I say? I pointed at the pockmarked wall. "A .25. Small thing to do so much damage."

We left the washroom. Back out in the sun I slipped on a pair of shades and scanned the stretch of boardwalk that ran east and west along the beach. In the parking lot, gathered around a blinged out Escalade, a half dozen Latino men were trying to look tough.

A flock of pelicans flew overhead, their shadows chasing each other across the sand. A trio of Latino women herded a group of squealing kids toward a playground of slides and swings.

I glanced over at Miguel and found him smiling as he watched the children. Something else we'd never share. During my brief, disastrous marriage there had been no kids. Sometimes you get lucky. The world could do without a Spider rugrat. Jason was all the kid I wanted. Though God knows there was nothing paternal about the way I felt about him.

An old woman pushing a shopping cart, full of battered shoe boxes and clothes Goodwill would have burned, rolled past us. She wore a heavy winter coat over a sweater that looked two sizes too big, and fingerless gloves. No dog, and she was white under layers of accumulated dirt.

The wheels on the cart wobbled, dragging through a drift of sand, nearly falling off the boardwalk and dumping its contents on the beach. I reached it first and hauled it upright. She glared at me and snatched the cart out of my grip. I raised both hands to show her I meant no harm. The movement pulled my jacket open, revealing my Beretta.

Her sunken eyes widened her hands tightening on her worldly possessions. This close, the smell of her unwashed body and clothes overwhelmed me. Her gray, lined face had paled even more until it looked like pitted concrete.

"What do you want?"

"We're not here to hurt you, ma'am." I wished we'd been able to come up with a better description of Momo and her white dog, but we'd have to use what he had. "We're looking for someone. A black woman. She has a dog with her and hangs around here..." I pointed behind us to the washrooms and the market behind it. I tried to ignore the *cholos* watching us. "The dog is probably white."

"Black woman," she snorted. "Probably a white dog. Young man do you have a clue?"

"Sometimes I doubt it," I muttered. I could feel Miguel behind me, getting restless. No doubt convinced he could do better questioning her.

"She calls herself Momo," I said. "We believe she used to associate with Isaac Simpson."

"Who?" No alarm in her voice. Nothing but indifference. If she knew who Simpson was, she didn't care.

"The man who died nine days ago in the washroom over there."

She drew away from us and threw alarmed looks over her shoulder. I knew she was going to bolt any second. I stepped in front of her cart, taking care not to touch it, knowing that would trigger panic. Miguel blocked her from retreating back the way she had come.

"We're not going to hurt you, ma'am," I said, speaking to her like I would to a wild animal. "We just need you to tell us if you know the woman, Momo."

"No, no." She started shaking her head violently, her lips working on other unspoken words, silent curses no doubt. Spittle sprayed out of her mouth. Standing as close as I was, I could smell her unwashed flesh and the foul rot from her mouth. What few teeth she had left were riddled with brown decay.

Behind me I heard Miguel doing his own muttering, but his words I could hear, though I'd rather have not. "... say to those with fearful hearts, 'Be strong, do not fear; your God will come...'"

I didn't need to be a Biblical scholar to know where those words were coming from. But I had no idea what he meant to do with them. Sooth her or scare her into compliance?

The old woman's agitation increased. Whether from Miguel's helpful words or our presence, like she said, I didn't have a clue. She moaned and shook her head violently, more spittle flying from her cracked lips.

I knew I didn't dare touch her or her cart. Already we were attracting attention. Out of the corner of my eye I saw Miguel flip his jacket open to show his badge to the growing mob from the parking lot drifting our way. Looking to find trouble or cause it?

The display of arms didn't help. The crowd grew and so did their hostility. Great, were we going to have a pissing contest here in the middle of the beach?

I knew things were going to get ugly if we didn't move on. With only two of us, crowd control was impossible. It would be nothing but stupid to get caught up in a riot out here. I signaled Miguel to move back. For one heart stopping second I thought he was going to refuse. Then whatever passed for common sense in his fundamentalist head took over, and he stepped off the boardwalk, right into the mass of gathering people, murmuring under his breath, "Though a mighty army surrounds me, my heart will not be afraid..."

He pushed through the loose crowd that thankfully fell away from him. Maybe they were as awed by his Biblical quotes as I was.

I studied the dozen or so men exhibiting the most suppressed rage. Cop haters always got my radar up. I wasn't all that surprised to see Eastside gang tats on several of them, and one or two Westside *placas*. Two rival gangs occupying the same space? Never a good thing. Tensions climbed and I could almost smell the testosterone. Miguel's back was up and he wasn't standing down for any of them.

I stood my ground too, and didn't leave the boardwalk until the old lady rolled her cart down toward the parking lot, and I was sure the bangers weren't going to follow her. Then I strode over to where an impatient Miguel waited.

I ignored his rage and kept my attention on the retreating bangers doing their cock-of-the-walk strut, bouncing fists off each other, mock wrestling. They stood beside the Escalade, flipped us the bird and watched us. I tried not to think how many of them were probably carrying.

"You see the ink?" I asked quietly so none of them would overhear us.

He was still angry. He glared at them, then swung around to turn his hostility on me. "Yes. Does it mean something?"

"Eastside, Westside they don't co-habit peacefully. I think we interrupted something."

"What? You think there's going to be more trouble than this?"

I thought of the death of Isaac Simpson and the way it hadn't made any sense. "I think maybe it already did." If I was right it might be only the beginning of a whole mess of trouble.

I turned to watch the gang bangers move as a group down the boardwalk, noticing how everyone got out of their way. They swaggered, sure of the fear they generated, not the least concerned a pair of Santa Barbara's finest were watching.

"Think you can ID those tats?" I asked.

"I got a good look at a few of them."

"Let's hit the station. I think I recognized a couple of those mutts. If I can verify my ID we might find known associates."

On our way back to our unmarked, Miguel glanced over at me. "What about the woman?"

"Momo?"

"We still going to look for her?"

"More than ever."

"You think she saw something?"

"I think she knows exactly what went on, and if I'm right, she may be next."

"You think they'll go after her as a witness?"

"I think it's more than that." I glanced over my shoulder to where the old woman had vanished. "Did you see her fear?"

"Of us?"

"Not us. We didn't mean anything to her. It was the bangers."

He shrugged. "So she's afraid of some rough looking guys. Who wouldn't be?"

"It's more than that," I said. "I think those 'guys' are taxing the indigents down here."

"Taxing them?"

"Extorting them. Probably for protection. And Isaac Simpson refused to pay, or couldn't pay."

Just before I keyed the car open, I spun away from it and nearly ran down Miguel. "Pit stop. I need to check something out with the manager."

Milpas market was busier than it had been the first time we stopped in. I didn't have time to wait for the till to clear so I pulled my badge out and pushed through to the counter. When Hardy saw us his mouth turned down. This time there was no amiable down-home-New Englander-just-jawing. I had spotted a teenage girl stocking cans down one aisle. I nodded toward her after catching Hardy's eyes.

"Get her behind the counter. We need to talk."

He called to the girl, who approached looking nearly as sullen as Hardy. When she said, "What is it, Dad," I knew why. Family dynamics didn't concern me right now.

"Take over here...?" I looked at her until she muttered, "Brittany."

"Brittany. Your dad will be busy for a few minutes." I turned to Hardy. "Got an office?"

He snorted. "No. We can go outside, in back where the ice machine is."

Out where the buzz of hungry flies and the cries of gulls competed with the sound of nearby traffic. The ice machine was in front of a narrow alley where a blue dumpster overflowed with a week's worth of garbage, explaining the flies.

Hardy planted himself in front of the ice machine, arms folded over his barrel chest.

"We need to ask you some questions," I said before his belligerence could ratchet up into outright hostility. "I need to know who has been hanging around your store in the last couple of months, whether they came in to the store or just loitered outside."

"I don't have time to be watching spics in the parking lot."

"Spics?" I leaned toward him, crowding his space. I hadn't said they were Latino. "Describe them."

"Spics. What can I say about 'em? Dirty Mexis, shaved like they just come outta jail. Tattoos. Those baggy clothes all the kids seem to wear. Sneering all the time." If he noticed he was standing beside another of his 'dirty Mexis' in the form of a cop, he gave no sign. Thick. I'd give Miguel points. He showed no sign the name calling got to him. His face was as flat as I knew mine was.

"What did they do besides hang around?"

"Pick on my customers. Call them names. Try to pick fights with the men, the women...I called the police but no one ever did anything. They'd ask if the Mexis could come in the store and when I said no, they said it wasn't trespassing then and they couldn't do nothing until they did. Lot of damn good payin' city taxes gets me."

"Did you ever see them interact with either Momo or Simpson?"

Hardy gave me a disgusted look. "They 'interacted' with everyone. Business is down since they showed up, but fat lot of good you guys did me. Want to tell me why that was?"

I made sympathetic noises, which didn't mollify Hardy at all. I jerked my head and Miguel followed me toward where our car was parked, baking in the sun. The Escalade was gone. I didn't turn around to see if the angry manager was watching us. I knew he was.

Miguel was getting better at reading me. "What's up?"

"He's lying."

He thought about that for a minute and nodded. "Okay, I agree. But about what?"

I drummed my fingers on the wheel staring over the dash towards the rolling waves beyond the beach, crashing and churning on the shoreline. "That I don't know." I rammed the key into the ignition and cranked the engine on, immediately turning on the air. A blast of hot air was soon replaced by welcomed coolness.

"He's afraid of them."

"Anyone would be, if they're smart. But we're going to put a stop to it."

"How are we going to do that?"

"Haven't quite figured that out yet, either."

"But you will." He sounded skeptical.

"Yes," I said, slamming the car into gear and booting it out of the parking lot. "I will."

Back at the station we pulled out the latest briefs on gang activity in our area and started leafing through them, looking for the bangers we had spotted on the beach or at least some familiar tattoos. It wasn't long before my suspicions were confirmed. The tats I had seen were all Eastside with the exception of two, who were confirmed Westside bangers with long sheets.

I took the briefs with me, then left for lunch around twelve-thirty. Over a corned beef on rye, I ran down what I knew so far. Bangers were up to something. Two opposing gangs showing up in Eastside territory, albeit right on the border between the two sides. Why? What would bring two warring factions together? Nothing good, I was sure. Add to the mix one dead, black indigent. Head shot, which suggested execution. So who executes a homeless old guy with no criminal ties? I went back to what I had told my class a good cop looks at. Opportunity? They had that – I'd seen them down there myself and had corroboration that they'd been there before. Means? I'd never known a banger that didn't have a surplus of weapons at his disposal. Motive? I was stretching there. Extortion? Common, but usually aimed at store owners or neighborhood dealers, not penniless street bums. Who expected them to have money? Or was there something darker at work here? There had been an increasing number of crimes against blacks by Hispanic gangbangers in the L.A. area. No one wanted to talk about it. Creating yet more racial tensions in a city that always seemed to be on the edge of another race riot was never a good thing. But the facts were there, buried in police reports from all over Los Angeles.

Bottom line: if there was anything to my suspicions, however flimsy they were, then it was even more imperative we find Momo. Both for her safety, and for our case.

That afternoon I contacted our gang specialist, Sergeant Thomas Paige, and caught him on his way out to a confab with some city people about handling graffiti showing up around town. He had about five minutes to spare and I had one question I needed answered above everything else.

"What about recent activity in the beach area?"

"Been an uptick all over the county. Assaults are up, a lot more violent muggings and home invasions."

"All gang related?"

"Far as I can tell." Paige was a laconic Angeleno who talked like he had a mouthful of nails. "Even a slew of shots-fired calls, nobody injured though. Word is there's talk of some new drug pipeline being set up with cartels and local bangers."

"Here in town?" Shit, that's all we needed, more drugs flooding the street.

"Haven't figured that part out yet."

"Keep me in the loop." I left him to his meeting and went in search of Miguel so we could get on with our own work.

Miguel and I returned to the beach and spent the rest of the afternoon interviewing everyone we found. A few talked of seeing an old black woman and her dog. But no one knew where they were. We saw the woman with the shopping cart, but she grew agitated again when we questioned her, so I was forced to back off without learning anything new.

There was no sign of Eastside or Westside bangers hanging around. Too bad, I was itching to get my hands on one of them. Find out just what they were doing hanging around the beach together.

At five we called it a day. I picked up my Toyota and headed home.

This time I cooked; chicken on the barbecue with a variety of cold salads Jason picked up on his way home from school. We sat in our cleaned up backyard, now bursting with flowers and bushes – another successful effort on Jason's part who, it turned out, had quite a green thumb. When he had first mentioned wanting to plant a few things in the yard I had indulgently said sure, figuring he meant to throw a few pots of marigolds or daisies out. Instead, he had bought a whole slew of garden equipment, bags of dirt and very smelly fertilizer. Within a month my scruffy backyard had been turned into a colorful oasis that was more of solace than I would have imagined. Or maybe it was sharing it with Jason that made it special. I didn't analyze it too closely. I simply enjoyed being out there with him.

After we ate, I lay back in the lounger with my feet up on

Jason's lap. Idly, he massaged my soles and calves, working his way up my bare thighs, first with his fingers, then his lips. He grew more focused, leaving a trail of heat along the inside of my calf, tracing the knobs of my kneecap then nipping the skin above my right knee. I spread my legs, bracing one foot on the patio stones. His mouth was hot; I shivered under his touch. "If I do this…" he nibbled again, then followed it with his lapping tongue. A wave of desire so hard I groaned washed over me. "…I can make you do that."

My dick pressed painfully against the denim shorts I had changed into after my shower. "And if I do this…" he continued his torturous path up my inner thigh until his lips caressed my swollen balls through the fabric. I sighed and closed my eyes as he worked my fly open. I wound shaking fingers through his thick hair. One of the first things Jason had done, even before the garden came, was talk me into replacing the old chain fence that separated my property from the other two houses at the end of my cul-de-sac. Now we had true privacy in our little retreat and it wasn't uncommon for us to take advantage of it. Though even with the fence, there was still that slightly kinky feeling of doing something forbidden. I had never been one for public sex, but with Jason I found I stretched my boundaries. "Oh, yes," he sighed, his mouth pressing into my balls and I rocked, thrusting my hips up. "Look at what I can make you do."

His hot breath caressed my erection, then the tip of his tongue licked precum out of my slit, his lips exploring and enclosing the swollen head with wet heat. I moaned and pressed the back of his head down, wanting him to swallow me to the root. My nerves thrummed and my balls tightened in preorgasmic tension. A strange vibration started at the base of my dick and grew. It was several moments of unbelievable bliss before I realized Jason was humming, and the vibration from his throat was going straight to the core of my cock.

I shouted out his name and shot my load. He swallowed and it felt like he was taking my whole dick right down his throat, milking me dry. I collapsed back against the lounger struggling to get my breath back.

He crawled up my body and I hugged him close, petting his back.

"Where the hell did you learn to do that?"

He grinned against my throat. "Would you believe TV? Some sex show on *here!* They were talking about how to give mind blowing head."

"Wow, finally paying through the nose for cable pays off." I nuzzled his throat. "You're a keeper, Jason Zachary."

"Yes, Sir."

Darkness fell and fireflies come out, enchanting us. We shared the lounger and one more beer before retreating into the house to watch one of our favorite Lauren and Bogey movies.

After the final credits rolled, I bounced to my feet. "Got something for you. Stay here."

I hurried into our bedroom where I scooped up the things I had picked up today on my side trip to Santa Barbara. I came out carrying them in both hands. He watched me approach with his usual intense scrutiny. No one I knew could stare down a person like my Alex.

I handed him the Maxpedition backpack first. He turned the desert-tan bag over in his hands, examining all the various pockets and compartments it had.

"You're serious about this trip, aren't you?"

"I'm always serious about hiking. Here…" I handed him the Merrell boots. "I measured your work boots—these should be a perfect fit. Comfortable, too. You won't get blisters in these babies."

He felt the weight of the boots and looked pleased. "Could kick some serious bear ass with these things."

I had made the mistake of telling him there were black bears in the Wilderness area we were going to. Bears and mountain lions, too. Now I had an even harder thing to say to him.

"Uh, can I ask you something?"

His gray eyes met mine and he frowned. "You know you always can. What is it, Jay?"

"Can you… can you not take your gun with you on this trip?"

"You know I don't like going anywhere without it," he said softly.

"I know, and I respect that, Sir, but do you really think you're going to need it up there? It's only for a few days…"

His frown deepened. Finally, all he would say was, "I'll think about it."

I let it go. He'd either do what I asked or he wouldn't. Nagging him would only lead to punishment and while I usually enjoyed that, sometimes he picked something I didn't like one bit, like sleeping on the couch, away from him. I wasn't going to push the matter.

I tugged his hand, pulling him off the leather couch. "Come on, try it on."

He shrugged the backpack over his broad shoulders and let me help settle it into place.

"How's it feel?"

"Comfortable. Balanced."

"Wait'll it's full of supplies. You'll get a good workout from it."

He patted his belly and grinned ruefully. "Maybe work off some of this, you think?"

I replaced his hand with my own, stroking his stomach through the thin T-shirt he wore. His muscles clenched under my questing fingers and he sucked in his breath. "I love every inch of you, Sir, don't ever think otherwise."

He grabbed my hand, shoving it against his swelling cock.

"Maybe you should try the boots on," I whispered as our eyes met, his shiny with deepening desire.

"Maybe I should."

But he made no move to do so. My hand squirmed around his growing erection, matching the one I had never quite lost since he had come home.

"Go get yours," he ordered. "We're going to do something together."

I hurried to obey and pulled my boots out of the front closet, following him into our bedroom.

"Strip," he said.

Again I obeyed, and soon stood in front of him naked, my cock already standing out from my shaved pubic area. He followed suit then put his new boots on, ordering me to put mine on. Within seconds we stood facing each other, dicks thickening in anticipation, clad only in our hiking boots.

He leaned forward and slid my collar around my throat, clamping my nipples in the slender chains attached to the brass ring. Pain lanced straight into my groin, I closed my eyes against the sudden rush of remembered desire.

"Arms behind your back."

I did as he ordered, the movement sending new bolts of pain through my pinched nipples to the base of my cock. I was leaking precum now. He smoothed his fingers over my engorged helmet, making it slick and strokeable.

"Who do you belong to?"

"You, Sir. Only you."

He used the soft leather restraints to cuff my hands behind my back. The last thing I saw before he slipped the leather hood over my head was him standing in front of me, wearing only his brand new Merrell's, his swelling dick rising out of his thick bush of red hair. Then darkness enfolded me and I was plunged into a world of smells and sounds and touch. Oh God, how he touched me. Pleasure and pain all mingled into one.

It was a long time before we got to bed that night.

I was late next morning. My fault. I had kept Jason in shackles for what turned out to be nearly two hours, proving once more that what he did to me was far beyond what any other man had ever done. We had collapsed on our double bed well after midnight not waking up until the phone dragged me out of bed, long after the alarm would have gone off. Jason mumbled and burrowed back under the warm covers while I sat on the side of the bed, trying to shake sleep off as the voice on the other end went on about how much I really needed new aluminum siding for my house. It was a measure of my half-awake state that I didn't hang up on the jerk for a full minute.

"Whassat?" Jason slurred and winced when he cranked one eye open and peered at me over his pillow. "It can't be time to get up."

"Fraid so." I pulled the covers off his shrinking body, barely pausing to admire his trim, hairless form. "We have to hurry. We're both running late."

He groaned but did as I ordered. We shared a shower to speed things up, kissed at the front door then dashed to our respective cars. I broke a few speed limits on the way in to the station. Both Miguel and Nancy were already there, and I thought I caught a knowing smirk from Nancy before I buried my head in the pile of reports on my desk.

"We need to find Momo," I said shortly.

"I agree," Miguel said. "I put a BOLO out on her this morning. Patrols are looking for her as we speak."

"Good." I filled him in on my speculations of the day before.

"Racially motivated hits?" Miguel looked troubled. "I've heard of it happening in L.A. but not here."

"I guess some things are too good to keep to themselves." I knew I sounded cynical, but after nearly a decade of being a cop

I'd seen enough to make anyone a cynic.

I transcribed the field reports from our conversations with Hardy and the nameless woman, then I pulled up the chrono report I'd started the first day of Simpson's murder. This covered everything Miguel and I had done from the original 911 call, including my wildest speculations on why the crime happened, right up to this morning's entry. Most such speculations turned out to be false leads, but every so often something would spark, and I'd find the trail that would lead me to a killer. I thought I might be on that trail now. Part of me hoped I was wrong, but that was the part that still believed in basic human goodness. For the most that had been beaten out of me by reality.

I finished up and added the pages to the murder book, pausing to look over the crime scene photos again. One close-up shot clearly showed the pair of entry points where the .25 caliber rounds had penetrated Simpson's head. The picture was so clear I could make out the dark stippling around the entrance wound that meant the weapon had been held only inches from the target. Whoever had shot Simpson had wanted to make sure the job was done. It spoke of a cold calculation. Simpson must have known what was happening to him. Had he understood it? Had they taunted him before the execution? I tried to envision the faces of the attackers. I didn't have a handle on them yet, but I was getting closer. I went back to studying the autopsy report.

Faint ligature marks on Simpson's wrists suggested he'd been restrained, probably with hands. So what did that mean? Two men? Three? Simpson wasn't a small man, he might have been old and scrawny, but I suspect he put up a struggle at the end. So my guess was three men, two holding him in place, and the shooter. I thought of the bangers Miguel and I had chased off the other day, the ones we had ID'd when we returned to the station. Would any of them be capable of such a heartless murder? At least two of them had jackets full of violence and assaults, with and without deadly weapons. So my guess was, yes, they were more than capable.

Fideo hadn't been among them, but that didn't mean he didn't know what his posse was up to. I could safely bet my pension he knew everything his barrio brothers did.

Back on my computer I pulled up our crime database. I also dug up Fideo's rap sheet. Looking over his KAs, I found a slew of other bangers. Some of his known associates had their own paper, some didn't. I could give them the benefit of the doubt and figure they were clean, or be realistic and guess they just hadn't been caught. I found a list of likely suspects and printed copies of all of them. When that was done I glanced over at Miguel.

"Want to talk to some *cholos*?"

"You find something?"

I grabbed my jacket off the back of my chair. "I'll tell you on the way."

I'd printed out an extra copy of the chrono and handed it to him once we signed out a car and were heading to the first address. My gang expert had ID'd the most violent of the Eastside bangers as a shot caller. The man who gave orders.

Before we went door knocking, I turned to Miguel. "Your Spanish is a lot better than mine. Jump in whenever you want. We can't force anyone to talk, we don't have enough for warrants or probable cause, but we may be able to spook something out of them." I glanced down at the printouts in my hand. "I want to tackle the younger brother first. He's been in a lot less trouble and may not be as familiar with the system. If we can rattle his cage, he may drop a few tidbits we can use on the older sibling. In fact..." I tapped my finger on my upper lip. "Why don't you take him? I'll keep his older brother..." I looked at the jacket, "Ramiro, occupied."

"How do you want me to handle him?"

"Play on his ego. Ask him what he and his homies have been up to. Make him feel like an important part of the set. Ask him if he got jumped in yet, like you're jealous. He's only fourteen, his machismo is stoked, so stroke him; he might buy that from you. Don't just listen to his answers, watch him. Take it for granted he's lying about everything. Ask him the same question two or three different ways. People always make their lies way too complicated to remember them for long. Watch his body, it'll tell you when he's lying for sure. The eyes can be a dead giveaway. Watch the position of his legs. If he looks like he wants to bolt, you're getting to him."

"Yes, sir."

"Then let's go nail us some...bangers." I'd been about to say assholes, but that might not sit well with my straight-laced, younger partner. "And drop the sir. We're equals out here, and if you carry that stuffy military attitude in there, you might as well wear a target."

"Yes, s—ah, Detective Spider."

He still sounded like a raw academy boot. I let it go. It would come in time, or it wouldn't. He was the master of that decision.

It took less than ten minutes to reach the first address. The streets were a mix of well cared for Spanish-style, white-walled homes and a few rundown three-story walk-ups. Statistically at least one of them would be a grow-op and there'd be a meth lab in the 'hood, too. There weren't too many neighborhoods these days that didn't have one or the other. We climbed out of the Crown. I checked the pancake holster under my left armpit, verified its accessibility then glanced at Miguel, who nodded. Together we approached the immaculate, green-trimmed stucco bungalow. A pair of potted orange and red flowering plants flanked the steel-barred door. My gaze restlessly scanned the front of the house, watching for some sign we'd been spotted. No flutter of curtains, no curious eyes peering out, no glint of a metal barrel taking aim on us. Nothing on the street but vehicles. No black Escalades in sight, though.

We took up places on either side of the door. I rapped on the wood and announced ourselves. "Santa Barbara police. Open up."

Nothing. I listened, then knocked again. Harder.

"*Es la policia,*" Miguel called.

Feet scuffled on the other side of the door. I felt Miguel tense, taking a step back, freeing his gun hand. I did the same and we were both rigid with watchful tension when the door cracked open enough to let a thin female face peer through.

"*Quien es? Que quiere?*"

"*Es la policia, Señora,*" Miguel said. "*Necesitamas hablar con usted por favor.*"

"*No, por favor vallanse, no puedo hablar...*"

"*Señora, tine que, no nos vamos a ir, hasta que hablemos.*"

"*Dejenos!*"

When Miguel told her to come out and talk to us, she shouted to leave them alone. *Not going to happen, lady.*

"*Señora, no puedo hacer eso.*" Miguel spoke softly. Only I could see the tension in him, his feet planted firmly, hands not on his service weapon, but ready to act in a split second decision.

"You have to talk to us, *Señora,*" I added, as though saying it in English was going to make her more amenable. But without probable cause to enter the place, we needed her to come outside. We didn't even know if any one of the sons we were looking for was inside.

Then the matter was solved for us.

From inside the house a door slammed shut and the woman's eyes went wide and she darted a look behind her, her face blanching. "*No, ese...*"

"*Señora...*"

We all heard the commotion in the back of the house a minute later. A deep-throated barking was barely interrupted by a string of Spanish curses.

Miguel beat me around to the backyard, arriving seconds before I got there. Definitely needed more exercise. We found a heavily tattooed Hispanic man halfway over a beaten down wooden fence. His legs dangled on the other side. He'd been trying to climb back. The hundred pound Rottweiler in the yard next door had foiled his escape. It clamped jaws the size of dinner plates around the guy's ankle and was dragging him over to the other side. He saw us and his curses grew more violent. When he fumbled in his belt I shouted and dropped into a shooter's stance.

"Don't even think about it, asshole," I yelled.

They never listen. He pulled a silver plated revolver out of his waistband, but instead of aiming it at us, he pointed the barrel down at the dog.

"Don't!" I screamed seconds before a shot split the air. The dog yelped and Miguel dragged the shooter off the fence, laying him out on the ground where he kicked the gun out of his hand, and slapped cuffs on the still cursing man's wrists.

He hauled him upright and slammed him against the fence that rocked under the combined weight of the two of them on one side and the hysterical dog on the other.

Cursing and struggling, he wasn't giving up. Miguel shoved him again. "Shut up or I'll toss you over there, and let Fido finish the job."

I had to admire my partner's quick wits. The cuffed guy subsided into sullen silence and glared at both of us under the dome of his tattooed, hairless head. Movement near the back door drew me around, Beretta still in hand, to find the woman we had talked to earlier standing in the doorway. There was a worried look on her lined face that already bore a lot of worrylines.

"Don't hurt him, officers. He's a good boy—"

We ignored her as we hauled the disarmed 'good boy' past her into the house we had tried to enter earlier. She trailed after us, wringing her hands. "Are you arresting him? You can't arrest him, he hasn't done anything."

I made a quick study of the visible parts of the house. Nothing suggesting illegal activity, but we'd have to wait for the warrant to search deeper. In sharp contrast to what Miguel and I were there for, the house was inviting and homey. The rich smell of cooking meats and sharp spices filled the small space. The stovetop was covered with simmering pots and pans.

Miguel shoved his arrestee down onto a sofa and began to list off the charges, first in Spanish, then in English, "Resisting, carrying a concealed weapon and if I'm guessing right, a non-registered weapon – if you're still on parole that compounds those charges – discharging a weapon, assault of a police officer, animal cruelty...that'll do for starters. I'm sure we can add more as we go along. Where's Antonio, Ramiro?"

"He not here," Ramiro said sullenly.

I stepped up beside Miguel and leaned over, planting my arms on either side of Ramiro's head. He flinched back from me. "Where is he, *cholo*?"

His sullenness grew. "*No mames. Vete a la verga.*"

I was in his face. "You kiss your mother with that mouth, *pendejo*?"

He tossed out a few more choice curses, leaving Miguel with a flaming face and an angry set to this mouth. We were marching him out to our vehicle for transportation back to the station for booking when a teenage boy appeared out of a back room.

"Antonio," his mother cried. "*Ese, vuelva a su cuarto.*"

The younger son ignored her just like the older one had. He stared at us, his hostility ratcheting up until I knew he was going to do something stupid.

"*No lo haga, el niño,*" Miguel spoke softly, his hand tightening on Ramiro's cuffed wrists. I could see he was getting jumpy. "Stand down, *ese.*"

Antonio opened his mouth to tell both of us where to get off. This time his mother took direct action. She latched onto the kid's ear so hard I swear I heard cartilage pop. Antonio yelped and tried to pull away, but she hung on grimly. Ramiro started struggling again, and I was tempted to ask her to take him in hand, but he subsided after a couple of sharp tugs on his handcuffed hands.

The old woman let loose with a string of epithets that had even my ears burning. I had to admit, I was curious. If these punks had this at home, how had they ended up getting jumped in by a bunch of losers like Eastside? I guess it just proved the sad truth that the lure of the street was stronger than a loving family could fight. I took over babysitting Ramiro and signaled my partner to take a crack at the much-subdued Antonio. The three of them headed into the kitchen where I caught a glimpse of the kid angrily slumping in a ladder back chair before his mother smacked him upside the head and clearly told him to sit up. He did, glaring at us as though we were to blame for his predicament.

I turned my attention on the banger proned out at my feet. "Want to talk to me, *ese*?"

"*Chinga tu madre*," he growled.

I tsked-tsked him. "And with *su madre* right there." I shook my head. "That's just plain nasty. You do know once we run ballistics on that little peashooter you tried to take Rover out with and we match it to the gun that killed Isaac Simpson, your ass will belong to the state for the rest of your life. No more *sopas* from momma." I sniffed the air pointedly. "No more *buñuelos* or good *cervasa*. You ready for that?"

Miguel was coming back, looking smug. I jerked Ramiro to his feet. "*Decir adiós,*" I said softly for his ears only.

We nearly made it to the front door when he pulled at my hold on his arm.

"*No se me.*"

"Then tell me who it was."

"*Consiga éstos de mí.*"

I ignored his demand to take the cuffs off. Instead I kept pulling him out of the house. His mother and brother followed, the former squeezing her hands under her breasts, the latter continuing to hold his sullen look. Through the open front door I watched a pair of black and whites pull up and discharge four unis who swarmed the house. I went to hand my prisoner over to one.

"*Se* Bala," Ramiro snapped doing his best to stay out of the other cop's grasp.

"Who's he?"

"Bala. *Se* Bala. *Yo no sé su nombre.*"

Liar. Someone knew his name. I looked at Antonio, then at mom. Mom answered.

"Fideo Esteban Gutierrez, *él es malo.* He is not a good man," she said with clear bitterness. "I tell my sons to stay away from him. Do they listen? Now you see? You see what this *ladrón* has done to us."

"Where can we find this Bala, Fideo, whatever?" I knew exactly who Fideo was. The asshole who capped that kid and Gillespie. I'd love a second chance at slamming the scrote into Quentin. Maybe I was about to get it.

With a little help from his mother, he finally told us.

Fideo had put the green light out on Simpson when he refused to pay Fideo's crew his tax. Word down from the *Eme* was to clean *mayates* off the streets. Sadly, that meant I was right about why an African-American was targeted. Clean the 'hood of the undesirables.

The unis stuffed him into their car, secured our evidence and sped away. The second patrol unit stayed behind. We would go and write up a warrant and search the place, then we would go and find Fideo. This time, I wanted to make sure the charges stuck. Fideo was going down on my watch.

All in all, a good day's work.

I always felt revved to another level when I was hot on the trail of a killer. It was beyond an adrenaline rush. It was colder, more determined. I could taste it. Ultimately much more satisfying.

Given what we already had, I knew we'd have little trouble getting a warrant. I left Miguel in charge of writing it and I went in search of Thomas Paige to get his take. He'd grown up in South Central L.A., his mother an El Salvadorian refuge and his father a steel worker back in the days when that meant something.

Then it hadn't meant anything, which apparently was why they ended up in one of the poorest, most gang-ridden areas of a city riddled with violent gangs.

We'd talked on a few occasions over the years when I had gang-related issues. He was a brusque man, not given to much small talk, but even with his reticence I had learned he had spent eight years within the sphere of the Cuatro Flats crew as a young man, and my impression has always been that he escaped being jumped in by the proverbial skin of his teeth. It wasn't something he talked about to this day. But whatever his past, it had made him our best gang expert and with our growing problem in that area, he was a boon to our small police force.

So the fact he was an abrasive asshole wasn't normally held against him. I'm sure there were a few of my fellow officers who would no doubt say the same thing about me.

Once I left Miguel with instructions on what I wanted, along with the admonition that I would be double checking his work when I got back, I took my box of donuts and a Venti black Columbian and headed over to Paige's desk. He glanced up at my approach then went back to a binder opened on his desk. Once there I could see that he was working on the latest gang briefs. No doubt updating them for our use.

"Got a minute?" I slid the donuts and coffee over the desk at him.

Paige's dark face showed his Aztec roots, and his flat brown eyes never seemed to miss anything. He barely glanced at either me, or my offerings. He chewed on a toothpick. I remember seeing him with a cigarette in his mouth all the time before the laws cut out that vice.

"Heard you broke the Simpson case."

"Got a lead I think is solid. Got some loose ends to tie up. Who's the Eastside head OG?"

His narrow lips pursed and his eyes vanished in a mass of wrinkles around his canvas rough face. I pegged the guy as at least fifty-five. Sometimes I wonder whether I envied him, or his presence horrified me. Would this be me in twenty-some years? And if it was, would that be a good thing or a living nightmare? I knew he was twice divorced, with kids he never saw.

"Been a guard change lately. Chalo got sent up to Q and his homies are in a flux."

Translation: an internal gang war to rearrange a new pecking order. "How far has it gone? Any top contenders yet?"

"Couple come to mind." Paige dipped into the box and helped himself to a cinnamon dusted. I took out a honey glazed and chewed. Though Jason had sent me off with a stomach full of fresh vegetable omelet, I still indulged in more sweets than I'm sure were good for me. Jason had been making noises lately about starting his own backyard vegetable and herb garden, and I was torn between amusement at his domesticity and fear that this was one more irrevocable step in the road to a permanence I was still leery of embracing.

I knew Jason didn't share my doubts. He was more than ready to go to whatever level I deemed acceptable. He would have married me in a heartbeat, but that was a big 'whoa' moment for me. I'm not sure I could ever take that final step again. Would that eventually drive us apart?

Back to the moment. "Name the top two."

"Castano deSilva, calls himself Random, and another *cholo*, Fideo Esteban Gùtierrez, aka—"

"Bala," I filled in. Now it was coming together.

"You're familiar, then," Paige said.

I nodded. "We made our re-acquaintance a couple of hours ago when I busted one of his soldiers at his mother's place. A Ramiro Jorge. He spilled Fideo's name. The mother filled me in on the rest. Needless to say she was not pleased with her son's affiliations. I almost nailed the bastard on that drive-by last month."

"I heard about that. Pisser."

"Tell me."

"I'm hearing rumors there's a major cannabis influx from a new source coming to town. Fideo might be involved."

"I've got one of his top soldiers in lockup. I'm going to bring younger brother in, too. Their *mami* is one pissed lady. She might be worth talking to. Get simpatico with her."

Now I had his attention. He sat up, dusting cinnamon powder off his fingers. "What charge did you manage on him? Is it going to stick? What do you think his mother can tell us?"

"I think she might surprise us all. Especially if she thinks it will help save the youngest." I went on to tell him about seeing Ramiro and his crew down at the East Beach rest stop soon after Simpson's death, how I had pegged it as an assassination. That got a nod from him and the sage, "Yeah, the mofos have decided to do Hitler's work for him and get rid of the undesirables. I'd heard the rumblings they were going to start extorting the beach side indigents, with a particular hard on for the African American ones. I think I know your victim, too. He was a mouthy dude, didn't back down."

"Guess it got him cleansed," I muttered. "But maybe they were talking more than ethnic cleansing. Maybe they're talking about how to divvy up the dope, too."

Then I told him how Miguel and I had found Ramiro trying to flee with an illegally concealed weapon and had gone on to shoot the dog next door. "I booked him and we're getting a warrant as we speak. With luck we'll scoop up some more juice to hold him on. You want to talk to him? Maybe you can turn him on this Fideo, and we can really have a good day's work. You know the players better than I do."

He took out another donut, this one raisin studded, and chewed thoughtfully. "I just might take you up on that."

I stood up, leaving the box of donuts on his desk. "Why don't you do that while my partner and I serve that warrant? If we come up with anything I can let you know while you're in there chatting him up. You come up with anything, you can let us know."

"See if you can extend that warrant to include narcotics in your search."

"I'll try. See if a judge will agree." I had my doubts about that. We had him on weapons possession, but hadn't found any sign of drugs or drug paraphernalia in our surface search of Ramero's crib. I fully expected any judge we approached to be reluctant to give us a blanket warrant to go on a fishing expedition.

Paige nodded, seeming to share my doubt. "Give it your best shot."

"You going to talk to him? Maybe you can persuade him to share."

He extended his hand across the desk. "Be glad to. What room's he in?"

"Interrogation room two." We shook. "Have fun."

"Just another fine day on the force." He lumbered to his feet, jerked his belted pants up over a sizable paunch, then adjusted his crooked tie. Though his efforts didn't do much to improve his disheveled look, it did nothing to diminish the power he projected. The man was a legend and knew it. "I'll let you know however it goes."

Before leaving Paige's desk, I phoned Miguel and told him how I wanted the warrant amended. He assured me he'd have it done ASAP.

Back at my desk, I had barely stripped my jacket off when Miguel came over waving his warrant. "I just heard from a patrol unit down on Por la Mar, in the park down there. They spotted Momo."

I took the warrant from him and grabbed my jacket. "Come on, you drive. I can look this over on the way."

I had to say, I was impressed with his writing skills. Most rookie detectives didn't have a clue, nor did all the courses in the world seem to help them. I scanned through to the end of the document detailing everything we hoped to find at Ramiro Jorge's mother's house, in the kind of minute detail the legal system required. I folded the papers up and tapped my knee with them. "You have some kind of legal training?"

"Pre law," he said stiffly.

"Going to be a lawyer?" When he nodded I asked, "What changed your mind?"

"Other lawyers."

"Yes, they can have that affect on you. The Lieutenant was pre law, too. I think she had the same epiphany."

He grunted, never taking his eyes off the road.

"Let's check out this Momo sighting," I said. "We can round up a judge later to go over this for us."

We rolled onto Por la Mar Drive, about a block from the beach proper. I spotted the black and white pulled up in front of a small, grassy park. Two uniformed officers stood on either side of a stoop-shouldered black woman who dragged a ratty, tag-along piece of luggage in one hand and a small, round white and tan long-haired dog on a tartan-colored leash in the other. She appeared to be arguing with them. When Miguel and I drew nearer, the older of the two unis touched his hand to the brim of his hat and murmured, "Ma'am, here are the detectives to talk to you. You just tell them what you told us, and everything will be all right."

She turned shrewd eyes toward us. Her face was a mass of wrinkles and seams with patches of wiry hair sticking out of her head at odd angles. She had a mouthful of broken and rotting teeth. "You two goin' to stop them boys what done Sly?"

"Sly? Do you mean Issac Simpson?"

"That was his slave name. His God name was Sly."

She tugged on the dog's leash and the pair headed toward the beach. Miguel and I fell in step with her. "What can you tell us, ma'am?" I asked. "We want to catch these boys and make them pay for what they did to Mr. Simps – Sly. Can you help us?"

"Don't know what you think I can do." She kept walking, and for a woman who had to be at least in her late sixties, she was agile. Even her dog had to trot to keep up with her. "They come around ev'ry day, no one do a thing. Not then, not now."

"We're here to do something, ma'am," Miguel said gently. "You have fought a good fight, you have finished the course and kept the faith. Now you must tell us what you know, and find peace."

I had no idea what he had just said to her, but her eyes lit up. "Do you think Sly be at peace?"

"I do, ma'am. I surely do. God teaches us that all we need to do is come to him as innocents and we are welcomed into His kingdom," Miguel said. He had her enthralled. I watched their interplay with fascination, knowing that at this moment I couldn't touch this guy. He was golden.

"Can I be at peace, too?"

"You can." Miguel took her arm, ignoring her filth encrusted clothes, and stopped her. "You know what you need to do. Peace is yours, but you need to ask for it."

"I'm asking—"

"You have to ask Him."

Her mouth tightened and she jerked on her luggage. "Him? Did He help us when those boys came after us ev'ry day? When we begged that man to help us, did He come? No, he just sent them with guns and they shot Sly." Tears leaked from her rheumy eyes. "They was gonna shoot me too, but Butterfly chased them off."

Her fond eyes looked down at the dog who was rubbing his head on the grass. Its white plume of tail curled over its back, and from what I could see the dog looked to be in better shape than its owner, who might have weighed a hundred and ten pounds wet.

"Well, we plan on putting them someplace where they can't ever hurt you or Butterfly again." Miguel crouched down and fondled the dog's head. "We already have one in custody. We need your help to put the others away." He glanced at me, then at her. "Will you do that? Will you help us?"

"How can I help?"

"You saw these men, right? Can you describe them to us? Could you help one of our people draw a picture of them?"

"Will you come down to the police station and do a line up for us?" I asked.

Panic filled her face so I backed away, leaving Miguel to calm her. Clearly he had the rapport with her. When he straightened to sooth her, I dropped into a crouch and fell to petting the hairy animal, which wiggled in what I assumed was ecstasy at my touch. At least the damn dog liked me.

The dog's reaction seemed to calm her. She even offered me a smile, which I returned. I met Miguel's gaze.

"She'll come?" The dog licked my hand, and it was all I could do not to wipe the slobber off on my pant leg. With a final, gingerly pat on its head I stood up, straightening my shoulders and smoothing my jacket. Miguel nodded.

"Good, good. We'll have someone pick her up—"

"I'll bring her down."

"Now? No, that's not possible." I wasn't about to sit in the unmarked with this woman and her dog. Miguel shook his head.

"I'll come back for her."

"That's better. Get a food voucher when you get back to the station – treat her to lunch. Make sure..." I glanced down at the fawning dog rubbing its head against my pant leg. "Make sure Butterfly gets something, too."

We left her in the safe hands of the two unis after Miguel promised them he would return within a half hour. We were both firm in our instructions that they were to make sure she didn't get out of their sight.

Back in our Crown I drove this time. "Good work," I said. "Think she'll be a good eye witness?"

"I think she'll do fine. She's a strong woman."

"Let's hope so. I don't want those mutts to walk because she flaked out at the end."

"She's doing this for her friend. She won't flake."

In the end, she proved him right. She picked Ramiro out of a line up, and when we finally tracked down and hauled in Fideo later that day, she picked him out of the line-up within seconds. She gave us a decent description of the other gang bangers who had been harassing both her and Simpson and we got warrants for them, too.

I was right. The judge signed off on the original search for weapons, but held off on the drug search 'for the moment', so we had to pass on that while we searched the house top to bottom.

Found a second weapon, a sawed off, and a couple of switchblades we took into evidence. They'd all be tested, and might tie our boy into other crimes. I could only hope.

All in all a damn good day's work.

I bounced through the door at the end of the day. Alex wasn't home yet. Good. I wanted to get my surprise ready for him. I put the champagne on ice and pulled the pair of lobsters out of the cooler I had packed them in at the fish market in town. I readied the big steamer on the stove and a second, smaller one for the corn we were going to have with the lobster. By the time I heard his truck pull into the driveway, I had everything ready.

I lit two candles on the dining room table, dropped the squirming lobsters into the pot, then hurried in to get changed. I knew Alex would grab a shower before anything else, so I had time. Skimming on my skintight leathers I added the black mesh shirt that showed off my shaved chest and made me look a lot buffer than I was in reality. At least it was Alex's favorite by far, so, whether I believed it or not, it didn't matter.

I hit the kitchen just as Alex padded in barefoot, hair still damp. He bussed me on the mouth and briefly cupped my ass in his big hand.

"Good day at work?" I asked.

"Yeah, it was actually. Nailed the guys involved in a shooting a few weeks ago. That was one case I wasn't sure we'd ever clear."

"Good for you. Who were they?"

"Nobody you need to concern yourself with." He sniffed the air. "What's that smell?"

"Dinner," I said and picked up a potholder. "Go on, take a seat. You can open the champagne. I'll be there in thirty seconds."

"Champagne?" He peered into the pot at the now brilliant red crustaceans. "Lobster? You win the lottery when I wasn't looking? What's up?"

"I'll tell you over dinner."

When I came in carrying our plates, the two shell crackers,

and the steamed corn on the cob, plus pots of butter for both of us, Alex was seated with the champagne open and the flutes filled. He waited for me to set his plate down and raised his glass to me.

"To whatever this is about." We sipped and he raised one eyebrow. "Okay, now tell me what it *is* about."

"I got my end of year marks."

"And?"

"I got a 4.0 on my biology finals."

I beamed, waiting for Alex to react. He stared at me, unblinking, and said nothing. I waited, barely able to breathe. Our eyes were locked. This was what we had both said we wanted when I decided to go back to school. It was what I'd always wanted, but been too strung out and stupid to go after. Was he not happy for me?

"Alex?"

His face lit up with a look of the purest joy I think I've ever seen on him. "I knew you could do it. Didn't I tell you that you could do it?"

"Yeah, you did, Sir." I ducked my head, suddenly shy. "Come on, eat before it gets cold."

I grabbed my lobster cracker and deftly used it to split the claw, dipping the flesh in melted butter and savoring the richness. Before I met Alex I'd never even imagined ever eating, let alone cooking, lobster. There were a lot of things I'd never imagined before meeting him. He must have seen my adoration on my face. He grew quiet and sipped his champagne.

"Better finish up here quick. We're not going to make it to dessert, you know."

He was right. We didn't. Thank God I hadn't made any. Who knew there were that many uses for simple dairy butter?

Later, in bed, my face nestled against his chest, idly playing with the damp hair on his chest, I looked up to meet his smiling, satisfied gaze. "Does this mean our hiking trip is on?"

His arm tightened around me. "Of course. I promised, didn't I?

"You'll have fun. You'll see."

"You're there. It'll be fun." Still, he sounded skeptical. I was going to have to work extra hard to make this trip special for both of us. Especially if I ever wanted to do it again.

"You'll see, Sir. I promise."

"It smells funny."

Jason looked up from unloading our gear – all of mine newly purchased and unused, well, mostly unused – from the back of my Toyota pickup. "What does?"

I sniffed. "The air."

"How does air smell funny?"

I sniffed again. Jason watched me quizzically. There was something missing. Or was it something there that hadn't been there before? Dust. Green smells, like the smells from our backyard when Jason was busy digging up one of his newly planted flowerbeds. The warm sun on my cotton covered arms – Jason said we needed to dress for the weather that might come, that the mountains often got cool, even in late June. All I could feel was sweat trickling down my spine and pits. I hoped he was right, otherwise I was seriously overdressed and was going to be a roasting turkey soon. Jason was close enough that I could smell him too. And that was a huge mistake. Everything about him always brought memories of what we had together. What I had never had with another man.

I turned away abruptly, taking another deep breath and trying to will down my arousal. To distract myself, I took out our digital camera and captured Jason getting his own gear on. He threw me a goofy grin, then stuck out his tongue. I laughed, snapped some pictures, went to tuck the camera back in my pack, when he took it from me.

"My turn," he said and took a half a dozen pictures of me looking around the trailhead we had parked in. I stared up at the folds of hills and steep slopes covered with trees so densely packed I had to wonder how we were going to get through them. From our level I could see several well-traveled trails leading into it. A few dusty cars were already in the lot, but no one was in sight. I guess they were already inside the park, doing whatever it is people did up here.

Whatever it was, I was soon going to find out. I was still skeptical, but I'd come too far to back out now. It would disappoint Jason, and suddenly that was more important to me than whether or not I was comfortable. There had to be an upside to this vacation, if only being alone with Jason with no outside distractions for a week. That had to be worth some discomfort. We'd never spent more than a day or two alone, without one of our jobs or school interfering, separating us. I'm surprised taking a vacation had never occurred to me before.

"It's all that fresh air," I muttered, drawing the smile I was looking for from him. His smile was always a burst of sunshine, even on the darkest day. I sometimes wished I could smile like that. "It can't be good for you. Germs and viruses and God knows what all waiting there to be breathed in."

Jason stepped close to me. He handed me the camera with a grin. "I think it's healthier than city air."

"Don't believe it. Full of bugs and other unspeakable things."

"I've breathed in bugs," he said, eyes dancing. "Really, it's no big deal."

"Thanks, I think I'll pass on that experience." More and more it was becoming clear I was in an alien world. A world Jason was intimately familiar with. I wasn't used to being in that position. I wasn't sure I liked it. No, I was sure. I didn't like it. I also knew I tolerated it for Jason. Nancy had been right. What that man did to me.

Jason was still grinning when he handed me my backpack. While I shrugged it on he pulled his iPhone with its GPS locater out. Sometimes I wondered if buying it for him was an indulgence. I spoiled him rotten. I knew it, but I still couldn't stop doing it. I knew we weren't going to be here long enough to get lost. He was also quick to assure me he had a really good sense of direction and never got lost, even without mechanical help. He could have his toys because they gave him so much pleasure. Even more so when I was the giver.

"That's all of it then," he said. "We should lock up and head out."

He glanced up at the cloud-flecked sky. A cool breeze flowed off the upper slopes playing around the Tilley hat I had crammed on my head. I fumbled my shades out and slid them on, looking up to find Jason still watching me. I was still thinking about the sign we had seen on our way up here, warning about bears for the next seven miles.

"Remember, it's only eight days," he said, as though reading my mind.

I wanted to ask him how many bears could we see in a week, then he licked his lips while I was staring at his mouth.

I looked away from him, not wanting to see his tongue slide over his moist lips, think about it wrapped around my cock, doing that humming thing. I scanned the trailhead where we would leave my Toyota while we spent the next eight days hiking and camping in the forests of the Matilja Wilderness area. Already several cars occupied the unpaved lot that wasn't much more than a wide place in the road. While I cooled my over-heated libido, a Jeep pulled in amid a cloud of dust and rattling gravel. It discharged a trio, two women and a man. A hulking great German Shepherd jumped out after them. It shook itself and took up a place beside the man. The oldest woman might have been Jason's age. The other two were younger, maybe eighteen. Both women were classic Californian blonde beauties. The man could only be described as Hollywood cute. I let my gaze linger on his basket then looked up to find Jason watching me. He flashed me a knowing smile, and bent to check the laces on his Merrell's.

The trio passed near us.

The dog wandered over our way and before I could say anything, Jason was crouched down tousling the thing's ears and thick ruff. The dog grinned at him, showing an impressive array of teeth.

The dog's owner stopped between us. The older blonde smiled at me "Hey," she said.

I nodded silently. Jason straightened and stood, his hand still on top of the dog's head. "Hey, where you from?"

"Portland," she said. "We're only here for six days. We usually come for longer, but this year Brad wanted to go to Big Sur, so we stayed there a week. What about you, where do you live?"

I could see Jason was a little taken back by the girl's loquaciousness. Jason wasn't a chatterbox. It turned out this girl was. It also turned out she didn't need any encouragement to keep talking, like having someone answer her mostly rhetorical questions.

"I love this place," she gushed. "I've been coming here since I was ten. Daddy used to be a park ranger, so I got to spend all summer here. I'd live here if I could. Don't you just love it?"

"Er, yes." Jason threw me a silent plea, which I answered by smoothly stepping up.

"Pleasure to meet you, miss," I said, taking Jason's arm. "But we have to finish gearing up." I touched the brim of my Tilley. "Nice meeting you. Nice dog. Shouldn't it be on a leash?"

I knew that would piss them off and it did. The guy puffed up like a bantam, but was smart enough not to make a big deal about it. He muttered something under his breath before stalking away from us back to their Jeep. Jason gave the dog one final pat then came back over to me. He looked after the animal wistfully.

"I didn't know you liked dogs," I said, touching his arm again, not liking the way he looked at it.

"I love them. Used to have one when I was a kid. We called him Buddy. He died when I was seven. Mom wouldn't let us get another one. Said they were dirty."

The sorrow in his voice was palpable. "Why didn't you get one when you grew up? Went out on your own?"

"Where would I keep a dog? That old dump I used to live in?" He laughed, but there was pain in his voice. Pain for what he had lost? Or pain for what he might have had in another life? I knew he blamed himself for the falling out he had with his family. I wasn't quite so forgiving. I placed the blame for that solely on his unbending family, who couldn't accept a beautiful son because he was "different." I knew I had to forgive them, for his sake. Because despite it all, he desperately loved his family. He'd been so happy when his sister had made overtures to him. That those overtures had come about because of the monstrous things I did to him, didn't exactly warm my heart to them. They had been there for him when he wouldn't let me be. I had come back after all the dust had settled and he got clean. Without my help. As someone who didn't count in Jason's life at that time. A place I didn't like being.

He sighed. "It wouldn't have been a good place for a dog."

But it had been good enough for him? I wished I could have taken him in my arms, but not out here. Not in front of these people.

"Good point," was all I said. And it was. Until he had moved to Goleta to be with me, Jason had lived in a studio dive that didn't even boast a real bed. Even a Chihuahua would have been cramped there. Still, seeing the way his eyes lit up when he looked back at the Shepherd, I decided to nip that one in the bud.

"That dog should be on a leash," I muttered. "Not running around bothering people. If she's a ranger's kid she should know that."

"Yeah, I guess," was all he said. Subject closed.

I took advantage of his distraction to surreptitiously watch the trio unload their Jeep and prepare for their own hike. The man reached up to pull a large framed pack off the roof of the vehicle, exposing the brown skin of his belly. The muscles on his arms flexed and bulged as he wrestled several more pieces of gear to the ground. Apparently even the dog had a pack. At one point the younger woman looked over at us and smiled flirtatiously. I nodded in return. Jason flushed. I watched them with a cop's eye. It was second nature; something I couldn't turn off even if I wanted to. Fortunately, Jason was one of the few people I knew who didn't let it bother him. He said he enjoyed the intensity of my attention. Said it made him feel special.

That worked for me. He was very special.

He came to stand beside me. His shoulder brushed mine. "Like what you see?"

"Would it bother you if I did?" I never took my eyes off the young man.

He thought about that for several seconds, I glanced at him and could see his mind working. Then he shook his head. "No. I don't own you. I've always known that. I wouldn't like it if you did fuck someone else. I'd hate like hell to have to go back to using skins. I like having you bare. I like the way you make me feel."

We had made an agreement once we had both been tested and declared virus free, that we would only keep on having the bareback sex we liked so much if both of us stayed on the straight and narrow, and didn't fuck other people. So far, so good. To this point there wasn't anyone else I wanted to fuck.

I wasn't quite so sanguine about the thought of Jason being fucked by anyone else. Something that had gotten me into trouble before.

"What about you?" I asked. "Do you like what you see?"

He shrugged easily, his tight shoulders rolling under his cotton lumberjack shirt. "Sweet basket." He made a show of studying the man and smiled. "But not my type."

"What is your type? You better say me," I growled. "You're mine. You know that, right? You better remember I can find your ass anywhere. I got you Lojacked."

His smile when he met my gaze squarely was smug. He touched his throat where he would wear the collar I had given him nearly seven months ago. That he only wore when we were in private. I knew I was being possessive. Was that good or bad? I studied him openly, but saw nothing that suggested Jason was irritated by my words. Instead, he seemed pleased.

"Yes," he said quietly. "I remember."

I felt a lightness in my chest and managed a grin. Again, I

would have swept him into an embrace, but we were just a little too public for that. We were so lost in each other, neither one of us watched the foursome disappear down the nearest trail. At that moment a pair of hogs roared up the unpaved road and slammed to a stop less than a yard from my bumper. I glared at them as the two riders swung off their bikes and dragged visored helmets off their heads, shaking out loose, shoulder length hair. One, the bigger one of the two, was Anglo with a robust beard, the other one, younger, was Latino. They ignored both of us.

"You ready?" I asked. My skin still felt slightly tacky from the insect repellent Jason had slathered on both of us as soon as we got out of the truck. Apparently only a fool went out in this area without it. One more reason to suspect I was in the wrong place. But I had committed to this and wasn't going to show weakness by backing down, as much as I wanted nothing more than to go home to civilization. I looked over at Jason again and sighed. Wasn't going to happen. I was in this for the duration. Eight days. Surely I could do that.

I watched the two bikers warily. These were two guys we weren't going to be scoping out. I wasn't interested in getting into a rumble because one of us looked at some asshole wrong. Besides, I had agreed to Jason's request to leave my duty weapon at home, when he said it bothered him to know I was carrying. He had made a good point that it would be awkward to wear it all day long along with my pack, and I didn't dare leave it in the truck or tent when we hit the trails. So if things got nasty, we were both unarmed, something I wasn't sure could be said of this pair. I couldn't see any visible sign they were carrying, but that didn't mean squat.

They both pulled packs out of the bike storage and vanished down the same trail as the foursome. Within minutes we followed all of them.

The first stretch of path was across open land that sloped gently uphill, through fields of green, scarlet, gold and blue plants that Jason helpfully identified for me. Lupines, California poppies, wild rose and monkey flower—and something that looked suspiciously like marijuana. Jason hastily assured me it wasn't, then he laughed, "At least I don't think it is. We can smoke some to find out."

That earned a stern look from me. I didn't like reminders that there had been a time when Jason indulged in a lot worse things than marijuana.

The air was full of buzzing and trilling and sharp rustling sounds as things fled and bounced out of our path. Bees and butterflies wafted from bloom to bloom, sometimes mistaking my head for something of interest.

Jason added a new warning, "Stay on the paths. If you come across a branch or large rock in your way, step on it, not over it. Always be aware of what's on the ground around you."

"Why? What am I looking for?"

"Snakes. More specifically rattlesnakes. Probably Western Diamondback around here."

"You forgot to mention this earlier."

He shrugged. "Snakes are less of a problem than people realize. They want to leave us alone, and they will if we don't blunder into them."

"I can stay away from them just fine."

"You'll be okay, hon."

From then on my eyes were glued to the ground, watching for menacing coils waiting for my unwary foot. Flying things became a bigger problem. After I'd swatted the fifth curious bee from checking out my obviously flower shaped ear, Jason took pity on me. He handed me a small, unmarked spray bottle, which I used to douse myself with a pungent mist. It must have worked; the bees stopped pestering me.

"What is this stuff?"

"Something I made up. It's all natural," he said, swatting aside a pernicious vine that tried to entangle our ankles and take us down. "It's meant to go along with the bug lotion we used earlier. Mosquitoes are bad enough, we don't want to mess with ticks.

Give you lyme disease."

"And we leave the city for this?"

"Hey, back to our roots. Where we came from."

"Maybe you came from it." I was feeling playful, not a normal state for me. "My family's from Kansas, grandpa's outta the Bronx, you know. What do we know from wilderness?"

When he met my eyes we both grinned. He looped his arm through mine.

"Now I know where my tough guy came from."

"Yeah," I did my best to growl in a totally phony Bronx accent. "And don't fuggetit."

"Never."

Ahead of us, the path took a series of twists and turns as it headed up into the distant hills. The lower hills rolled up into green furrows that folded to gray that Jason told me were the true Wilderness areas. "Devils Heart Peak, the Sespe Condor Sanctuary," Jason said. "We can't go in there. It's protected land. I'd sure like to see one of them, though. Magnificent birds."

I looked up at the sky marbled with streaks of white. I pulled off my hat and wiped my forehead. A warm breeze whispered over my almost naked head. It felt good. "Maybe we will."

Over our heads a broad-winged bird floated, not moving its wings at all. As I watched it move in the same direction we were going, a half dozen smaller black birds came out of the trees ahead of us and dove at the larger bird, which folded its wings and dropped toward the ground. The black birds followed. They looked like the bird a killer had sent his victims during a puzzling case I'd had last year. The case where I had met Jason. Ravens. That's what they had been.

"Why are those ravens attacking that bird?"

Jason shook his head even before I finished the sentence. "Not ravens," he said. "Crows. They're mobbing that red-tail hawk. They think it might raid their nests." All at once he grinned. "You know what they call a flock of crows?"

"No," I said. "I'll bite. What do you call a flock of crows?"

"A murder."

"A murder of crows? What the hell kind of name is that?"

He shrugged. We watched the crows harry the hawk until it vanished into the trees a hundred feet above us.

"It'll take us a couple of hours to reach that," he said, pointing at the dark mass of greens, where the large bird and his tormentors had gone. "We'll start looking for a place to pitch the tent around four. That good for you?"

I wasn't sure about any of this, but I nodded and tried to think positive thoughts. Truth was I hate not being the one in charge, and Jason knew that. I also knew he was trying to make it easy for me, but there was a part of him that was enjoying this role reversal too damn much. I might just have to reclaim my status once we made camp. But I'd have to do it without any of my gear. I didn't have so much as a pair of cuffs with me. That's okay, I could assert my ownership without them. I had before. I jammed my Tilley back on my head and followed him.

After another hour of moving steadily uphill over increasingly rugged terrain, the brand new pack that had started out at forty pounds had mysteriously blossomed to at least a hundred. I was beginning to have serious doubts about my ability to do this. I wasn't the model of fitness I had thought.

I remember Nancy's remark about my domesticity. Was that what it was? I was getting soft under Jason's tender care?

That pushed me to extend myself. I'd be damned if my own body was going to fail me. The stiff breeze that was now blowing down on us wasn't enough to cool me off. Sweat poured off my face, my sleeves were saturated from wiping my forehead. Finally we started passing larger trees. Some slender green leafed trees, others twisted with age, still others slender with pale trunks, crowded the trail. One good thing, we were moving downhill again and my legs got a much needed break. Light faded and overhead flashes of sun broke through the interlaced canopy sporadically. After the brightness moments ago, I had to blink several times to see where I was going. So it was hardly surprising when I stumbled over something in my path. I twisted around sharply and only a last minute grab at a thin tree trunk kept me from pitching on my face.

Jason was at my side immediately. "You okay?"

I shook off his solicitous hand and straightened, trying to see what had tripped me. All I could make out was a tangle of undergrowth and fallen branches all woven together forming a thick mat. The air smelled heavier in here, full of rich earth scents and decaying vegetation. A somnolent buzzing filled the dimness surrounding us. There seemed to be fewer bird calls, and those I heard were deeper in. Nothing moved around us.

"Is it always this quiet? Where are all the birds?"

"It's midday, they aren't very active in the heat. Like everything else, they siesta to save energy."

"Doesn't sound like a bad idea to me," I muttered.

"There's water up ahead. We want to get across it and back up to higher ground. We can rest then."

I nodded and calculated our path. But I was hopelessly out of my element. I couldn't see where we had come from or what might lie ahead of us. Distantly, I thought I heard the sound of running water like Jason had said. Or it could have been the wind through the branches. There was a constant mutter all around, like surf. The water sounds grew louder as we made our way downhill.

"Watch your step, this area is steep."

Fortunately, there were trees and tree branches in abundance to provide hand holds to keep me from rolling down the ever steepening hill side. The underbrush grew denser too, tangling my new boots up and forcing me to slow to barely a crawl. But finally we broke out into a rocky creek bed where water danced and laughed over smooth sun-bleached rocks and the odd waist-high, bone-white boulder.

I was dismayed to realize Jason meant for us to cross the water without a bridge. I was glad for my new hiking boots. The rocks were slippery and unstable and only the good grip the boots gave me kept me from falling and breaking something. By the time we made the other side I was drenched up to my knees.

And cold. The water was like ice.

"Meltwater." Jason grinned at my discomfort and urged me on. "Almost there. Just a quick climb up and we can sit down. At least you got cooled off, right?"

Once he stopped me half way up the steep brush-covered slope and I froze without a clue to why. I heard soft bird songs, but that was about it.

"Blackback Woodpecker," he said, head cocked as though to hear something I wasn't aware of. Then something screamed and I jumped. "Scrub jay. Noisy, but a good early warning system."

"Warning for what?"

"Er, things."

"Jay," I said warningly.

He shrugged. He wasn't happy, but he said, "Bears. Cougars. People," he added hastily.

Bears again. I sighed. "Are you sure it was a good idea to leave my weapon behind?"

"Oh, that. Sure," he said laughing. "It wouldn't have been much help anyway."

"What do you mean? I'm a good shot. You know that." I was surprised that he was expressing doubt in me. Normally he knew better.

"I know you are. But a handgun isn't going to stop a charging bear. An elephant gun might. A bazooka. Not much else will."

"Oh, that's reassuring."

He slipped his arm around my shoulder and stroked my cheek. "Nothing's going to happen, Sir."

I grabbed his hand. "I'm the one who's supposed to say that."

"Yes, Sir." He smiled and looked down. His cheek had a streak of dirt on it. He looked like a chastised little kid caught being bad. I leaned forward and kissed him.

"Get us out of here," I said. "I need a drink."

By the time we scaled the miniature mountain back up to level ground I was beyond beat. The coolness of my wet legs had vanished, replaced by clamminess and sodden denim. I found the first fallen log and slumped onto it, not caring when the moist bark broke off under my butt and covered my lightly clad legs with dark, fragrant pieces, or the dampness that soaked into my ass.

Jason thrust a canteen into my hand and I guzzled the cool water down a parched throat. I sighed and handed it back to him. He took an equally deep drink.

"You did good, Sir." He studied my face and frowned. "How do you feel?"

I tipped my head back and closed my eyes, letting my hands dangle between my legs. The muscles in my thighs felt hot and tight. "Tired," I said, knowing I would never have admitted that to anyone else in the world. "I never quite realized how out of shape I am."

He tucked his canteen back onto his pack and knelt in front of me. I peered down at him through half-closed eyes. When he started massaging my legs I groaned.

The next ten minutes were sheer pleasure, greater than anything I'd ever experienced. He worked every muscle in my leg from my ankles to my butt. By the time he leaned back and flexed his fingers I felt limp.

He grabbed my hand and pulled me to my feet. "We need to keep moving. We can't pitch camp here. It won't be much longer, though. We need to find one of the water outlets. They mean we can camp."

The spot he eventually stopped us in didn't look much different than a dozen other areas, but I had to take his word on it that this was "perfect" as he said, with enthusiasm I was incapable of sharing. There was a water spigot, so we filled up both our canteens. Jason had warned me more than once that we couldn't drink from any water source but these. As if. I don't drink out of things where fish fuck or animals shit. We had included some water purification tablets in our packs, but Jason said he didn't want to use them unless it was absolutely necessary.

According to Jason, one person could assemble the tent we bought. Good thing too, since I'm not sure how much help I was. We ate a cold supper that night, which included splitting a banana and a peach he had sliced up and stored in a baggy. Neither of us had the energy left to build a fire and cook anything. After making sure no traces of food remained out to tempt prowling wildlife, we slipped inside the tent that was barely as big as our bed at home. He insisted we strip and put on the long johns he had brought against my will. I'd never even owned a pair of the ridiculous things, but he said it wasn't smart to sleep nude like we did at home. So I pulled them on and grumpily climbed into the sleeping bag, only slightly mollified when he joined me and we spooned.

I had forgotten all about reasserting my position and found sleep overcoming me almost immediately. A crescendo of crickets and tree frogs followed me down into darkness. But it was the soft sound of Jason's breathing in my ear that comforted me most.

I woke to the delicious feel of Alex's cock pressed between the crack of my ass. At some point he had pulled my long john's down. His mouth slid over the back of my neck, nuzzling and licking me behind my left ear.

Fingers twisted my nipple ring hard, sending a jolt of pure pain and exquisite pleasure straight to the root of my cock. I groaned and arched against him, letting him know I was fully awake.

Without a word he pushed his fat dick past my tight anal ring, slamming up my channel with a grunt. He rode me hard and fast, rocking into me, skimming his fist around my cock and bringing me to a numbing climax seconds after he came inside me.

After he withdrew and I rolled over to look up at him, he gave me a lazy, sated grin.

"I see a good night's sleep agrees with you," I said.

"Slept like a baby." He reached for his glasses.

I looked down at his limp cock. "Sure don't wake up like one."

He ran stiff fingers through my short hair, tilting my head back so he could study my face before kissing me soundly. "No, I don't. What's for breakfast, boy?"

I scrambled into clothes and climbed out of the tent. Alex was at my heels, tucking his pant legs into his boot tops like I had told him, to keep out bugs and prickly seeds. He left his plaid shirttail out and his sleeves rolled up over his muscular arms. I stepped into the woods to take care of business after warning Alex to watch out for poison oak. It was barely dawn. The crisp morning air was cool and alive with bird song. Without even trying, I heard an orange-crowned warbler, and a mountain quail, along with the usual complaining jays. The air carried a bevy of odors from all around us. Pine resin from upslope, sage, creosote and mulch from the meadows beyond the riparian woods we were in. Somewhere, the smoke from a fire. We weren't alone on the mountain. Like you could actually be alone anywhere in California these days. As long as they weren't parked next to us, and they didn't make a stink about two guys sharing a small tent, I didn't care.

I saw Alex with the camera, taking candid shots of me as I got things ready for our breakfast.

I pulled my backpack down from the tree I had stashed ours in and rummaged through it. Digging out the battered cooking pot I'd hung onto even after years of not using it, I got a fire going and soon had coffee brewing; if you can call dumping a mound of coffee into the pot and covering it with enough water to give us each a cup brewing coffee. Dehydrated eggs and the last of the fresh fruit we had carried in with us was breakfast.

He made a face when I served him the coffee. "Sorry, no Starbucks up here." I waved toward the slope we had climbed up yesterday. "Before we strike camp we can go down there and splash water on our faces."

He grimaced.

"Get used to a whole new level of clean." I grinned. "Good thing I like the way you smell."

He grimaced some more and buried his nose in his tin mug. But I could tell he was pleased. I hoped he liked the way I smelled, too.

Packing up took at least fifteen minutes longer than it would have taken me on my own, but I knew better than to make Alex feel helpless or incompetent. Once our gear was on our backs and I made sure everything we'd brought in was coming out with us, I did something I should have done from the beginning. I scoured the forest floor until I found four walking sticks. When I handed two to him he looked at them, then at me dubiously.

"They're improvised Nordic walking poles. If I'd been thinking I'd have picked up the real thing." He demonstrated how to use them. "Trust me, climbing up and down hills will be a lot easier with these. Gives you better balance. And they're a great all body workout. Get those lats and core muscles in shape."

He tested his like I'd showed him, seemed satisfied and waved me to go ahead of him.

"I'd like to follow the water, if that's okay with you." I hefted my brand new Nikon binoculars that Alex had bought for me. "See a lot more around water."

He nodded and flexed his legs a few times to stretch what were no doubt sore muscles from yesterday's hike. I added an incentive.

"I think there's a pool further up. We can stop and do a quick cleanup if you're interested. Just no hanky-panky. Chances are we won't be alone for long."

"I'll save the hanky-panky for tonight, then." And there was dark promise in his intense look. I got hard just thinking about it.

"Well, Sir," I said softly. "Let's get on the road so tonight comes sooner, why don't we? We have a long way to go today. I'd like to try for at least ten miles."

Our time was slow in the beginning. I knew Alex was probably stiff from his unfamiliar workout yesterday and face it, I was too. What with school and the demands of taking care of Alex and our home, I hadn't done as much hiking lately as I would have liked. We both needed to get our sea legs.

I paused frequently, ostensibly to scan the overhead limbs and nearby bushes for elusive birds, but also to give us both a break. At one point, I followed the chattering call of a mountain quail and found a female and her newly hatched brood. When I pointed them out to Alex he gave me a big dopey smile as a reward. Even hardened police detectives can be charmed by half a dozen one-ounce balls of fluff scurrying after their more sedate black and gray mom.

Ahead of us, golden sun streaked through a break in the trees. Dust motes and flying insects danced in the still air while nearby, something croaked. As the day lengthened and the heat mounted, cicadas began their electronic singing.

It wasn't long before I cracked open the bug lotion and we paused long enough to cover each other in the gel. My hair was plastered to my scalp. Even Alex had sweat collecting under his armpits and trickling down his face.

"Almost there," I muttered when I heard the change in pitch from the steady whisper of moving water to our left. "Want to head down?"

He nodded and I led the way downhill. A gangly, brown shape flew across our path, darting under a dense cluster of gray-green brush. Twigs rattled, then quieted as the rabbit passed. Then just as we started down again the most God awful scream rent the air.

We both froze, hearts trip hammering behind tense rib cages. The sound was not repeated. Belatedly, I realized what it was.

Alex started off the path toward the sound. "What the hell was that?"

"The rabbit. They scream like that."

"A rabbit? You're telling me that was a rabbit?"

"I know. It spooked me the first time I heard one. Thought some kid was being murdered. But trust me, it's nothing."

Alex came back, grumbling. I thought I caught something about cities being a whole lot safer. There the only thing screaming were people, and he knew how to deal with that.

It took us another twenty minutes to find the pool, a collection of water ranging from a few inches to several feet deep. It only took another five to get down to our skivvies and plunge in to the icy bath. I shuddered and braced myself to duck my head under, holding it for the count of ten, then lunged to the surface and shook myself like a dog. Alex did the same, gasping for breath when he came back out of the water. We ended up sitting side by side on a large boulder at the head of the pool, dangling bare feet in the water. Sun reached us through breaks in the leafy canopy. A faint breeze danced over our bare skin, cool at first, then as we dried it grew pleasantly warm. Across the pool a scattering of rushes and cattails swayed in the soft, gentle wind. A frog croaked and dragonflies buzzed the smooth surface in search of lunch.

Alex lay back on the rock, hands laced behind his head. His eyes were half closed.

I rolled onto my elbow to stare down at his sculptured chest with its dark, jutting nipples. When he lay on his back, the extra flesh around his middle was less obvious. I stared at his navel, and the line of hair there. Glancing around quickly to make sure no one else was around, I followed the swirl of reddish hair covering his chest with two fingers and arrowed down to disappear under the waistband of his jockeys. Knowing what was under there in no way dampened my desire to see it again. I swallowed against the sudden rush of desire.

He grabbed my hand before I could go any further.

"No hanky-panky, remember?"

"This isn't hanky-panky," I murmured, lightly stroking the outline of his swelling cock with the hand he still held. "This is." I leaned over and pressed my mouth against his pubic bone where a pulse beat and quickened under my lips. I licked his water-cooled skin before straightening. "See the difference?"

The swollen head of his erection poked out of his underwear. A single drop of fluid leaked from the slit. Before I could take it any further and damn the consequences, he scrambled to his feet and without warning, cannonballed into the deepest part of the pool. A geyser of ice cold water erupted, covering my newly dried, and sun-warmed skin.

"Cool your jets, mountain boy," he said when he returned to the surface.

I wiped water out of my eyes and squinted through a prism of water droplets at him. Rainbow drops of water sculptured his body. God, he looked good. I don't care that he thought he was getting soft. I didn't care that he didn't look like a swimsuit model or that he thought he had to wear his shirts untucked to hide his growing love handles. I just wished I could prove that to him.

Well, maybe this week, away from the distractions of home and work, would give me a chance to convince him. We weren't going to have any other diversions but each other.

Things were still so tentative between us. I always sensed Alex held back, afraid he would lose control again like he had in the beginning, when his jealousy had boiled over into violence that he still hadn't forgiven himself for. It didn't seem to do any good to tell him I wasn't afraid of him, that I craved his touch, even his pain. He gave me some of both, but in the end, always held back from giving me all of what I needed.

I hated that. I wanted the Alex I had fallen in love with back, unafraid, sure of what he did and knowing it was the right thing. The Alex who never had to second guess his actions.

But how the hell did I convince him of that?

Jason had no idea how much I wanted to drag him into the water with me and fuck him hard and rough, screw anybody who might stop us. But I held back. Like I held back a lot these days. I wanted to release the fever that burned in me whenever Jason hung from my sling or my leather restraints, but when I thought of reaching for the lash or the strap or the candle, a spark of fear flared in me. What if I couldn't stop, like had almost happened that day so long ago when I had beat him black and blue, and all for something he hadn't even done. I had discovered that day I was capable of stupid things, at least when it came to this man. Things I never wanted to visit on him or me again.

I knew he wanted my lash, just as he craved the pain of my domination, and I gave it to him, to a point. It was that point that was driving a wedge between us. I knew it. Jason knew it. Could we fix it? I knew I wanted to. But the fear was still there, untapped and unexplored. Unacknowledged in most cases, since I refused to admit the weakness of fear to anyone, even Jason.

Wading through the frigid water, I scrambled up on the rocks and grabbed my clothes. Jason followed. He pulled the bug repellent out and slathered more on both of us. We were silent as we dressed and hefted our packs onto our backs. I shoved my Tilley over my still wet hair, grabbed my walking sticks and headed, first along the banks of the fast moving stream, then climbing back up to the forest floor. We paused frequently while Jason scanned the trees for something he saw or heard. He would point out and name a bird, and I would try to catch a glimpse of it. Even when he passed me his binoculars, I never had much luck. All I could see was a richness of green, in every shade. I couldn't tell one tree from the next. All the green clustered around the trunks and covering the ground looked the same. Occasionally, a flash of color would blur across my field of vision, but never long enough for me to really see it.

Jason would give me a name – yellow warbler, house wren, plain titmouse, which made me wonder, were there fancy titmouse – or was it titmice? And what kind of name was titmouse, anyway? None of it was familiar. Where were the gulls or the pigeons or even the black birds that were ubiquitous in the city? Instead of becoming more familiar with time, everything grew more and more alien to my city trained eyes. Even in Kansas City I'd stayed inside the urban zone until my ill-advised marriage led us to California. My wife, Barbara, had never been an outdoor girl either. So even then we had rarely gone beyond the city limits, unless it was a trip to L.A. where she could shop and have dinner out somewhere down on Melrose, or someplace else trendy that she heard about in *L.A. Weekly*. "In civilization," as she'd often said.

I pretended enthusiasm for what Jason loved, hell I pretended to see what he was pointing out. My eyes just didn't work like his. But it was fun to listen to him chatter away, even if I didn't understand half of what he said. Jason had been a shy, very unsure, undisciplined sub when I'd first met him. He had blossomed since then, taken control of his life, even as he handed control of his body over to me.

When he stopped talking and moving I almost plowed into him. I had to grab his hips to keep from knocking both of us over, losing one of my walking sticks. He barely noticed. He had his glasses to his face, staring intently into the area above us. I tried to see what he was seeing. I might have seen a flicker of movement but that was all.

Finally he lowered his binoculars. He glanced back at me, his face aglow.

"A Northern Parula. I've never seen one before."

"One for the life list, then." I knew all about the life list he'd been building for years. A list of every bird he'd ever seen. I guess birders got pretty excited over those things. Personally I couldn't see the attraction, but I didn't need to. It was enough that it made Jason happy and lit up like it did.

The discovery seemed to give him renewed energy. He scrambled to the top of the ravine leading us through the trees over what he said were trails, though I couldn't always see them. All through the trees we heard jays screaming. They had to be one of the most vocal birds I've ever heard. Bad tempered too, it turned out.

Memories of our cool dip faded as the strain on my overworked muscles grew. Even with the walking sticks I was losing my balance more often on the uneven ground. Finally I called for a break. I leaned the sticks against a massive oak trunk. Gulping down mouthfuls of cool water, I wiped the sweat off my brow and began doing stretches to loosen up my muscles, knowing our hike wasn't over.

I barely saw a flash of movement out of the corner of my eye. I've got fast reflexes – to be a living cop in a city like Santa Barbara you have to – and I ducked and looked for what was attacking me, damning myself for not carrying. For being out here unarmed. The shadow came back, screaming, and I barely had time to recognize the jay before I had to duck again. Cursing, I grabbed my walking stick and swung it through the air. This time instead of attacking me the damn bird landed on a branch above my head and scolded me.

It didn't help that Jason was bent over, barely holding in his mirth.

"What?" I growled, not sure who I was maddest at, him or the bird. It seemed like they were both having a good laugh at my expense.

"She must think you're getting too close to her nest."

"Well I have no interest in eating her or her fucking eggs—" The bird dove at my head again. "But if it's going to bother her that much, I'll leave."

I don't back down from punks or tweakers or armed psychos, but I found myself retreating through a leafy forest while a three-ounce bird screamed at me. I'm convinced the damn thing was laughing at me the whole time. I know Jason was.

Finally, we left the bird behind and Jason stopped giggling. He sidled over to me.

"We should think of finding a place to pitch camp. I'd like to make a fire tonight. I've got Mexican rice with beef, or Thai satay. Your pleasure."

"My pleasure would be to cook up that fucking bird and chew on her bones."

"I thought you didn't want to eat her or her family."

"I changed my mind."

That set him off again. After a while I had to join him. It was damned funny, when I thought about it. He was still smiling when we set off. An hour later we finally found a spigot of fresh water and a spot hidden by a cluster of trees that Jason said would suit us. I was a little more help this time. The tent was up, our supplies looted and a fire started in the firepit in short order. Jason explained that there was currently no drought, so fires were okay. "But then," he added, "if it wasn't, we wouldn't be here. Too dangerous to be up here during a fire season."

Far off, a dog barked. I thought of the unleashed Shepherd we had seen and figured the trio of young people were nearby. Hopefully not too near. I really didn't want this night to be interrupted. I filled the two lightweight pots we had carried with us while Jason set up the grill. I had been amazed at the amount of stuff we were able to fit in our backpacks. Enough for hot meals, if you didn't mind freeze-dried, which turned out not to be as bad as I thought it would be. Even with limited gear and ingredients, Jason produced a meal that filled me up and left me full and sleepy. I found a comfortable spot on a broad tree stump where I could lean back against a fallen tree and stare into the fire that Jason built up once the grill was cleaned and put away.

Normally, our evenings at home were spent in front of the TV watching one of my classic movies or, on the rare occasion, something newer that Jason ordered from Netflix. I used to control what we watched all the time, but since his taste had matured I let him pick a movie – sometimes.

Once the fire was going he came over and sat on the ground between my legs. I rested my hands on his shoulders, every so often squeezing them, massaging his collarbone and neck with my thumbs and fingers. The fire was mesmerizing. There were a couple of patches of sky visible through the canopy overhead, mercifully free of birds or other impertinent animals. Jason's head tilted back. He stared avidly up. Every so often his gaze would wander my way; he always found me watching him instead of the stars.

"This is nice, isn't it?"

"Mmm," I murmured, not really wanting to break the silence and talk.

Nearby, an owl hooted, a solemn, eerie question thrown into the darkness. No one answered.

Jason tilted his head sideways rubbing his cheek against my thigh. I stroked his ear, tracing the outline of it, then slid around to cup his chin. He turned his head abruptly and took my thumb into his mouth, sucking on it gently. I closed my eyes at the rush of desire his simple touch could evoke in me.

Sometimes the depth of feelings I had for this man scared me beyond measure. It would be so easy to lose myself in him. I'd never surrendered myself to another person that way, or any way. This was serious. This was something forever. I think that made me more nervous than anything that had come before this. It made me wonder how easy it would be to walk away and spare myself future loss of control. What you can't control, you can't own. How much safer it would be to reclaim myself by giving him up.

Not going to happen. The thought was fierce and cold. He must have sensed something because he drew away from me, turning all the way around to look up at me. His eyes were clear and guileless.

"Alex?"

"Nothing." I urged him to sit back, returned to stroking his soft skin, feeling the rasp of day old beard on his chin, knowing I would feel the same. Without another word I bent over and touched my lips to his. I flicked my tongue out to taste him. He tasted of wood smoke and coffee and Jason.

Part of me wanted to drag him into the tent, fuck him roughly and silently to erase the thoughts in my head. I didn't move. Instead I kept circling his chin and throat with my fingers, lingering on his mouth occasionally, feeling him suck one digit or another. The forest filled with the sounds of night. Crickets serenaded each other, tree frogs sang. Something buzzed in the canopy overhead. Every so often something small and hard would smack into the trees or fire and burst into flame. I tried to see what the kamikaze creatures were but couldn't. Finally Jason said, "June bugs. Don't let them land on you. They bite."

"Oh, do they. Another dangerous critter. This place is more hazardous than the streets."

Jason smiled. Under my fingertips he was humming again. I was rock hard and painfully constricted in my jeans. But nothing on earth would have made me move at that moment. The torture was exquisite.

He knew I was hard. He couldn't help but know it. I must have felt like a furnace against his skin. His head moved from side to side, managing to caress me with gentle pressure. Soon, the dampness from my precum would seep through, and he would know how far gone I was.

Seconds before I had taken as much as I could and was going to drag him to his feet, he turned over onto his knees, pressing his mouth against the wet spot over my denim covered cock. His hands came up to knead my thighs. I was intensely aware of his delicate touch as he slid the button of my fly open and eased the zipper down over my swollen cock. Then his wet, hot tongue was on my slit, lapping up precum, circling the glistening head. His lips closed over my prick. I moaned and opened my legs wider, silently urging him on. He obeyed and swallowed me to the root, his agile tongue slipping wetly up and down my veined cock, then swallowing me again. When he tugged on my jeans, I rose off the stump and he pulled them down, moving away from me long enough for him to jerk them over my hips. He pushed stiff fingers up under my balls, playing with the perineum, exploring me. I raised my hips off the tree trunk inviting him to investigate deeper. He did with enthusiasm. But without taking my boots and jeans off he couldn't go further, and I didn't want his mouth off me. He continued pumping along the length of my erection. His tongue stroked the sensitive underside of my dick and tasted my precum. I moaned and thrust into the heat of his mouth. This time when he started humming deep in his throat, I lost it. My fingers dug into his scalp, rocking him mindlessly up and down on my cock again and again until I came, pouring cum down his throat which convulsed as he drank me in.

I shuddered when he pulled off me, resting his head on my leg. I stroked his short hair, loving the crisp texture.

The owl was back. I lurched to my feet, tucked myself back in and zipped up. Reaching down, I pulled Jason up with me. I wrapped him in my embrace, nuzzling his throat, sliding my tongue into his mouth, tasting myself. "Let's put things away," I said. "Call it a night."

He went over to tend to the fire, I packed up all the gear, putting the food in the lightweight bear safe, making sure there were no traces of food anywhere that might attract the wrong kind of attention. Finally, everything was put away and we retreated to the tent. Again we found ourselves spooning through a night of deep sleep, waking in the same position we had fallen asleep in.

At dawn I tried to move on top of him, wanting to finish what we had started the night before, but every muscle in my body, except my swollen cock, was aflame. Before I could stop it, I groaned. Instantly Jason was leaning over me. He knew immediately what was wrong. He gently pushed me onto my stomach and held me down when I tried to sit up.

"Lie still." Not used to Jason ordering me to do anything, I froze. He took advantage of my confusion and, stripping my long johns off, massaged my calves, kneading and prodding my stiff muscles hard enough to cause agony, slowly working up until he was digging his fingers into my buttocks. My erection was long gone. He wasn't gentle; I ground my teeth but didn't beg him to stop.

Finally he sat back on his heels. "I'm going to make coffee and pull together some breakfast."

I flipped over onto my back and lay there enjoying the absence of pain. If Jason hadn't been so quick to leave I might have tried to finish what I had started, but he was gone, so reluctantly I climbed into my clothes and followed him outside. I drank two cups of atrocious coffee and chewed on dried fruit and breakfast bars while sitting on my tree stump. Jason bustled around the campsite putting everything away and packing up. He took both canteens down to the water spigot and was filling them when the squirrels first appeared. Two of them, tag-teaming each other through our encampment, one gray, one black. The gray had a massive plume of a tail, nearly white, the black one had a wispy thing, more rat tail than squirrel. Did that make him a squirrel loser? An animal nerd? Watching them, I finally understood the phrase greased lightning. Those things moved *fast*.

Up a tree, over intertwining branches, down the walls of our tent. I could hear the scritch-scritch of their tiny claws on the tent canvas. The gray launched himself into the air, bouncing off the top of the tent, sailing over the black squirrel's head and landed smack in the middle of my lap. Needle sharp claws scrabbled for purchase on my jeans, digging into my still tender balls. I tumbled backward, startled at the assault. Before I could sit up the animal was gone, flying off me, landing on the tree trunk above my head. I stared up at it. I swear those beady little eyes glared back at me. Pissed that I was occupying his space, interrupting his rumble? His tail flicked over his back, froze, then flicked again. And again. The black scampered away. The gray chittered at me.

"Bring it on," I said. I cupped my balls and readjusted them, trying to ease the bruising pain the squirrel assault had caused. "You going to chase me around next?"

The squirrel chirred little squirrely curses.

"You know in any other place I'd have my gun with me," I said. Gray stopped chittering, cocked his head at me then started up again. Not impressed. "It's a Beretta 9 mil and while some pundits will tell you the Glock is a finer weapon, I do very well with my Beretta. I'm a trophy-holding marksman. If it was with me I'd have your little squirrel brains plastered all over that tree trunk you're sitting on."

"You're threatening squirrels now?" Jason came up behind me and slid his arms around my waist. For a moment all three of us, two men and a squirrel, were motionless. Then the squirrel flipped his tail over his head one more time, gave me one last evil eye and vanished up the tree.

"The magic Spider touch," Jason said solemnly, then his face split into a huge grin. I couldn't help it, I smiled back, sore balls forgotten.

"Tell me, are there any more demented animals I should know about who could possibly be after my testicles? Manic-depressive mice? Am I going to be mobbed by a battalion of butterflies? A squadron of shrews? A murder of crows?"

"A quartet of quarrelsome quail," he added helpfully. "A round of rowdy robins... "

"A medley of mad mooses?"

"Mooses? I don't think you'll find any of them around here."

"Okay," I said. "No mooses, moose, meese, whatever. But—"

Barking broke through our levity. This time it sounded a lot closer than before. It had a frantic edge to it. My cop senses went into alert. The dog hadn't seemed the hyper type when we'd first seen it in the car lot, assuming it was the same dog.

I stood up. "Let's finish up here and go."

This time it took us less than ten minutes to pack up and hoist our gear on to our shoulders.

We headed toward where the barking had come from. It didn't come again.

Bird songs followed us as we made our way upslope, the dog forgotten. The landscape changed, the trees became less deciduous and more coniferous; lodgepole, fir and towering ponderosa pines, interspersed with the occasional jack pine, and the even rarer aspen. My massage must have worked; Alex was striding along behind me, keeping up to me as spry as I'd ever seen him. In fact there was almost a spring to his step. I really hoped he was enjoying himself. It meant a lot to me that he grow to love the things I did. Not only so we could share, but so he'd understand the love I had for the simple things, like a vigorous hike through forest trails, perhaps seeing a bird I had never seen before. I wanted to be able to talk to him about these things and know he understood, even if he didn't share my birding quirks.

But even though I'd known Alex now for nearly eight months, he remained an enigma to me. Would there ever come a time I understood him? Or would that ruin it all? If I understood what made Alexander Spider tick would the mystique be gone? Would he become just an ordinary man? I looked up at him, at his broad shoulders and still narrow waist. I stared at the hollow of his back, where his spine merged into the top of his ass, a spot I loved to lick on my way to other treasures. Whenever I did he always made the softest gasp as though I had applied an electric charge to his skin. Ordinary man? There would never be anything ordinary about this man.

I caught up to him and when he looked over at me, I captured a quick kiss from startled lips.

"What was that for?"

"For being you."

"Oh, well, that's not much of an accomplishment. I can do that in my sleep."

Still, he seemed pleased, and the Alex I had first met would never have given even that much away. Detective Spider was a man who kept things close to his chest.

"How far do you plan to take us today?"

"At the rate we're going now, I think we can do twelve miles. I'm hoping to do better tomorrow. How are you feeling?'

He thought for a second. Another Spider trait, he never answered even a simple question quickly. Eventually he nodded. "Good. Better than I expected."

"I'm glad. You're tough, Sir."

"You mean I'm better adjusted."

"I had to get acclimated, too. I haven't done this sort of hike in…" I thought hard and was surprised at the answer. "Years. Long before I met you."

"Why did it take you so long to come back?"

I shrugged, not liking it when the conversation turned to the life I had been falling into when I first met Alex. "Circumstances," I said uneasily. "I like having companionship when I'm hiking. For safety reasons it's best not to be alone."

I saw the spark of his jealousy and hastened to add, "Never with anyone special. Just…friends." Friends I had succeeded in driving away with my reckless behavior and the growing frequency of my drug and sex binges. The kind of friends I had attracted then weren't the type to indulge in communing with nature except in the most basic, chemical and lust driven sense.

Ahead of us came the sharp snap of a tree branch. Scuffle of heavily booted feet and soft guttural voices. Alex tensed beside me seconds before the two hog riders we had encountered in the trailhead parking lot strode into view. They stopped when they saw us.

I don't know if they made Alex as a cop, but their tension jacked up and hardened. It was Alex who broke the tableau. He stepped forward, hands spread at his side. Assuring them he wasn't armed? Was that a good idea? Then again, making them more nervous by having them think either one of us was dangerous also wouldn't be good. I decided to trust Alex. He knew these kind of people better than I did.

The taller of the two, a dark giant, who had thick hair swept back off his forehead, his cotton shirt open to reveal a thick mat of hair over a heavily tattooed chest, took a step ahead of the smaller man, standing partially in front of him. The Latino crowded in behind him. The leather jacket he had been wearing the first time I saw him was folded up on his backpack. I was glad they hadn't shown up a minute ago. I can't imagine what their reaction would have been to us kissing.

Then I noticed something. The two were standing close, not quite touching, but closer than men usually stood together, way inside any kind of personal space. And I would have sworn the bigger guy had taken a protective stance over the other one. The same time I was studying them, they watched us. A light seemed to dawn on all of us at the same time. Their tension relaxed. I offered the smaller man a genuine smile. One sub to another.

The Latino looked Alex up and down with active interest. "Been here long?" he asked with studied casualness and only the barest touch of accent.

"Couple of days." Clearly, they hadn't noticed us in the car lot.

The dark giant stepped forward and held out his hand. "Hawk. This is CJ."

We nodded. I relaxed a bit more; Alex didn't. Alex was all protective cop. "Alex and Jason," he said.

Hawk's gaze drilled into Alex. "You a cop?"

"Yeah."

"LAPD?"

"Nah, Santa Barbara. Homicide."

"Nice town," CJ said and all of us nodded. Suddenly he seemed uneasy. "Say, you being a cop, maybe you heard it, too."

"Heard what?"

"Last night? You hear anything?"

"No." Alex and I traded glances. "Hear what?"

It was obvious Hawk hadn't wanted to say anything but now he frowned and said, "I heard a gunshot. So did CJ. You?"

Alex stiffened. "No," he said slowly. "We didn't hear anything, did we, Jason?"

"Nothing." I think both of us had gone out like lights after the blowjob I had given Alex. I know I hadn't heard anything else until Alex's pain-filled groan this morning.

"When was this?" Alex went right back into cop mode. "Could you tell where it came from? A single shot? Multiple? Any idea what caliber—"

"Whoa. Don't go all cop on us," Hawk seemed put out. Not used to cooperating with the police? Most bikers didn't have good experiences with the law. "I heard a single shot, that's all. Up here, good luck trying to figure out where a sound comes from. Could have been the next ravine over, could have been a mountain away. Sounds are weird up here, y'know?"

Proving he had some experience with this area. He was right, the configuration of the land and the dense tree growth could both muffle and amplify sound, and completely distort its source.

"You ever hear a gunshot before?" Alex asked.

They both nodded and CJ added, "We're from Boyle Heights. Hear lots of gunshots."

"This was a single shot," Hawk said. "Probably handgun, decent caliber. Maybe even a Glock or Sig."

Alex was impressed, then wary. "You know guns."

"Military," Hawk said. "Army grunt for three years. Got to Private First Class then I got dumped on account of Don't ask, Don't tell."

"You heading down the mountain, then?" Alex asked.

"Got to. Work tomorrow. 'Sides, ain't neither of us armed, I don't want to be around if some crazy ass-nut job is on the loose. Man could get hurt that way."

I could see Alex's mind turning. "Well, do me a favor. When you get down, stop at the ranger's office, give them a report. Tell them Detective Alexander Spider is up here but they may want to send one of theirs up to look around."

Hawk shrugged then nodded. "Sure, guess I can do that." He and CJ turned back down the mountain. "Good luck."

Once they were out of hearing I turned toward him, puzzled. "You didn't tell him you were unarmed. Shouldn't the rangers know that?"

"I never tell anyone I'm not carrying. Not a thing I want others to know."

"Should we be worried?"

He shrugged. "A single gunshot hardly constitutes a crime spree. There are shooting ranges up here. Someone might have kept their weapon on them when they went outside the range. It's legal to pack now in national parks. Some idiot could be playing around, fired accidentally. It happens. We'll keep our eyes open." He tugged my hand and pulled me against him. "Besides, you're safe with me, you know that, don't you?"

I enjoyed the embrace and he was right, I did feel safe. "Sure."

"Then let's go. I need to stretch these legs out before they go stiff on me again."

"Well, I'm always available for a massage."

"I'll take you up on that later."

We concentrated on making good time. Around noon we stopped for a quick lunch of trail mix, dried fruit and a generous amount of water. With our packs lightened, our pace picked up. I tended to keep us close to water when I could, where I was more likely to spot interesting birds.

And they were out in abundance. Late spring, early summer was a good time for birding. Birds still in breeding plumage, nests full of newly hatched eggs and a lot of mouths to feed meant more activity, which meant a better chance of spotting them. A tiny gray Bell's vireo made an appearance, then a pale olive Willow flycatcher. Alex stoically followed me, feigning an interest in each bird as I spotted it when I knew he had no real interest. But he was here with me, and seemed to be enjoying the walking part of our hike. He had complained to me lately that he was spending way too much time desk bound at work and when we both came home from our busy days, sometimes the last thing we wanted to do was get physical. We needed to change that. I'd have to suggest doing something like this more often. Get us both back into shape.

We crossed over another ridge, and this time the sound of rushing water below was strong. Alex could tell just by the look on my face that I wanted to go down, though the slope looked steeper than previous ones.

First, he parked himself on a fallen tree stump, pulled off his pack and patted the spongy surface next to him. "Let's take a break. Drink." He pulled out his canteen and drank deeply. I followed suit, then pulled out a sealed plastic baggie of trail mix. We chewed on that for a while, enjoying the cool breeze that flowed over our sweaty skin. He took his hat off and set it on his lap.

We capped off our canteens, knowing we'd have to find some more on the other side, but for now the lighter load was a relief.

Taking a firm grip on my walking sticks I walked over to study the ravine before we took the plunge. I could see the beginning of a few easy paths down, but in two cases the paths dwindled and became dense, impenetrable brush. We might be able to bull our way through, but why bother? There were other, more efficient ways to get down there.

I pointed out the path I had plotted in my head. It switched back and forth, using tree trunks as guides and hand holds on the way down. If I calculated right, we'd probably end up about fifty feet north of our present position. Below, the steady whispery roar of fast moving water could be heard. Even from here I could see a lot of dead fall. Trees had come down, probably last winter, and hadn't been cleaned up by the forest crew who would remove most of them as potential fire hazards, leaving a few as nursery logs for new growth.

"Be careful at the bottom. It will probably be slippery, and might be unstable, too. Last thing we want is for either of us to get caught up in a dead fall. Those things can be nasty. It's not long after the last thaw upstream. The water's likely to have eroded the banks or loosened some of the stones. It could be a mess down there."

It was a good thing we both had sturdy boots. We took our time; I went first, making heavy use of my walking sticks to test the ground in front of my feet, frequently adjusting my path to avoid loose or tangled spots. Even with all my precautions I did my share of slipping and sliding, catching myself at the last minute on anything I could grab. Sweat poured off my face and down my back, sticky and rank, attracting hordes of insects, who ignored the bug spray I had put on hours ago. Behind me Alex cursed and slapped at his own tormentors.

Snags and masses of collapsed trees and tangled limbs forced us further and further upstream. I kept throwing Alex encouraging smiles, but he seemed okay with the exertion. Whether that was stoicism or he really was adjusting even I couldn't tell. I sure as hell couldn't ask.

We were three quarters of the way to the bottom and a good seventy feet from where we had started when I fell. Both of my walking sticks caught on something and were wrenched out of my hands. The action threw me off balance and I stepped back to catch myself. My feet skidded on the wet, tractionless slope and I went down, bouncing and rolling until I came up against a tree trunk with a solid oomph. Alex was kneeling beside me in an instant.

"You okay? You hurt? Can you get up?"

Except for my dignity, I was fine. I let him help me to my feet where I stood slapping mud and decaying plant matter off my khaki pants. My knees were saturated and the dampness was seeping through to my bare skin. All I succeeded in doing was transferring the stinking mess onto my hands making them wet and cold and dirty, too.

"I'm fine, thanks," I said after checking myself out for injuries. Besides a bruised ego, there were none. I grimaced down at my befouled hands and pants. "Maybe I can wash up a bit down there."

He nodded and went to retrieve my fallen staffs. We kept climbing down, with a little more care this time. My little tumble had reminded us that we were vulnerable up here. There were no EMTs standing by or Red Cross stations anywhere near here. We had to take care of ourselves. Finally, we reached the edge of the stream, a rocky stretch of fast moving water that roared and whispered over what looked like a giant's game of marble toss. Like someone had been playing with a handful of rocks, then had grown bored and left them scattered willy-nilly behind him when he left. Pebbles the size of pea sand made the streambed treacherous, large boulders as big as smart cars guided the flowing water into pools and mini rapids. I found the deepest area and gingerly waded in. Even though I was prepared for it, the icy water was a shock. I endured as long as it took to rinse my clothes and hands clean then I hurried across and pulled myself up onto dry land. I perched on a large flat rock waiting for Alex, who chose a shallower fording spot. I took advantage of the break to scan the surrounding trees, spotting a pair of towhees as well as a hunting falcon far above us, over the treetops. Still no sign of the one bird I'd love to see, the California condor, still one of the rarest birds in the world.

The climb back up proved easier. We found a steady supply of trees and sturdy brush to grab onto. Within ten minutes we were back on relatively level ground. I was pleased to note that neither one of us was winded. We shared a grin and a drink, then set off.

As we walked I looked up at what little sky I could make out. It was well past noon. "We have at least another four hours or so we can travel if you're up for it."

"I'm good."

The next stretch of terrain wasn't too challenging. We made great time. Better than I'd hoped. I was sure we managed a good nine, ten miles. We stopped at a water spigot and topped up our flasks as well as filling up our stomachs. After crossing another cutback I knew Alex was flagging again. Not wanting him to have to admit he couldn't go much longer, I stopped and stretched, touching my toes to stretch out overused muscles, feigning a groan.

Alex's hand was on my back before I straightened. "Everything all right?"

"Yeah, I'm good." I grimaced and shrugged my backpack off. "I don't know about you, but I'm ready to call it a night."

He looked around warily as though expecting something to come charging out of the deepening shadows that grew and swallowed the forest around us. "This a good place to stop?"

I swung around, checking out the landscape. Then I pointed north, to where an old growth tree must have come down recently, leaving a clearing only now being repopulated with young ponderosa and jack pines, all rushing to be the first to reach the sky, to overshadow its slower growing rivals. The winner of that race would grow to massive proportions over the decades, unless some disease or misfortune brought it down prematurely. But right now it was a good place to pitch our tent. A protected opening in the tangled forest.

It took us next to no time to get the tent up, our packs stowed and our cold supper in our stomachs. Before total darkness fell, we crawled into the tent and sealed it up behind us.

I moved to pull on my long johns. A hand snaked out of the darkness and stopped my hand.

"No you don't," Alex whispered. "Not yet."

He swept clothing and sleeping bag aside and held me down with his greater weight. Not that I was fighting. Not for real, at least. A little struggle is good for inducing passion. I bucked against him, pushing at his chest with both hands, forcing him to take control of me. He did it so easily.

"Little tiger. Do you really think that's going to stop me?" He pinned my arms over my head and traced a line of liquid heat along the underside of my right arm, nuzzling my pits then nipping my throat. I turned my head to meet his mouth, but he evaded me. His laughter vibrated through me, rooting itself at the base of my cock, which swelled and pressed painfully between my belly and his. He nudged my knees apart, and his thick cock probed my ass.

"Who do you belong to?" he growled, his lips against the fluttering pulse of my throat. When I tried to answer him, he jammed his mouth over mine and swallowed my moans. "Open your legs," he ordered.

I obeyed and he rose up on stiff arms, thrusting the tip of his cock past my tight ring. I opened wider, raising my legs to brace them on his shoulders, trying to thrust up, to drive him inside me. He pulled back.

"Not yet. Stay still."

Again I obeyed, though every nerve in my body demanded I get him inside me where he belonged. He didn't speak another word. I knew without him saying it that he was going to take his time tonight. This wasn't going to be a fast, hard fuck, but a slow seduction that would set us both on fire, a flame that could only be quenched when we both lay spent and panting on our makeshift bed.

Right now I didn't care if a tree root dug into my hip or there were stones under my head. All I could feel was him, over me, teasing me with his thick cock and crazy tongue. His dick slid along mine, digging into my belly, then moving further down again, finally slipping between my open legs to probe at the crevice behind my balls. His mouth traced patterns of heat over my face, throat and upper abs, tugging at my pierced nipples, then soothing them with his warm tongue. Time stopped until we were both struggling to breath. Our hearts throbbed in furious tempo. With a final grunt he rammed his dick up my ass with one thrust, and I threw my head back and howled as my orgasm slammed through me. The tent filled with the scent of sea and musk. I shook as he rammed me again and again, until he drove into me one more time and came with a long drawn out groan.

He collapsed on top of me. I don't think either one of us moved for several minutes. Or maybe it was hours. But finally he pulled out of me. I curled around him resting my head on his shoulder when he tucked me under his arm.

"Who do you belong to?" This time it was barely a whisper.

"You, Sir."

We fell asleep, sweat and semen gluing our bodies together, surrounded by the scent of our exertions.

At one point I stirred to find Alex gently wiping me down with one of the wet cloths we had packed. I mumbled as he stroked the cum off my chest and soft dick. He paused long enough to kiss me lightly before I slipped back into a deeply satisfying sleep that I didn't wake from until the strident call of jays woke me the next morning.

The space beside me was empty when I finally struggled awake. I dragged on my clothes and stumbled outside, blinking against the sudden rush of light. Alex had taken down the bear safe and breakfast, in the form of dried fruits and jerky. After taking care of business, I returned to find Alex had dismantled the tent and draped our sleeping bags and long johns over nearby tree branches to air them out.

We ate quickly and packed our gear in companionable silence. I was pleased that Jason didn't feel the need to chatter away when there really wasn't anything to say. I was content. This vacation was proving beneficial beyond anything Jason had promised when he asked for this. I was glad now that I had ignored the niggling doubts I'd had.

New energy filled me as we set out on our fourth day of hiking. My grip on my walking sticks felt surer than they had since we'd started out. I still followed Jason, though it was a position I didn't like. But he knew how to move out here. I didn't. Not liking it wasn't going to change that simple fact.

We'd be home soon enough, and things would go back to the way they should be.

One thing I didn't mind, I had a fine view of Jason's tight butt, remembering how it had felt last night and so many other nights before that. I'd never had a more enthusiastic lover. Before Jason there had been a lot of others. Not one of them stood out in my mind. There were only a handful I ever returned to for encores. I hadn't even been aware how empty my life had been until Jason stumbled into it. I still remembered the first time I had seen him, waking up in bed with a dead man he didn't know, then being arrested by my partner and me. How vulnerable he had looked. Scared. With good reason, too. He'd spent nearly two weeks in jail going through God knows what – I had never asked and he didn't volunteer – before I realized he couldn't possibly be our killer. Most men would never have given the cop who put them through that the time of day afterward, but Jason wasn't like that. Even then I had known there was something there I wanted to know better. Something special.

He had felt the same thing. The memory of our first date lingered even now and had the power to make my knees weak, and my cock hard.

Jason glanced back over his shoulder and the look he gave me was full of what I could only describe as joy. I couldn't help it, I smiled back. Where did he get it from? That boundless fucking optimism that allowed him to get knocked flat on his ass, get back up and bounce back. Without being bitter, or full of rage at the unfairness of it all. I always used to wonder whether I could be so good, and I knew the answer. It wasn't one to be proud of.

Ahead of me Jason stopped and brought his binoculars up, peering up into the canopy full of light and shadow. I followed his look and saw movement. Something larger than most of the birds we had seen so far. I could see his excitement through the set of his shoulders.

I came up behind him, and without speaking, let him know I was there. After a few minutes he dropped the glasses to turn glowing eyes on me.

"Did you see it?"

I nodded, then admitted ignorance and asked, "What was it?"

"Great Horned Owl. I've only seen one other before."

"Rare?"

"No, just not urban birds. Nocturnal, too." He held up the binoculars. "Want to take a look?"

I took them and raised them to my untrained eyes. At least I had an idea where to look. And there it was, a big mottled brown lump staring balefully back at me as though it caught me looking and was not impressed. I pulled away and met Jason's quizzical look.

"Is that something else I need to watch out for? He going to come down dive-bombing me too?"

Laughing, Jason took the binoculars back. "No. Trust me hon, he's not interested in you or me."

A jay screamed nearby and Jason perked up. "Oh, look. The jays found it."

I looked up in time to see the brown lump being attacked by a trio of angry birds that weren't even a quarter the size of the owl. It didn't take long before the bird fled the screaming jays and vanished on silent wings deeper into the forest. I didn't blame it.

"That's what they were screaming about this morning, I guess," Jason said as we resumed our hike. "Told you they were a good early warning system."

We fell into what Jason assured me was a ground-eating pace. It seemed slow to me, but he insisted it would conserve our energy – we'd cover more ground if we didn't wear ourselves out by overdoing it. So we hiked up forested hills and down into twisting valleys, dodging low branches and tangled roots. Heat built as the day lengthened, bird calls were replaced by the hum of insects. They flew around my head. I kept my mouth shut, remembering Jason's story about eating bugs. Instead they went for my eyes and nose and buzzed in my ears, ignoring me when I shook them away.

Something slithered on the path in front of me. I froze, staring at the ground, trying to see what was under the round cover. When nothing moved, I prodded the ground with my walking stick.

Then I stopped. Shit, was I actually letting fear control me? Letting a sound send shivers through me and make my heart race? I didn't back down from armed *cholos*. Was I so out of my world I was overreacting to every little thing?

My anger made me snap, "How much longer are we going to walk today?"

He stopped and faced me. His face wore a look of concern. "Are you tired?"

"What? No! I was just wondering."

"I'd like to go another couple of hours. That okay?" he said it cautiously, as though afraid of offending me. Is that what we had come to?

I took him in my arms. "We'll go as long as you want. Just so you know," I brushed a strand of hair off his sweating brow, "I intend to fuck you hard tonight. If that's okay with you."

His smile was blinding. When he raised his face to me I kissed his open mouth, holding nothing back. His response was immediate, and left me wanting him then and there. I broke away and stroked his cheek.

"You do that again, I won't be waiting till tonight."

He blushed and pressed his face against my chest. "Whatever you want, Sir."

Satisfied, I put him away from me. "Two more hours, then we make camp."

"Yes, Sir."

I heard the rush of water just over an hour later. We traded looks and the same thought must have crossed our minds. I reached the first pool just after Jason. He knelt down on a flat rock and dipped his hand in the clear water. Standing, he shook his hand and looked over his shoulder at me.

"It's not too bad."

That was good enough for me. I dropped my backpack and hat and started stripping. Jason watched me, making no move to follow suit. I was down to my skivvies; his eyes became pools of desire, almost as deep as the water I was about to enter. When I slid my fingers under the waistband he licked his lips. I stopped, my fingers brushing the smooth, wet head of my swelling cock.

"Am I doing this alone?"

He hurried to strip, took a deep breath, closed his eyes and did a cannonball into the middle of the pool. I counted to three and followed him with a yell. I came up flinging my head to clear my eyes of water and found myself staring into Jason's face, inches from mine.

Without a word I grabbed him and yanked him against me.

The water around us was cold, but he was furnace hot. I plunged my tongue down his throat, then covered his face and throat with kisses. He moaned, grabbed my ass, pulling me tight. His heart hammered against my chest.

Something crashed in the bushes behind us. We jerked apart and looked around. Nothing. The next look we shared was bemused, and a little bit pissed.

"How 'bout we wash up and get to the top," I said. "It's about time to make camp."

Like always, he obeyed. After splashing around and washing as best we could with no soap, we dressed and made our way to the top of the ravine. It took another twenty minutes to find a suitable site to pitch our tent. After looking around, Jason said we could have a fire tonight, then he went in search of firewood. I went through our packs, digging out the cooking gear and a freeze-dried beef stew, and laid out the tent for Jason to put up when he returned.

While I waited for him to come back I moved around our camp, studying the forest around us. I tried to see it through Jason's eyes. What was it about this place that he loved so much? Why did he come alive here in a world that was so alien to anything I'd ever known? From the first time we had met I had always feared another man would come between us. Had I been looking in the wrong place for my rival? Was it out here? In a world I didn't – couldn't – understand?

While I stood at the edge of the clearing something moved in the shadows. I tensed, my hand automatically drifting over to where my shoulder holster would have been if I'd been carrying my piece. It closed over air. I cursed under my breath.

Then, like a ghost, a deer emerged from the forest and paused at the edge of our clearing. Long legs moved delicately over the short foliage, big ears swiveled around nervously. I held my breath as a second, smaller deer followed it. This one was spotted. A fawn.

The two of them moved like wraiths across the open space, freezing when there was a sound from the direction Jason had gone. Both of their narrow heads shot up. In a heartbeat the deer vanished with a flip of their long, white tails.

Seconds later, Jason was back with an armful of wood. His face lit up when he saw me, and my earlier fears faded like the ghost deer. I caught him before he reached the fire pit and took the wood away from him. After dropping it beside the earthen pit I took him in my arms.

"What's this all about?" he asked.

I pressed my erection against his belly. "You have to ask?"

"No—" he gasped when I nipped his lip, then licked it. He moaned. "Alex."

"You missed the deer," I whispered, my voice shaking with my need. "I want to fuck you."

"What about the fire—" He narrowed his eyes. "What deer?"

"Forget about them. Forget the fire, too. It can wait. I can't. I need you."

With that I wrenched his jeans open, and dropping to my knees, took him in my mouth. He cried out as I ran my tongue up his shaft, sliding over the slit, lapping up the musky fluid leaking out. Then I swallowed him, suppressing the gag reflex, reveling in the familiar taste and feel of him. This was mine and no one else's. Something buzzed around my ear. I hoped it didn't bite me. I could tell from the sounds Jason was making that he was close to coming and I pulled off him. I wasn't done yet. I stood up and pulled him back into my embrace, wanting a lot more than having him come in my mouth, as pleasurable as that would be.

"Get that tent up, boy. I told you I'm going to fuck you and I'm not doing it out here where the damned bugs can eat my ass off."

"Yes, Sir."

I don't know if he moved faster knowing what was coming, but in no time the tent was up and the wood stacked for the fire. "Later," he said, with a soft smile.

Even so, I was in a fever by the time we crawled inside and sealed the flap behind us. We stripped fast and I pulled him down on top of me. He straddled my hips, our cocks sliding together over my stomach. Reaching between us, he wrapped his hand around both of them. Even in the dim light of the tent I could see the glazed look on his face as he massaged us, his thumb stroking the bulbous head of my cock and his. I shuddered with my need for him.

I urged him up on his knees, and at my hoarse whispers he impaled himself on my dick. He rocked on me while I pumped his cock. He was moaning now, soft sounds that turned into grunts as I drove myself into him again and again until I filled him with cum and he jerked and came in my hand.

Sagging, he fell into my arms, covering my face with kisses. He paused with his mouth over mine and whispered, "I love you, Sir."

Outside, an owl called a plaintive who. I rolled Jason over and kissed him before slapping his ass and pulling my jeans toward me. "Let's go build that fire. You can feed me now."

"Yes, Sir."

At dawn the next day I rebuilt the fire while Alex took care of his business. I got breakfast started;. freeze-dried scrambled eggs and sausages. After last night both of us had a heavy appetite. Following breakfast, we cleaned up the campsite, repacked and hit the trail again while it was still early. If we could keep the pace we had yesterday we might make twenty miles, our best day yet.

I also noticed a shift in Alex's attitude. When we had first got here, despite pretending otherwise, I knew he wasn't really happy. I think it was so alien to him that he felt out of place. I should have expected that. But I had really wanted him to love the same things I did. A ridiculous hope, I realized now. In fact, I think I always knew it had been wishful thinking on my part, but I wanted him with me anyway.

But now, now he seemed to be enjoying himself. He had even helped me get the fire going this morning and was out looking for more kindling to feed it so I could prepare our breakfast. When he came back with an armful of wood, his flannel shirt dusted with tree bark, a streak of dirt on his face, he was laughing. When I asked him why, he said, with wonder in his voice, "I think I saw a turkey. Are there really turkeys out here, or did I just hallucinate?"

"Wild turkeys? Yeah, they're being reintroduced," I said, smiling along with him. "Though there are some people who say they weren't native. I don't believe it. They've found evidence of them in the Pleistocene era. Wow. I'm jealous. First deer, now turkey." I stepped up to him and slipped my arms around his waist, leaning my pelvis against his. "Are you still sorry you came?"

"Sorry, no—" He caught my look. "Okay, maybe I was a bit."

"But it's good now?"

He hugged me back. "It's good. Now, are you going to feed me, boy?"

"Yes, Sir."

I was right. We made good time. We adopted a rhythm that didn't waste energy, filling up our canteen with water treated with our purification tablets, eating handfuls of trail mix while staying on the move. We were coming up on the point where we would have to turn back. One more day going in, then turn around so we could get back on schedule. We had a couple of days of leeway, but I knew it was better to have those days back at home. I wanted to write up a blog of everything that had happened in our hike – well, almost everything, I amended. I didn't plan on sharing our nights with anyone. I smiled at the memories. I sensed Alex was coming back. I hoped so. Ever since he had tracked me down in Los Angeles, convinced me he loved me and I came back with him, there had been a reticence in him. Small, but it was there. I loved the man who had come back for me, showing his willingness to change for me.

But still, he refused to touch me in the way I wanted—no, needed. He didn't believe me when I said I wanted his pain, his control. Instead he handled me like fragile glass, and while his touch always aroused me and I had never been more satisfied as a lover, I wanted my Alex back. The one sure enough in his needs to take control and bind me to him both physically and emotionally. Only rarely did he even use restraints on me anymore. I missed the days when he would put me in his sling or flog me to show me just how much I belonged to him, and him alone.

It wasn't my place to ask. He was my Master and it had to come from him. But oh, I missed it so when he was sure of himself.

Around us, the forest grew quiet as the heat of the day grew. Finally, we almost reached the point where we would have to turn around to make it back on our time schedule.

The next time we stopped for a brief rest I knew it was nearly time. Our eyes met. "Another half hour, then head home?"

I was surprised when Alex seemed reluctant to agree. I put my hand on his cotton-covered arm. "What, Alex?"

At first I didn't think he was going to answer me, then he shrugged and looped his arm around my shoulder, drawing me against him. I leaned my head against his chest, relaxing in the place I wanted to be most of all. I could feel the soft beat of his heart and his breath stir the hair on my head.

"You're not going to believe this, but I'm sorry to see this end."

My heart lifted and I raised my face to look up into his.

"Really?"

"Yah, really. Surprise, huh? But it's been good. When was the last time we got to spend this much time together, neither one of us being called away or answering to anyone else?"

I rubbed his chest and leaned up to kiss him. When we finished both of our hearts were beating a little faster. I laid my head back on his chest and inhaled his wonderful smell, playing with a button of his shirt.

"I love you, Sir."

"I love you, Jason Zachary."

I always knew he did, his actions told me so, but it was so rare for him to say it aloud. I never wanted this moment to end. If I could have suspended time right then I would have. Lived like a creature trapped in amber forever, the world a golden blur beyond me, where it couldn't touch me or him ever again.

We separated and Alex took my chin in his big hands. "You know how special you are, don't you, Jay?"

"Yes, Sir."

"Come on. Just a little while more. We'll come back. Maybe later this year. Or if not here, maybe someplace else. Hawaii. Canada. Would you like that?"

I tried to imagine us on a crowded beach at Waikiki and couldn't. Maybe one of the other islands. Someplace quieter. Or Canada. They had gay marriage. Not that I ever expected Alex and I would marry. I knew he never wanted to do that ever again, but to be in a place that let that happen and it was okay, that would be nice. "With you? Anywhere."

When ten minutes later he saw movement in a nearby tree, he was the one who pointed it out to me. It was a Western Wood Pewee. When I identified the common woodland bird he grinned.

"Tell me it's really rare and a once in a lifetime sighting."

"Of course it is. I'll call Audubon as soon as we get back. They'll wri—"

His hand on my arm tightened, stopping me in mid-word. In the silence an out of place sound came from ahead of us. An engine.

"What is it?" I asked.

"There's no road around here, is there?"

"No…" I frowned. "Not for another twenty miles at least, and not in that direction. What do you think it is?"

I could almost see Alex, my doting lover, vanish, replaced by Detective Spider, the über efficient and unemotional homicide cop. Alex had spoken sometimes of how his gut was good at giving him early warnings, that even when everything seemed good, when his gut told him otherwise, he'd learned to listen to it.

Is that what he was doing now?

"I don't know," he finally said. "But I don't like it."

Neither did I. The hairs on the back of my neck stood up. But I followed him when he left our path and headed south, away from the path we had planned to take. Towards the rumbling engine noise.

The first thing I noticed was an unnatural looking clearing open up where there should have been dense forest. And this wasn't the result of a natural culling. That kind of occurrence would have left a lot of smaller, child trees ready to fill the gap. That hadn't happened here. Instead, it looked like a few select trees had been physically removed. There weren't any fallen giants anywhere, no understory at all, no broken or overgrown nursery logs feeding new growth out of their decay. This area had been clear cut. That meant heavy-handed human activity at work. An errant breeze brought the rank smell of smoke and diesel fuel over the more natural odors of things growing.

Goose bumps riddled my flesh as I watched Alex drop into a crouch behind a thick fir tree. Without a word, he dragged me down beside him. When I recognized the rows of nearly four-foot tall plants I knew we'd stumbled onto something that could get us killed. I couldn't begin to guess how many marijuana plants there were in the clearing. Hundreds maybe. God, maybe even thousands. Maybe more. Alex shot me a warning look and I shrank back into the shadow of a cluster of firs.

I knew enough not to speak.

Over the sporadic sound of a motor that sounded too loud to be a car I could make out another, more familiar sound. Running water. One of the ubiquitous creeks that criss-crossed the Matilija wilderness was nearby.

Alex heard it, too. Still without a word he led us toward the sound. Maybe he figured where there was water there was likely to be more growth to help conceal us. Conceal us from the owner of the truck and the illegal grow-op.

With less than a foot between us we slipped over the lip of a steep, vine and tree clogged ravine. Half sliding, half stumbling, we made our way down to the bottom. The rush of fast moving water grew louder and I remembered hearing that snow fall in the mountains had been higher than normal the last winter, so run offs would have been high. Like the other streams we had crossed, that meant more dead falls created by downed trees to trip unwary feet.

But this ravine was far worse than the last few we had traversed, and I knew where the trees that had been removed from the clearing above us had been put. The ravine was riddled with solid trunks that had water backed up behind them, creating treacherous pools that would have roots ready to tangle our feet, and enough current to snatch us away and sweep us into those dead falls. Once caught it would be damn hard to pull free. Drowning would be fast when you got knocked around and battered by limbs and stone. I began to wonder what was more dangerous, the rushing water below us or the men I knew would be armed behind us.

I wanted to tell Alex we needed to be careful, but I didn't dare speak. He wasn't rushing though, and for that I was thankful. I tried not to, but the sense of urgency I felt from Alex scared me and it was hard to move slowly when the dangers behind us were unknown.

My foot slipped on a tangle of ivy and roots nearly sending me headlong down the slope. Only a last minute grab at a leaning aspen kept me from rolling down the treacherous incline. The thin trunk bent under my weight but held, and I ended up on my rump on stony hard ground, slamming into it so hard my teeth clicked and I nipped my tongue, barely suppressing a yelp of pain.

Finally, we reached the bottom and crouched on the damp, but relatively smooth, surface of a large, glacier-carved boulder. On three sides water foamed and sucked as it hurried down the mountain on its hazardous way to the ocean hundreds of miles away. I watched a branch twist and bob in the current a few feet from my feet. It finally broke free and swirled away, only to be caught up by another submerged branch.

Alex looked back at me. The look we traded said it all. We needed to get over that rushing water. The other side represented more safety than this side did. But how to navigate the chaotic, fast-flowing water?

I looked up at the vault of cerulean above us. Clouds dusted the deepening blue of a mid-afternoon sky. We might have five hours of daylight left. We sure as hell couldn't be down here when night fell.

We backtracked to the shore and clambered over ground constantly shifting under our feet, slimed by algae and pea sand made unstable by the fast moving water. We were soon soaked to the knees, shivering and beginning to tire. But a quick look back showed us the way was clear. Maybe we hadn't been spotted.

Ahead, a natural bridge of stones led us finally to the other side.

Alex waited for me to come up beside him. "Check your phone. You got a signal?"

I did as ordered. The phone was seeking...seeking, but couldn't lock on a signal. Not surprising. Disappointing, but not surprising. We were too far down in a ravine surrounded by rock below and trees above, to pick up anything.

"We have to keep going," Alex said. His whole body was tense, only his eyes never stopped moving, continually scanning, looking everywhere for signs we'd been spotted. That we were being hunted. "Keep trying the phone. As soon as you get a signal give them our coordinates, tell them to move fast."

I nodded and slipped the iPhone into my shirt pocket, where it would hopefully stay dry and I could check it easily.

Alex spotted it first. Maybe it was his cop eye that let him see the anomaly. He grabbed my arm and pointed downstream on the side we had just left.

"Hold on, I need to go take a look at that."

"What is it?"

"I don't know. But I want you to stay here while I check it out."

Ice water squelched in my Merrells as I retraced my path back over to the other side. Jason was right on my heels, ignoring my orders to stay put. I'd deal with him and his disobedience later. Right now I had to investigate what I had spotted. I wasn't exactly sure what I had seen: a splash of color out of place, an odd unnatural shape. Jason might be good at finding the things that did belong, but I'd spent enough time in the forest now to see things that didn't.

I kept continuously scanning everywhere, my gaze making passes over both sides of the stream, and back the way we had come. Back toward the concealed grow-op we'd stumbled upon. I hadn't wanted to believe it. I knew a couple of them had been found in recent years, both run by Mexican cartel connected locals. I remembered the shot the bikers reported hearing. Could it have been linked to that? There were other hikers up here. What if someone else stumbled on this? I never met a drug dealer who wasn't heavily armed. Why would this bunch be any different?

The midday air was somnolent, heat shimmered off the sun-baked rocks, shards of light danced off the restless water straight into the back of my eyes. I wished I could pull out my sunglasses, but I didn't want to risk missing anything by cutting down my sight. So I squinted and endured peering through my regular glasses. I glared back at Jason, reminding him he was supposed to stay back.

"What is it?" Jason repeated. "I don't see—" Then he did. "Is that a shirt?" His voice rose.

Plaid, red and blue, which had stood out from the green background as something alien. I was leading us now, my protective instinct kicking in. I didn't want Jason anywhere near this until I knew what 'this' was. Since I could hardly send him to the other room, I had to be satisfied to have him behind me. I waved him to stay and this time he obeyed. Maybe he was getting the same uneasy feeling I was.

A side pool of motionless water had been cut off from the faster moving stream by a twist of land and a pile of fallen branches that had washed down over the spring thaw and been caught up by a pile of rocks. Between the rocks and the fallen branches, an effective natural dam had formed. Like the pool we had played around in earlier in our hike, this water ranged from a few inches to knee deep in spots. Dark shapes darted through the depths. Trout? What other kinds of fish existed up here? I stepped closer to the mass of tree branches.

I could clearly make out the shirtsleeve now. It looked very similar to the one I was wearing, straight out of L.L. Bean's closet. I skirted the deepest part of the quiescent pool, testing the ground in front of me. Stones shifted underneath my feet; I slid, caught myself and pressed forward. Mud and rotting leaves squelched and gurgled under my already soaked feet. Over the whoosh of running water and distant birdcalls I heard a familiar sound. Familiar, but out of place here. But then everything was out of place to me in this alien world. I paused to listen. A low, steady seething of sound that seemed to fit with the lazy, rising heat.

Jason heard it at the same time I realized what it was.

"What's that sound?"

"Flies," I said, a ripple of ice racing down my spine. "Stay back—"

My foot fell through a tangle of brush and I went to my knees. Something viscous exploded under my hands when I tried to break my fall. The stench that burst out made my stomach lurch and my throat close over a gag that threatened to spill my guts on the already reeking mess under me.

I threw myself backward, yelling at Jason, "Get back! Don't come near me."

"What is it? That smell... Oh God, Alex—" Panic and nausea filled his voice. He spun away and vomited into the water.

I wanted to join him, but I had to be professional. Scrambling to my feet I backed away from the mass of decaying flesh, still mostly concealed by the snarled mess of branches and leaves that had formed a dense mat piled over the corpse. A grinning skull peered up at me through maggot eaten flesh. It was human.

"Get back!" I shouted again. This time Jason obeyed. I caught a brief glimpse of his pale face then I turned back to my discovery. It was easy to fall into investigative mode. Easier than having to face the reality of what I had found. My mind started flashing through what I needed to do. First I had to clean my hands off; I didn't dare touch anything with this noxious mess on me. Then I had to figure out where we were so we could find our way back when I got the authorities involved. Jason would help me there. I was now thankful I had given him that iPhone. It had both a GPS and a compass. Once I was sure I could get back here, we needed to secure whatever evidence might be lost if I left it here – once I decided what that was. I spared Jason another glance. His face was still colorless and when our eyes met we both knew the truth. Our vacation was officially over. Backing away from the corpse I crouched down over a pool of clear water where I dipped my hands and arms in, washing until I was sure it was all off. I knew the stench would stay with me for days. Might always linger, though that would be psychological more than physical.

"I need you to use your GPS to tell me exactly where we are. Can you do that?" I spoke slowly to break through his trauma. I had to repeat it twice more before his eyes cleared and he focused on me.

"S-sure. What do you want me to do?"

"I have to be able to get back here with the rangers. They'll have to walk in like we did. Or find how they got that truck or whatever it was in." I looked around, hoping for what? A clearing big enough to land a 'copter? Good luck. This place was as inaccessible as they came. Nothing but a human on foot was getting in here. "Can you do that, Jason?"

Finally he nodded and turned away. He fumbled out his GPS and with trembling fingers began working the instrument. Finally he was shaking his head. "I'm still not getting a signal."

I had no way to mark the site or cordon it off so I had to hope no one else would stumble across it before I could get back with the rangers and hopefully a coroner. But I had to think of the whole area as a crime scene, which meant I had to do a grid search. Normally I would have several officers assisting me. At least we had our digital camera. I pulled my pack off and opened the pocket holding the Canon.

Before I did anything else I checked how many images were left, satisfied when I saw it was still good for well over a thousand. That would serve my purpose.

Then I had to find something to collect samples of anything I didn't want to leave to the elements while I went down the mountain. That was going to present a problem...then I thought of the bear safe and knew it just might do the trick.

I looked over to where Jason hovered, doing his best not to look while he waited to see if he could help me. Brave boy. Not many people could sit around like he did, knowing a rotting corpse was practically under their feet.

I stepped toward him. He looked up in alarm, then calmed when I stroked his arm. "I need the safe," I said. "We need to take some samples back in case the site gets compromised more before I can get back here."

"The safe – you want to put *what* in it?"

"I swear to you, I'll buy us a new one, but I have to do this."

"I-I understand." He swallowed. "Is there anything I can do?"

"Just get me the safe and secure our coordinates. I don't want any problems finding the place when I come back with the rangers."

I took another step closer to him. I slipped my arm around him and held him while he buried his face against my neck. "I'm sorry, Jason. I know this week meant a lot to you. I'll make it up to you."

He shook his head savagely. "Not your fault. I'm just sorry for that poor person..."

I kissed his cheek and set him away from me. "So am I. Do you want to go up top? I can take care of this."

"No, I want to stay with you."

"I need to take a look around. You have to stay here and not touch anything. Go over there and sit on one of those rocks. I'll be as quick as I can."

He nodded and moved over to a large, flat, sunbaked rock that jutted out over the stream forming a natural seat. His eyes still had a vacant look to them. I wished I could have spent more time reassuring him, but time had suddenly become very important. Camera in hand, I set to work. I took photos of every angle around the dead fall concealing the body. Then I managed a few close-ups showing the skull and remnants of clothes. Clearly, the body had been buried in some way until recently. Insect activity wasn't advanced enough to be old, and the fact that larger animals hadn't found and scattered the remains also told me that. Maybe it had been buried under snow? I realized I might need Jason after all.

I approached him again and crouched down in front of him. "Jason," I spoke firmly, letting him know he had to listen to me closely. I didn't have time to smooth away his fear. I took my Tilley off and held it in front of me. "When would the snow around here have melted? How much do you think there would have been? Enough to fully bury a body?"

He raised his face to me, his look earnest. "Yes, probably. Even if the snow's not really heavy, it accumulates. It could easily bury a body, plus the rangers probably don't get up here as often once winter comes, if at all."

"So a corpse put here in late fall would stay here, hidden?"

He looked sick and I was sorry to make him think about the subject. "Yes. It could. Who do you think it is?"

"I don't know."

"Who could have done this? Or was it an accident?"

I had wanted to consider that possibility, but knew it was a false hope. I had seen the hole in the skull's forehead. Dead center kill shot. Execution style. Like Isaac Simpson.

But all I could tell him was, "I don't know, Jay." Sad commentary for a man who was supposed to have all the answers to the dark questions. "But it might have something to do with the drug dealers. Someone stumbles on them, they can get nasty."

His throat convulsed. "Like us?"

I squeezed his kneecap. "I'm not letting anything happen to you. Got it?"

He nodded, and even tried to offer me a sickly smile.

I went back to searching the crime scene, using one of my walking sticks to pry apart brush, lift branches and poke through piles of rotting wood and other debris. I quartered along the stream bank first, hopping carefully from stone to stone looking for anything else that looked out of place.

I looked back at Jason still sitting on his stony perch, watching me, hands dangling limply between his legs. His binoculars lay forgotten on his chest.

I turned away. Nothing I could do for him right now.

I saw the tan boot and denim pant leg first. Like the first body it had been buried under a pile of leaves and branches. Unlike the first body though, this one hadn't yet been decimated by insect activity.

Gently, I pushed the branches aside. But even before I saw the face I knew who it was. The man from the car lot, the one Jason and I had scoped out. The one with the dog we had heard barking last night and this morning.

Had it been barking at this man's death? Where were the two women he had been traveling with? With less caution now, I searched through the piles of wood and damp rot but there were no more bodies.

Perhaps that should have cheered me. But I'd been a cop too many years. I didn't know what had happened to those two young women, but I was pretty sure it wasn't anything good.

I expected Alex to take his time on his search. I tried not to pay attention to what he was doing and I avoided looking at the horror he had stumbled upon. The second time a dead body and Alex had figured together. The first time, with George Blunt, had been bad enough. This was unbelievably worse. The stench still clung to my nose and throat and all I could smell was corruption and vomit. Both made me want to throw up again, and it took all my will power to keep my stomach from emptying itself on the rocks around me.

I was startled when Alex hurried back to me, scooped the backpack I had set beside me and shoved the gear at me. He jammed his hat back down on his head. "Come on," he said. "We need to get back down to the rangers."

"What happened?" I cried. He was scaring me. "What's wrong?"

"There's another body. This one was recent. We need to get out of here. Now, Jason. I'll explain on the way, but we can't stay here—"

A sharp crack split the air. At first I thought a tree branch had broken off. Then I found myself lying on my stomach with a mouth full of dirt and water and Alex lying on top of me.

"What the fuck—" I tried to sit up but Alex held me down with an iron grip.

"Stay down! Don't move."

"What—"

"Shhh," he hissed and I shut up. He was a good forty pounds heavier than me and while normally I didn't mind having his weight on me, this time he wasn't trying to fuck me. When I got my head turned around enough to see his face, I realized he was terrified. That scared me more than whatever was freaking him out. His eyes frantically moved back and forth like he was looking for something that wasn't there.

Then the sharp crack came again and the dirt less than two yards in front of us exploded in a shower of stone chips, sand, and debris.

"Shit." I tried to scramble out from under him and move backward as realization slammed into me. We were being shot at.

Alex rolled off me but before I could do more than take a deep breath he jerked me backward, until we were crouched behind the large boulder I had been sitting on moments ago. With one hand he held me down, and at the same time he rose up on his other arm to peer over the top of the boulder. His hat lay under both of us, squished now beyond recognition.

I wanted to grab him and haul him down with me. What was he thinking? That was a man with a gun out there.

And I'd made Alex come to the park unarmed.

"Stay low," he said. "We have to try to get out of the open and into the trees."

"How are we supposed to do that?" We were sitting ducks if we moved out from behind this rock.

"As fast as we can. Keep a low profile and don't run in a straight line. And whatever you do, don't stop for anything." When I nodded he shook me. "Anything. Do you understand? You. Don't. Stop."

What was he saying? That I was supposed to leave him behind if something happened? I nodded because he clearly wasn't going to let me do anything else, but there was no way in hell I was running away if it would mean leaving him to face a man with a gun while he was unarmed.

I set my mouth but when it was clear he wasn't going to let it go, I nodded again. This time he must have been satisfied. He turned away from me and once more rose from his crouch to peer over the lip of our hiding place. A third shot pinged off stone. He flinched and dropped back beside me. When I saw the blood on his face, I panicked.

"Alex! Oh my God, you were hit—"

He grabbed my shoulders and pinned me to the rock behind me. "No. It's a stone chip. I'm fine."

I took a deep breath, knowing panic wasn't going to do us any good right now. Alex knew how to handle situations like this. He was a cop. I had to trust him.

I touched the wound on his cheek, smearing it. His glasses were gone. His eyes were hot and intense. He was all business now. The man I loved was buried beneath Detective Spider. "We're going to be okay, Jason."

I wanted to believe him. I needed to.

"Are you ready?"

I followed him as we first retreated straight back from the boulder, sloshing through shallow water over our stone bridge, trying desperately to keep our feet under us while we watched for the hidden shooter.

No more shots came. That fact did nothing to calm my fear. He kept me in front of him, I knew damn well what he was doing. Shielding me with his own body. We reached the first of the trees, but it did nothing to lessen my terror. It only grew as I realized that the trees didn't only keep us hidden but could help conceal the shooter, allowing him to creep up on us.

Alex knew that, too. He became hyper alert, I swear he had eyes in the back of his head. He made the hairs on my body stand up.

It was almost like being in the same room as a tiger.

Comforting if he's on your side, not so much if he's not.

My calves were aching from moving in a crouch across uneven, unforgiving ground uphill. We kept to the heavier planted areas, and every few seconds Alex would push me down and do his jack-in-the box routine. So far, whoever was out there wasn't taking any more shots. Did that mean he had gone? Or was he circling around, trying to get a better shot at us?

I was clammy, and had to force myself to breath deeply and not hyperventilate. My chest ached from the effort, and I was light-headed. We moved up the hill with terrible slowness, expecting at any minute to hear that deadly crack. And what? Do you feel a bullet enter you, or was it too quick?

Alex's hand on my back signaled me and I immediately dropped to my stomach. He moved, hand still holding me down, then the sound I had been dreading came again. Crack-snap of more shots. They whined past us. Alex grunted and jerked me back into a half crouch.

"Come on," he whispered. Before I could respond he was pushing me along in front of him.

Branches scratched and poked at every inch of exposed skin. I was bleeding and sweating in streams by the time we got to the top of the ravine. I risked a quick look back but I couldn't see anything.

Alex didn't wait around to see, either. He hustled me along, keeping off the trail, dragging us through the densest brush he could find.

Dead falls caught at our feet and it was all I could do to keep up with him. If he hadn't refused to let go of me I'm not sure I wouldn't have fallen down and stayed there.

I have no idea how long we ran, or crawled, depending on your definition. My lungs ached from trying to suck in enough air, I was being eaten alive by bugs attracted to my blood and sweat. I swear they were crawling all over my chest, even down into my pants and jock. I swiped at a persistent fly that wouldn't stop buzzing around my eyes.

We were both getting tired. I could feel Alex drooping in exhaustion, but he pushed on. Finally he shoved me into a heavy tangle of bushes and prickly plants, and leaned against the gnarled boll of an old fir tree. I sagged on the ground beside him, doing my best to catch my breath, knowing we couldn't stay long.

I looked over at Alex and didn't like what I saw. His normally fair, freckled face was almost paper white and his eyes were half closed. When I leaned over to touch his knee to ask him how he was, I saw it.

Blood.

It stained his hip and even as I frantically pulled his shirt up I saw more seeping out. He'd been shot.

I knew exactly when I'd been hit. The bullet burned into my side, tracing a path down and across my hip, slamming into the ground between Jason and I. No time to stop and look. I had to keep moving.

I bit my lips hard against the sudden rush of pain and nausea that came when I dragged Jason back up, pulling him toward the top of the ravine. We had to find someplace to hole up long enough for me to find out just how bad the wound was. Jason came along willingly. He had no idea I had been hit, and I planned to keep it that way as long as I could. Once we stopped, I knew he'd find out. I'd deal with it then.

I was lucky. I wasn't losing a lot of blood. I suspected it just nicked my side. With further luck it hadn't hit anything vital or grazed my intestine, which would fuck me up big time. I know we had a rudimentary first aid kit – Jason had been adamant about that – but whether we'd have the time to use it was another thing. Even if we did, I doubted a band-aid and a painkiller was going to be much help.

Still, I refused to think about whether even trying to use it would be a waste of time.

The burning grew and I found my breath getting short. A wave of dizziness and pain passed through me. I knew we had to find a place to stop, and soon. If we didn't I was going to pass out. I'd kept us off the more traveled areas but now I looked for someplace even more concealing. I spotted it in a yard high clump of dense greenery. Something prickly dug into my skin as I pulled Jason in after me, ignoring his protests. Inside, I was able to lean against a thick tree under a drooping pine bough and let myself go limp. If I could rest for a few minutes, I could go on. We didn't dare stop; we were too close to the shooter, and the marijuana he was protecting.

Jason knew there was something wrong even before he spotted the blood. He tore open my shirt and was nearly weeping when he examined the wound from all angles.

"Just a flesh wound," I said.

"You think I fucking care? I need to take care of it." Before I could protest he was digging through his pack and pulling out the first aid kit. He cleaned the wound with antiseptic that stung like a bitch, followed by bandages and tape, which immediately were saturated with fresh blood. He applied pressure to try to stop the bleeding and a bolt of raw pain shot through me. I bit my tongue to keep from groaning. That might set him off in a panic.

"I'm okay, Jason." I tried to sound strong. "It's a flesh wound. The bullet isn't even in there. It was a through and through. It barely hit me."

"Oh, will you stop it? Will you for once drop the fucking tough guy act? We need to get out of here. Can you walk? We still have our walking sticks. I can support you—"

It was one of the hardest decisions I had ever made, but I had to do it. I met his gaze and took his chin in my hand. "I need you to go get help. I'll only slow you down. You can get down in a lot less time by yourself, if you hurry."

"No! No way I'm leaving you here."

I'd known he would be stubborn. Good thing he was also obedient.

"Yes, you are. You have to, Jason. It's for the best for both of us. If you stay here, we're both in danger. I can hide in here. He'd have to be right on top of me to see me. But with two of us, we're more likely to be spotted. We both know you can move faster alone than dragging me around."

He opened his mouth to protest and I squeezed his chin tight enough to make him wince. "Obey me in this, boy. I insist."

"I...okay," he whispered.

"What did you say?"

"Yes, Sir." He went to pack up his backpack and got a worried look on his face. Then he broke the news to me, "I've lost the iPhone. I must have dropped it. I don't remember—"

"It's okay, Jason. You'll find your way back. I know you will. Now go."

"Alex—"

"Go. Now. No more talk. You're wasting your time. Just get out of here. Don't disobey me here, Jason. You know what happens when you disobey me."

He hung his head and whispered, "Yes, Sir."

But before he left he pulled off his backpack. Slipping off his canteen he set it down beside me. "You might need this."

"No," I whispered. "You'll need it..."

"I can find water along the way. In fact..." He cleaned out his backpack, then repacked it with nothing but some food bars. "I'm leaving everything. I can travel faster this way." He tried one more time. "Please, Alex. Don't do this."

I took as deep a breath as I could to steady my voice. "Obey me, Jason."

"Yes, Sir."

I watched him leave with an immeasurable sadness, knowing very well I wasn't likely to see him again. But he would be fine. I was sure of it. That knowledge alone would be enough to get me through what I had to do.

When I was sure he wasn't coming back I let my body lie back, falling to the soft, mulch-covered ground. I doubted anything I was lying on would be sterile, but I had my suspicions that none of that would matter soon. I had examined the wound as best I could while Jason cleaned it up, and before he bandaged it in a futile attempt to keep germs out. From the angle of entry and the path the bullet had taken through me, I strongly suspected my bowel had been perforated. It was only a matter of time before peritonitis set in. Time I had pretty well run out of.

I closed my eyes and willed myself to be calm. I had some time left. How much I didn't know. Enough for Jason to get down the mountain and bring back help? Assuming he got there in half the time it had taken us to get up here, we were still looking at two, maybe even three days before they could start back. No one was going to be searching these woods after dark. So, first light in three days they'd be on their way. Then what, fifteen, sixteen hours to reach me? How sick would I be by then? Almost five days? I knew it wouldn't be good.

Half sitting up, I dragged my backpack over, enduring the excruciating pain the stretching action brought. Once beside me, I ripped it open and drew out the tent roll and the thin thermal blanket we had packed in case it got colder than anticipated. The tent roll went under my head, I wrapped the thermal blanket around my already shivering body. Too early for fever. Was I going into shock? Whatever it was, I was going to have to deal with it on my own.

Once I had settled in, I pried the top off the canteen and let some water dribble into my mouth, just enough to moisten it. Then I recapped it and dropped my head back on the mock pillow.

I just hoped some damn bear didn't come along and cause trouble.

I had forced myself to obey Alex when every cell in my body told me to stay with him. He needed me. I couldn't leave him alone in this place—

But he had ordered me to go. I had always obeyed him, ever since he had returned for me and I had surrendered myself to him. I didn't know how to fight him. I had never wanted to until this moment.

I stumbled from the hiding place he had chosen and by pure instinct headed west, toward the car lot where I knew I could find either rangers, or someone who could help me

I kept a low profile, it helped that I was a lot shorter and lighter than Alex, and as long as I stayed in the heavier brush I doubt too many people would see me. The shirt I had worn was mostly browns and blue grays, the colors should blend in to the surrounding bush. I had another advantage, I had some bush savvy. Maybe more than the pot farmers had. I could hope.

I moved a lot faster on my own. I never would have admitted it to Alex, but he had slowed us down considerably. Now, with the memory of Alex, lying on the ground with blood seeping out of him, spurred me on. I made double time. I didn't bother finding more walking sticks. I could move quicker and more silently without them. Going down slope I could use tree branches and trunks to slow my headlong rush and keep myself from falling and bashing my head in. I was a lot less worried about my safety. It no longer mattered. Not as long as Alex was behind me, injured. I refused to think that he might be dying. I clung to the idea that all I had to do was bring help back and he'd be okay.

Still, I was getting nowhere fast. I trudged on, daylight waned around me and even when shadows cloaked everything around me, I kept walking. I walked through darkness into the next day, using my innate sense of direction to keep me on the right path. With images of Alex bleeding haunting me, I began to despair. So, several hours after dawn, when I first heard the sounds I didn't know whether to give in to my fear or find out who was coming and deal with them. Regretting my impetuous decision to leave the walking sticks I crouched down as something tore through the brush upslope from me, moving faster than I was and making a lot more noise. It sounded big. Man-size or bigger. Jesus could it be the bear Alex had always been afraid of? The more I listened the more I heard the snuffle-snort of an animal, not the softer breathing of a man.

My hand closed over a piece of fallen log that was as long as my arm and twice as thick. It felt reassuringly hefty in my hands as I made ready to surprise my visitor.

It broke through the bushes and crashed noisily toward me. I raised the branch, steadied myself and promised I'd get one good shot in for Alex. The breathing grew hoarser and I swear I heard whimpering. Christ, had they shot someone else?

I jumped out, staying low, hopefully out of the range of a shot if he got off a quick one. My foot caught on a twisted root and I tumbled to the ground, still clutching my makeshift weapon.

It whimpered again, then a snuffling whine accompanied a warm, moist nose stuck in my face. I looked up and blinked and found myself staring down the long, black muzzle of a German Shepherd.

The dog from the car lot.

I scrambled to my knees. The dog sat and whined again.

Alex had never told me the identity of the dead body he had found. I remembered we had heard a dog – this dog? – barking last night and this morning. Had it been out there looking for its dead master? If that was the case, where were the two women who had been with him? Oh, God, had Alex found all of them? Was that why he had hurried to get me out of there? Had the person who shot Alex also shot and killed those three hikers? But he had said "another body." That implied only one. Which one?

Blindly I reached out and dug my fingers through the dog's ruff. It whined and stepped closer, shoving its damp nose into my neck. The pack it had been wearing was gone. Lost or pulled off I guess. I pushed away from the animal. I didn't have time to console a lost dog. I had to find a ranger. I—

The dog went into sudden alert mode. The hair on the back of its thick neck rose and it turned its head back the way I had come.

"What do you hear? Is someone there?"

Clearly something was upsetting the dog. A low throat-rumbling growl emerged from the tense animal. My own hairs stood on end.

I had to move on. I tossed the wooden weapon to the ground and started downhill again. The dog didn't even hesitate; he followed at my side.

Not sure if that was a good thing or not I tried to ignore it. Like it or not, it looked like I had at least temporary custody of a dog. "Try not to make any noise, will you?"

He was silent. So far so good.

The day lengthened. I couldn't see the sun overhead, but I could feel its passage. Shadows deepened and I knew I was running out of time. Day two and Alex needed me to get help. I dare not stop for darkness or anything else.

My legs turned rubbery and exhaustion tugged at me. Even the dog, who still hugged my side, seemed spent. I guess we'd both had a few rough days.

We'd also gone as far as we could. Still, I didn't quit until I stumbled over a fallen branch and nearly took a header down a steep incline. Even then I pushed on, memories of Alex's face when he had sent me away driving me past reason. At last the ground leveled out, and the trees around us grew thinner. We were leaving the riparian area, and entering the upper meadowlands. We startled a pair of mule deer who darted away from us, the white flags of their tails flashing in the moonlight. It was a measure of how exhausted it was that the dog ignored them.

I glanced up at the half moon that bathed us in silver light. A rash of stars filled the sky, and if I hadn't been so sick and scared I would have loved nothing more than to lie down and watch them wheel overhead.

Instead, I sat, the dog huddling against me, shivering and making low whining noises even when I tried to sooth him. I prayed to God to give me strength. I prayed that Alex would be saved. I slipped into an uneasy, nightmare ridden sleep. I don't think the dog slept any better. More than once I woke up to find him churning his legs and whimpering. He was trapped in his own nightmares.

An hour before sunset, I stumbled into a campsite and found Danny and Niko, a couple from Dubuque. I scared the shit out of them. They recovered quickly and Danny gave me some coffee he had just brewed. Even black, nothing had ever tasted so sweet.

There really was a God.

Niko had a cell phone she handed to me without a word after I told her why I needed it.

And mercy of mercies, I got a signal.

Sometime after Jason left I dozed. I don't know for how long, but it was full dark when I woke with a start. At first I had no idea where I was, or what had happened to me. I lay on my back, still groggy, blinking and straining to see something, anything that would give me a clue. Disjointed memories returned. Jason had been there, here, then he was gone. Where? When?

There had been a body. No, two. The man from the parking lot had been shot. Why? Then I remembered the two women who had been with him. Had they been killed, too? Just because I hadn't found their bodies didn't mean anything.

I thought of Jason then. Would he get down off the mountain? I'd been so afraid he would disobey me in the end and come back. He hadn't and I was immeasurably glad. At least he had a chance.

I put my hand down on my side. Big mistake. Pain shot through me and I had to dig my teeth into my lip to keep from screaming. I clawed at the loamy ground and waited for the spasms to pass. When they did I was left clammy with sweat and shaking. I kept shaking even after the pain passed into a dull ache. The movement had reopened the wound. Fresh, warm blood trickled down my side. I knew the blood loss wasn't my real problem. I was sure the bullet had perforated one of my intestines and even now the infection would be raging. Eventually it would shut me down. It was only a matter of time before I got too sick to think clearly. Already shivers racked my body, signs of an oncoming fever.

I swallowed and only managed a dry rasp. God, I needed a drink. I had already finished the canteen Jason had left me. Where was mine? I turned my head sideways, ignoring the stabbing pain and located my backpack, less than a foot away. Even from here, in the dim light, I could see my canteen strapped to the side. The backpack's strap lay near my left hand, which was still clutching the ground. I gingerly pulled my fingers free of the dirt and inched across the needle and loam covered ground, brushing the canvas strap before falling away. I tried again. That was when I felt something pressing against my uninjured side. I froze, fingers barely touching the strap.

What the hell was that?

When it moved, I almost lost it and succumbed to gibbering panic that flooded my mouth with bile.

I reached gently for the strap, managing to catch it in two fingers. The motion rocked my body a little further off the ground, exposing more of my right side.

The pressure returned. Whatever it was it was moving, pressing against my back. I was able to determine its shape and the sour metallic taste of terror filled my mouth again. My heart slammed against my ribs and I forgot to breath.

It was a snake. Had Jason mentioned snakes? Yes, shit, he had. Double shit. Diamondbacks, he had said. I'm pretty sure along with warning me about bears and cougars and screaming rabbits, he had mentioned Diamondbacks. What the hell do you do if a rattlesnake crawls into bed with you?

Stay still. Not a problem. Moving was an agony and getting worse by the minute. What was more worrisome was the fever that was spreading. So far only small shivers wracked my body; I knew they would get considerably worse. How long would the snake linger? If the warmth of my body was attracting it, then probably all night. Would it leave when dawn came? How far off was that?

I lay half on my side, my spine twisted and my right arm stretched out, reaching for the backpack. I couldn't maintain this position indefinitely. Already my legs were cramping up and muscular spasms knotted up my spine. I hadn't wanted to breath, then I couldn't when my chest locked up. Sooner or later I was going to roll over on top of the snake. What would kill me first? The snake bite or the sepsis in my blood? I forced myself to take slow, deep breaths, past the pain, past the rigid muscles that locked my diaphragm in a knot. Every move produced excruciating agony and sent tremors along the length of my body. The bullet wound burned and the heat spread through my gut, along my twisted spine.

I dug my fingers into the soil, desperately trying to stabilize myself. The strap to my backpack dug into my hand, reminding me of how acute my thirst was. I could barely swallow; at the same time my bladder was full. The irony wasn't lost on me.

I was reduced to the purest sensations. Pain piled on pain, each one sharper and more intense than the last. I let it flow over me, struggling to control, if not the pain, my reaction to it. I thought of Jason then and what he craved from me. His love for me transmuted what I did for him into pleasure for both of us. Pleasure the like of which I'd never experienced with another person. I had never truly considered the depths of his trust in me. The doubt I had felt meant I didn't trust him or myself in return. I had been shortchanging and betraying both of us with my reluctance to take our sex games all the way.

My fist closed over the strap and with tiny, pain wracked jerks I pulled it toward me. I succeeded in fumbling the canteen off and used my teeth to uncap it, spilling fluid on my cheek and the ground under my face. I tasted dirt and the cold briskness of fresh water.

I didn't even know if drinking was good for me or not. I wasn't sure I cared anymore. I gulped it down greedily, feeling my fatigue fade, bringing an increased awareness of the pain that tore through me. Pressing my forehead against the damp ground, I squeezed my eyes shut and focused on control.

A violent shudder pulsed through me; the creature at my back coiled and uncoiled, I swear I felt the slide of cold scales over my spine as it settled back against my warmth. I fought down panic, knowing to give in to it would mean death.

The shivering and fever rolled over me, and I lost control of everything.

I shouted into the cell when I connected with the 911 operator. At first my words were a torrent of confusion. Only the calming voice on the other end broke through my incipient hysteria. Beside me the dog whined and paced around me, reluctant to leave, but just as reluctant to stay. Danny and Niko, young and scared at what they had stumbled into, hovered over me.

Finally, I took several deep breaths and forced myself to speak calmly.

"I need to speak with the rangers. We've found a body – two bodies!"

"Sir, calm down. What is your location? What are you reporting?"

"My partner and I are camping..." I frantically searched my memory for specifics of where we were in the nearly two million acres of mostly wilderness park land. "We're north of the Matilija Canyon area. My partner—" Christ, I wanted to say lover, husband, anything but partner. That sounded so indifferent, so sterile, but I couldn't muddy the waters here. "My partner is a Santa Barbara police detective. He's been shot. We need medical assistance. Right now."

"Give me your location sir, I'll dispatch an ambulance. Are the gunmen still in the area?"

"Yes, no, I don't know! You need to get the police in here, or the rangers. Or whoever. But send them now. And tell them there are drug dealers there, too. A marijuana farm—"

"What is your location, sir?"

"I told you! Matilija Canyon. We hiked in four days ago. Yesterday...no, day before yesterday, we were traveling along the creek bed north of Fox Mountain. Maybe ten, fifteen miles north. I don't know. I lost my GPS. We don't have time for this. He's shot. He may be...he's hurt." I couldn't say dead, I wouldn't say dying.

"Can you stay on the phone, sir? It's possible we can triangulate your relative position from your phone—"

"It's not my phone..." I looked at Niko helplessly. She stared at me for thirty seconds, then shook herself.

"It has GPS." She recited the phone number, which I repeated.

"You can track me?"

"I'm sure we can, sir."

"Please, hurry." God, I wanted to weep, but I had to be strong. Then she said the sweetest words I've ever heard.

"Someone will be dispatched immediately, sir. Please stay on the line."

I was so intent on doing as she told me I didn't notice the dog's growing tension. When his incessant whining turned to a growl, I threw him an angry look, only to find his ears flattened against this head and every hair on his body standing on end. Goose bumps crowded my own skin.

"What's wrong with your dog?" Danny asked.

I wanted to tell him he wasn't my dog, but I was too mesmerized by the intensity the Shepherd showed.

"What is it, boy?" I spoke softly, not wanting to startle him. "You hear something?"

A covey of quail exploded from a patch of scrub brush not fifty feet away from where we stood in the open, staring back at the dark line of forest we had just left. I crouched down and whispered into the still active phone.

"I think they followed me. I think they're here."

"Speak up, sir. I can barely hear you."

"They're here!" I hissed, then took off at a dead run straight downhill, still clutching the phone.

The dog flew ahead of me. Niko yelled and I knew they were chasing me, too. I was beyond caring that I was scaring them. I stumbled on. The moon wasn't much help in letting me see my way. I didn't dare look back to see if something more than my overactive imagination. Danny and Niko followed me. I stumbled, went down but kept moving, scrambling forward on hands and knees until I could get my feet under me again.

Short, scrubby red-tinged poison oaks and sumac flashed by. The creosote stink of chaparral grew stronger the lower we got in our race. The oily excretion the plant exuded clung to everything. It overpowered the stink of my sweat and fear.

The dog raced over to me once when I fell, and shoved his damp nose in my face, his warm doggy breath in my mouth and nose. He gave a short soft bark then bolted again. This time he didn't come back right away. When he finally did, he looked subdued.

I stumbled on. My legs grew leaden and my heart labored in my chest. I half fell, half dove into a small copse full of scraggly aspens and frantically checked that the phone was still connected.

"Are they coming? Tell me you're on your way."

"Yes, sir. We have you on GPS and your location is being monitored."

"Thank God," I muttered then froze. "But the phone isn't mine." I looked at Niko helplessly.

She backed away. "We have to go." She took Danny's arm. "There are men with guns. We can't stay here. They'll shoot us, too."

"Can I keep—"

Niko snatched the phone out of my hand. She shook her head. "I'm sorry..." The dog growled again and the couple backed away from both of us.

"Please—"

But they were gone, hurrying down the mountain, leaving me standing in a field with a manic dog.

I had a choice to make. I could go on, hoping to find someone else who would help or I could go back and bring Alex to safety myself. The only thing I knew for sure was I wasn't going to leave the man I loved more than life itself, to die alone in a wilderness he hadn't even wanted to come to.

Fuck that. I climbed out of the copse and headed back up the mountain. I was going to find Alex. Find him and bring him home.

Pure exhaustion drove me back into an uneasy, nightmare-ridden sleep. The ground underneath me rocked and swayed sickeningly. God, I was on a boat. I don't do boats. My stomach rolled with the pitch of the sea. I hastily gulped back my nausea, only to find my mouth was sandpaper dry. Water. I needed water to drink. Not to float on. I tried to sit up, but couldn't move. In fact, when I tested my limbs, I couldn't feel them. I blinked my eyes open but there was nothing but darkness pressing down on me.

Then I grew aware of the weight on my chest. And the voices. But not voices with words. Loud, aggravated voices, raging, then laughing, then raging again. It sounded like a nearby drunken party spiraling out of control. Where was I? Had I been rescued? Taken to a hospital?

Out of the loud voice a more chilling sound. A high-pitched scream of pain. Of somebody dying. It must be a hospital. The bed under me felt lumpy enough. But if I was in a hospital what was going on outside? It sounded like a rowdy party ready to blow up into a rumble. And that scream. I shivered. Someone needed to call the cops. Wait. I was a cop. The weight on my chest grew heavier. I was having trouble breathing. Pain blossomed in my gut. I needed to move whatever it was off before it suffocated me.

This time, when I opened my eyes, I saw what sat on top of me. Cold, unblinking reptilian eyes stared back at me from a brown wedge-shaped head the size of a dinner plate. When the snake's tongue flicked out and touched my chin I almost screamed. But I couldn't breathe, so no sound came out. The thing looked like it was the size of the Burmese rock python Jason and I had seen once at the Santa Barbara zoo. Since when did rattlesnakes get that big? Or heavy? The weight was increasing, pressing down on my rib cage so hard I swear I heard the bones creak. It was impossible to draw a deep breath. Then it was impossible to breathe at all.

How the hell had it gotten from behind my back on to my chest? Outside, beyond my sight, the wordless voices went on, laughing and shouting, with a growing edge of hysteria to it. The scream came again. Louder. More frantic and terror filled. Couldn't they see me? Couldn't they *hear*? Couldn't they see the fucking snake that was now the size of a car? Then there was a new sound. One that struck even more terror into me.

The staccato sound of the snake's rattle, like bones in a tin cup. It opened its mouth to reveal a set of scimitar shaped fangs glistening with yellow venom. The massive triangular head reared back, flat black eyes like buttons never leaving mine. I jerked my arms up to block the strike but I couldn't move. I opened my mouth to yell, hoping someone out there would hear.

No sound emerged. I squeezed my eyes shut and waited for the strike.

The weight vanished. My eyes flew open; the rattlesnake was gone. So were the screaming voices. My body was shaking so hard my vision was vibrating. I was still lying in the dirt under the pine tree, one hand clutching the canteen. The pressure behind my back was also gone. Daylight infused my shelter, flowing in with soft, damp mist. Now the only sounds I heard were the distant voices of countless birds and insects waking up.

Christ, I had been hallucinating. Was it the fever? Delirium? Had the infection advanced that far? I realized I had no idea how much time had passed. What day was it? Could I trust anything I experienced, or was it all suspect now? And was that a bad thing? Maybe hallucination and delusion were better than full awareness of what was happening to me.

Coward, I sneered. *You lie here feeling sorry for yourself? Who knew you'd be so weak in the end.*

I dragged the canteen over and pried the lid off with my teeth. There was little more than a dribble of delicious warm water that barely wet my lips. It wasn't enough. I'd need more, and soon. I realized with despair and disgust that I had lost control of my bladder at some point. My jeans were dank with piss. Was that what had driven the snake away? I would have laughed if the effort hadn't hurt too much. Talk about telling someone to piss off.

Something crashed in the bushes beyond my meager shelter. Jason came back? God, I hoped not. I wanted him gone from here and not putting himself at risk by coming back, thinking he could save me. Then the crashing stopped and a male voice hissed, in Spanish and broken English. *"Callate. Tiene que estar aqui en algun lugar. Yo vi sangre. Le di y no pudo aver ido muy lejos."*

"If he's around here, then where the fuck is he?" a second voice snarled. "What the hell you thinking, taking potshots at them before we got close enough to surprise 'em?"

"Chinga tu madre, pendejo."

"De seguro vienen a los mendigos policias con la estupides que hicistes. Agaramos dos esta vez, que no, una para cada uno. Vamonos, no cres que es dulce."

I felt sick. They had taken the two women we had met earlier, just as I'd expected. The ones traveling with the dead guy. His next words made me cold.

"Entoces para que tubimos que decasernos tan rapido? No habia terminado."

So the girls were dead, too. I didn't want to think what their last moments had been like. Bad.

"We gotta get out of here. No telling who heard those shots, you goin' all psycho on me. Let's harvest this shit and clear out."

"Es muy temprano, Sabes Dominguez tenemos que esperarnos otro mes," the second male voice said. I had no idea who Dominguez was. Probably their cartel handler. I knew they'd be moving soon, now that heat was coming down on them. They knew they'd lose the crop if they waited. His next words confirmed that.

"Que es lo que van a decir si encuentran esta mierda?"

"We take it now, before they find us, that's what," the Anglo growled. "Should have shot that damned dog when you had the chance. Damn thing almost took my foot off 'til I scared it away. You see that fucker run? What a pussy."

The Latino guy muttered something about not waiting next time. Like there was going to be a next time.

"Bitches are a lot easier to handle then, that's for sure." The Anglo one laughed. "That slut pissed her pants when I nailed her old man."

I wanted to believe they were just more hallucinations, voices from a fevered mind. Then I heard the sound of a magazine being ejected and slammed back into a gun and it sent ice through me. They had automatic weapons. I was unarmed and they were almost close enough to breathe on me.

God help me, I hoped it was all in my head.

Try as I might, I couldn't keep my eyes open. And I couldn't stop shaking. Hard shaking. Bone crushing shaking. My jaw was in agony from trying to keep my teeth from chattering and giving me away. My tongue felt mangled from being worried by my uncontrolled teeth.

The voices faded, then came back stronger and louder. Only this time there were at least a dozen. Christ, how many of them were there? I'd met homicidal pairs, but never committees. My confusion grew. Cotton under my cheeks, the unmistakable scent of the laundry soap Jason used on our bedding. I was back home. How had that happened? Had I lost consciousness and been rescued? By who? Jason?

But where was he? I looked around as best I could but I was still paralyzed. Only my head could move, and what was visible threw me into deeper confusion. It smelled like home, but it wasn't our bedding. Neither Jason or I would ever use flowery pink sheets. The last time I had seen sheets like that – I realized I wasn't at home. At least, not my current home. I was back in the house I had shared briefly with my wife, Barbara, nearly five years ago. The house she had thrown me out of when I had come out to her, and asked for a divorce. There had been nothing amicable about that divorce, either. She never forgave me for lying to her so completely from day one. Only the fact we had no kids, and she had a better paying job at her law firm than I could ever hope to achieve, saved me from losing everything. As it was, she took the house, sold it then moved to New York where I heard she married another corporate lawyer and now had her two point five kids and the champagne lifestyle she had always wanted.

None of which explained why I was back in our marital bed unable to wiggle so much as a toe. She was in the other room. I knew it. But, and this made no sense at all, Jason was there, too. Just out of sight, barely audible, but I would know his voice anywhere. So was my partner, Miguel Dominguez, which made even less sense. The two of us never socialized, even over lunch. Their murmuring voices were added to the cacophony of other voices shouting and laughing. The party was back in full force.

Then somebody I recognized appeared. Nancy, my old partner and new boss. She bustled through the door – door ?– and walked by me. In total confusion I called out to her. She ignored me and vanished through another door that was ablaze with flashing lights and growing disco music. The music grew loud enough to almost drown out the voices. I swore I heard Jason among them, laughing and talking away a mile a minute, something he rarely did with anyone but me.

Nancy was back. I shouted at her and she turned toward me, sneering. "Don't you know it's rude to expect people to always do what you tell them to? Who do you think you are? Jason's out there, you know. Having fun. I bet you hate that, don't you? He's not supposed to have fun without you."

"That's not true," I protested but she ignored me. She vanished again before I could tell her she had it all wrong, about everything. Then she was back. "You always were a hard ass, weren't you, Lieutenant?"

She giggled, a light tinkling sound that was like nothing I had ever heard from her and frankly, couldn't imagine her doing. Somehow it unnerved me more than anything else that was happening to me.

I must be hallucinating, or dreaming, or something. Maybe dying. Was that it? I was lying in the dirt on top of a mountain dying because I forgot to duck in time? How stupid was that? And here I was. The man who always controlled everything couldn't even stop the fucking voices in his head. Couldn't stop himself from pissing his pants. Who lay here shaking like a newborn kitten. Who had lost control of everything.

She wouldn't give up. Nancy came back. This time in full uniform, her Lieutenant's bars and shiny new badge all spit and polished. She leaned over me, head cocked as though listening to something only she could hear. Finally she met my eyes.

"You're dying, you know? How does it feel? Like shit? You think you're getting a shitty deal? Imagine what it's going to be like for Jason. You leaving him again. Not a good track record, there, Spidey-man."

"Fuck, don't call me that."

"Spidey senses all wonked out on you? That's cause you're dying, Detective. Hate to be the bearer of bad news," she lied, sounding gleeful. "But you've bought the farm. Dead man walking – or crawling in your case, I guess. Going to meet your maker, and won't you be a sorry sight at the pearly gates—"

"Shut up! Shut up! Shut—"

The barking brought me crashing back into reality. The music and voices faded, along with my old domestic domicile, to be replaced by the savage barking of a dog then the crash of something fleeing through the bushes outside my shelter.

"What the—"

Several shots went off in rapid succession, pinging off trees and stones, followed by more shots and some choice, guttural curses. Then silence. Fire filled me, my gut burned. I flashed between furnace hot and arctic cold. I was shivering so hard I was actually moving with the vibrations across the ground. My mouth was beyond dry. My eyes would barely open, they were so gummed up. Even when I forced them apart, my eyeballs vibrated and nothing would come into focus.

It was true. I was dying. But suddenly, I was damned if I was going to die in here like a sick animal crawling under the porch to pass in shame. I reached out and grabbed a handful of loam, digging my fingers below the carpet of needles and twigs and getting a grip. I pulled myself onto my stomach. The pain in my gut flared into white, hot agony that didn't subside as I dragged myself toward the tunnel of faint light I was sure marked the opening of my living tomb. There must be a moon, since I was sure the sun had gone down long ago.

The pain pulsed behind my eyes and through my clenched jaw, but I persisted. Sweat poured off me, my hands grew slick with wet loam that I belatedly realized was a mix of blood and sweat. I had torn my fingernails off leaving bloody trails behind as I dragged and pulled myself out from under the pine boughs.

I could barely hold my head up, in fact it kept rolling forward, digging my chin or my nose in the rich, fecund needle covered loam that smelled of decay and mold. I was chewing on dirt and pine needles, vainly trying to spit them out of a mouth that was bone dry.

Nausea gripped me and I vomited, though nothing but a sour bile came up. The stomach spasm sent raw bolts of pain so pure it transcended my fear. I screamed, but it emerged as a pathetic croak. Still, too loud. Something was out there, listening.

"What was that?" They were back. The two killers. Mutt and Jeff.

"Sounded like a bear to me. Let's get out of here—"

"Weren't no bear. You think you're in some kinda Disney movie?"

"Fuck it was."

"It was a dog, *chocho*."

"Dog don't sound like that."

"Maybe you hit it. You ever think of that, *pendejo*? You shot at the damn fool thing often enough."

"Hope so, that was a mean looking *chingada*."

The voices faded as the two of them moved off, or maybe it was just another psychotic delusion. I didn't stop to think. Thinking was wasted now. All I could do was act. I dug in and pulled myself along. I tried to use my feet to push, but any movement below my chest brought breath-stopping torture and sent me tumbling toward a blackness I knew would be permanent if I let myself slip into it. As comfortable and pain free as it might be, I wouldn't give in like that. Not yet. Maybe my control of everything else, including my mind, was gone, but I could still control this.

There was no dramatic moment when I broke free of my prison. The ground under me was still loamy and covered with tree debris. I tried to avoid the myriad of sticks and things that dug into my hands and face, nearly poking out my eyes more than once. I was covered in scratches and the bug repellent Jason had lathered on me generously was fading. The bugs apparently found me delicious. Flies persistently buzzed around my face and the bloody wound at my side. Whenever I stopped moving they would swarm the torn flesh and fight over the feast. Their buzzing grew in intensity. It was all I could do not to scream. The inflamed flesh was so tender even the minuscule weight of their bodies, the tickle of their feet was agony. But any movement on my part to shoo them off brought equal pain. And the pain was spreading, everything from my neck down was afire. Each time a fresh spasm passed through me I shuddered, and dug my bleeding fingers into the ground, squeezing my eyes shut to try to ride it out. Each episode left me weaker and weaker.

I tried not to think about what the flies were doing. I'd come across my share of decomposing bodies, riddled with maggots. Laid by the sort of flies that were now lighting on my wound. Is that what they were doing? Turning me into a fly feast?

Then something worse. Squeaking. Mice? Rats? Squirrels don't eat flesh. What else did up here? I never paid any attention to Jason talking about the wilderness animals he loved. I had no idea what was sniffing around me looking for a free lunch.

I pushed on, fleeing from my pain, from the terrible future

that awaited me.

Knowing that soon I wasn't going to be able to move at all.

As long as I was in the open I could keep moving fairly quickly. But once the forest canopy closed over my head, I was forced to slow to little more than a crawl. At least that's what it seemed like to me. I reluctantly pulled the miniature flashlight I had pocketed, knowing it would give me away instantly if I was spotted by the killer. I did my best to keep the beam shielded, focusing it on the ground at my feet. Even so, I tripped often and banged into more than one fallen branch, leaving my shins black and blue.

The dog had vanished a long time ago.

I should have slowed down. I was going to hurt myself, or worse. But the knowledge that Alex was up there, at the mercy of the elements and that monster, spurred me past all caution. It would have been nice to wait for the authorities, but they were going to take too long. I didn't even know if they would venture in this far in the dark, or would they set up a perimeter and insist on waiting for dawn?

I wasn't sure Alex had until another dawn, not if he was being hunted.

The nighttime forest was alive with its own sounds. Creatures sang, the wind shivered through the branches overhead, and once a female Great Horned owl called out. Soft rustles fled from me and once something larger crashed through the heavy brush away from me. When I raised the flashlight to get a look at the terrain ahead of me, I would catch glimpses of brilliant eyes watching me. But nothing showed itself, for which I was grateful. The last thing I wanted was a run in with something big enough to cause bodily harm. I kept hearing things move in the darkness. Just out of sight.

Maybe it was the dog coming back. Maybe it was something worse.

The air had grown cool, which was another good thing. It kept my body from overheating and with any luck would keep the local reptiles quiescent.

I came across the bear sign soon after. I found it by literally stepping in it. Something squished under my Merrels and I stepped back, shining my flashlight down around my feet. The scat was fresh, black and runny. Not a good sign. Fresh meant the bear was still in the area, black and soft meant this particular bear was feasting on flesh someplace. Probably carrion. Breaking a thin twig off, I prodded the nearest mound. It broke apart, releasing a pungent odor that further confirmed what it was.

I scanned the ground around the scat and the hairs on the back of my neck stood up. A second, smaller mass of scattered excrement. This bear was female, and she had at least one cub. Shining the light around revealed the trail leading north, uphill. I stepped into it and had to crouch to fit inside. Wide enough for two men to walk side by side, but not stand up. A bear trail.

I backed out fast, hyper alert now. My skin was literally crawling as my nerves jumped in anticipation. Fight or flight. That's what survival always came down to. Over the whisper of the wind exhaling through the tree branches above me, the passing of tiny rodent feet seeking shelter and food as they scurried through the underbrush, I strained to hear anything that would suggest I wasn't alone. No further sign of the bear sow or her cub. Small reassurance. I knew they were near. That scat they had left couldn't have been more than a couple of hours old. No telling how old the meat was they were eating. The light was too low to see any detail of the clumps of hair I had seen buried in the shit. But there had been fur, so that was a relief. I'm not sure I could have handled the suspicion that the bears had found a human body.

I checked my wristwatch. Ten-forty-three. Dawn was hours away. I had to find shelter, preferably off the ground. Good luck with that. I was physically fit but climbing trees was not among my skill sets.

I slipped through the shadowy trunks, using the ambient moon and starlight, and occasionally my flashlight to search out one that had branches low enough to give me something to grip.

After nearly half an hour I found one I thought I could manage. I stood underneath it, contemplated what I was about to do next. Pulling a handful of granola out of the bag in my pocket, I chewed, stalling. For what? Someone to deliver a miracle to me? God to show me a way to save Alex? *Get real, Zachary. No one's going to save you or your man except you. So stop wasting time.*

With a deep sigh I took one last look around, checking for the bear. Even if I couldn't see or hear one, I knew she was out there, probably on the prowl for food for her and her cub.

Rule number one in bear country: you don't want to mess with a mother bear and her cub. Ever. All mother animals will defend their young, bears have a particularly savage way of doing so. Rule number two in bear country: you don't want to mess with a bear and her dinner. Bears spend most of their awake time browsing for sugar-rich berries, tubers and other fat inducing foods. All designed with one thing in mind – build up bear body fat for the long hibernation in the upcoming winter. Cartoon movie makers got more than one person mauled or dead because they wanted photos of the cute bear taking their treats – and the bear tried to take a lot more. Female bears have a special need; most of them are pregnant when they den up. The cubs are born while their mother sleeps. That takes a lot of body energy, and it all has to be taken in before they den up. When mama bear finally wakes up in spring, she's hungry and very cranky. Four hundred pounds of cranky bear is not something I want to meet anywhere. Rule number three? Leave before you have to invoke rule number one or two. Or climb a tree when leaving isn't an option.

I slung my binoculars around my back, nestled against my backpack and wiped my hands on the legs of my jeans. I was sweating, and it wasn't just from exertion.

I didn't climb far. Settling into the notch of the tree maybe four feet off the forest floor. I felt like a fool, but not enough to climb down.

Tomorrow, I had to forget all about the sow and her cub. I had to find Alex. I wasn't sure who I feared the most, the bear or the homicidal maniac who had already tried to kill us. Granted the man was armed, and had already killed at least one man and shot Alex, but then I'd also seen proof what an enraged bear was capable of, too.

It was a pity I couldn't arrange for the homicidal killers to meet my bears...that was when my mind started spinning out crazy possibilities. As sleep evaded me, my mind went flying far afield. Maybe I was on to something. The guy who had shot Alex wanted me, too. I was a threat to him. If I gave myself up as bait could I draw him in to a confrontation with the bears? Was I willing to gamble that he wasn't versed in wilderness lore? Wasn't bush smart? Maybe that was just wishful thinking, and I was stereotyping, but drug-growing goons with automatic weapons and murder on their minds didn't strike me as being too savvy about local fauna.

The plan that started forming then required that I be right, because if I wasn't, Alex and I were both as good as dead. I couldn't stop shivering and it wasn't only from the cold. I knew no one would be coming up the mountain until day broke, no matter how dire the emergency. I did my best to get comfortable, wedging myself in as securely as possible to keep from tumbling the few feet to the forest floor. My face was pressed against the rough tree bark, which kept flaking off and falling down my shirtfront. My skin itched and I blinked furiously to clear the dust out of my tearing eyes.

The owl called again. She was hunting, I heard a sharp squeak that terminated abruptly, signaling a successful hunt. It made me think of the man after me. I doubted he was doing anything under cover of darkness, but I had to be ready at first light to go on my way. And with luck, put my plan into effect. I'd have to move fast. Both of us were running out of time.

I huddled as best I could, curled up tight to conserve body heat. Even so I was soon shivering; clenching my jaw to keep my teeth from chattering. The need for rest, fought with the fear, that if I dozed off, I'd fall or do something to alert anyone or anything in the area that I was here.

Eyelids that weighed several tons now slid closed, and I

tightened my grip on the tree branch. Pinesap stung the myriad scratches I wore from my travels. I pressed my eyes shut. Let me just rest for a few minutes. My shivering got worse.

My last conscious thought was: how bad must it be for Alex? Then even the rough feel of the tree limb under my cheek faded and I felt a welcomed peace fill me.

I blinked and snapped my eyes opened. I was no longer in the tree. I was lying on rough ground that smelled of loam and rotting vegetation and something else. Something familiar. Confusion reigned. Had I fallen? But the tree I had climbed earlier wasn't there. So where was I? Then I recognized the statuesque fir tree Alex had hidden himself under when he had ordered me to leave him. How had I gotten back here? This was where I wanted to go, but it should have taken me several more hours to reach it.

Eagerly I turned, looking for him, only to find the shelter formed by the tree boughs was empty. Had he crawled away? Maybe he hadn't been as badly hurt as we thought. How ironic would it be if he had passed me on our journeys, me to come back to him, while he made his way to safety. But that didn't jibe with the way he had looked when I left him. If he'd been well enough to walk we would have gone together. No way I would have left him, orders or no.

I scrambled across the enclosed space. The ground was torn up. Raw earth now threw off the smell of sewage and compost. The earth under me squirmed with insects and worms. Clots of something dark and sticky covered the ravaged, heaving earth. Where was Alex? He'd lain here; I could still see the outline of his body in the disturbed dirt. Worms crawled over my outstretched fingers. I cried out and shook them off. Then need and curiosity overcame my revulsion.

I got down on my hands and knees and crawled over the ground. I was quickly covered in a viscous red fluid. I was swimming in it. Blood. That had been the unfamiliar smell.

Where the fuck was Alex?

Panic suffused me. On hands and knees I tore through the nearby brush, ignoring the growing stench of blood and the swelling buzz of feasting insects. Alex! I wanted to scream his name, but when I opened my mouth, no sound emerged. Moving was like plowing through neck deep water. I was going nowhere at a dead crawl. The buzzing increased to a roar. I half stood, bracing against a resin-covered tree trunk and threw myself past the screen of branches into daylight—

And awoke seconds before I tumbled off my tree limb. Wildly I clutched it, pressing my face against the rough bark, scraping my already raw skin. I was hyperventilating, and had to force myself to breath shallowly, until the panic attack subsided.

A dream. It had only been a dream. Several insects buzzed around my head, clearly the source of the sound in my nightmare. I batted at them, then had to catch myself a second time to stop from falling. Nearby birds were beginning to awaken. I couldn't see any lightening of the sky, but knew it must be coming soon.

With stiff muscles I scrambled to the ground, bending and stretching to loosen my limbs up. I glanced toward my planned route and saw it was mostly uphill. It would be a hard slog, but I knew I was in good shape. Unlike the sedentary Alex, I spent several hours a week keeping fit. I did it for Alex and for myself, since I always wanted to be at my best for him. And now it was going to pay off for both of us.

I made my careful way out onto the trail, keeping an eye out for bear sign, and always alert for the human menace that stalked these woods. I would have even welcomed the dog's return, but he was evidently long gone. Hopefully, he hadn't had a run in with the bear and her cub. I trusted that he knew better.

Over an hour later I came across my first bear scat of the day. Fresh. It was scary how fresh. In the growing daylight I could make out some dense black hairs and scuff marks that the large pawed animals made, as they bulled their way through dense brush. Common sense told me to go the other way, to put as much distance as possible between me and the she bear. But common sense wasn't going to help Alex or me out of this mess.

I was beginning to think only luck, and maybe God, was going to do that.

I was in the middle of another captive nightmare. Was I even capable of having a rational thought anymore? A pig was hunting me this time. The snuffling and snorting form hovered on the edge of my reality, which was stretched very thin. Was it drawn by my blood? The sound of my hoarse breathing? Could it hear my heart laboring in my chest, every pulse sending waves of pain through every nerve ending in my dying body?

I knew pigs ate flesh. There had been a couple of well-known cases where killers had used that nasty fact to dispose of unwanted corpses. Would a death by animal attack be a swifter, more merciful one than what I knew faced me if I died from sepsis and the fever that raged in me, burning up my brain and my sanity?

It was harder and harder to force my mind to focus beyond the pain and delirium that was a constant presence now. My open wounds were crawling with flies but I was beyond trying to drive them away. It took too much energy and it didn't stop them.

The pig got closer. Was it my imagination or could I feel its hot, fetid breath on my oversensitive skin? Coarse bristles rubbing against my head? I knew it was beside me even before a warm, wet nose nuzzled at my face, exhaling on me seconds before a tongue came out and slopped over my mouth and nose. Then it whimpered.

Whimpered?

I opened my eyes. Instead of a nightmare creature about to chew me apart, I was looking up the nose of a worried looking dog. The German Shepherd. The one Jason and I had seen in the trailhead where we had parked the truck. The one we had heard barking just days before I found its master's dead body.

The dog whimpered again and gently nosed my cheek. Warm, doggy breath blew over me. When I uncurled the fingers of one hand, the dog licked it, then rubbed its massive head against my fingers. Wanting to be petted?

"Good boy," I managed to say.

The dog wagged its tail.

"Too bad you're not Lassie," I croaked through a throat so dry it hurt to talk or swallow. "I could send you to get help. Timmy's down the well, grandpa."

I started laughing, knowing it was hysteria, but still not able to stop. Fortunately, my laughter was little more than a whisper. The dog heard it, and tentatively nosed my cheek again as though it wanted to understand.

There was a crash and muffled Spanish curse moments later. The dog flattened beside me and a low rumble came out of it. The Shepherd was growling, its ear pressed flat against its broad head. I guess it didn't like our neighborhood pot growers, either.

"No, Timmy, huh?" I whispered as shivers took control of my body and I started convulsing, gasping for breath as my chest spasmed in a desperate attempt to pull in air.

My eyes were open, but my vision was fading. Soon, the dog was little more than a black and tan blur with only darkness beyond it. At the same time the voices in my head grew in volume and persistence. The screaming partygoers were back, joining with animals roaring and something inhuman screaming.

I was only vaguely aware of a weight settling beside me, pressing against my chest, calming the violent tremors and bringing a strange peace to me. If I was going to die out here at least I wouldn't be alone.

I was making good time. Between my grim determination and my previous exposure to these trails, I ate up the distance between us. I stopped only long enough to drink when I came across a water outlet. I refused to think that I might be too late. That I would find Alex beyond hope or already dead. That would be unbearable. Alex was my life. Maybe that sounds pathetic, to live through another person so completely, but I couldn't imagine life without him. If that meant facing his killers and following him into death then I wouldn't go down lightly. I would make them pay for what they had done to us.

It was weird, but I found myself missing the dog. I had been glad when he came back and was still there the next morning, but then sometime during the day he had wandered off. He'd done that before and always came back. This time he didn't. The next morning he still hadn't returned and I had to write him off. Too bad. I hoped he would be okay. I couldn't waste any time fretting over him.

Right now I had to find that bear and her cub. Once I'd located her, maybe I could set the next step into motion. That was just as dangerous as tracking down the two of them and risking the sow's wrath. I had to find an armed killer and trick him into following me without getting myself killed outright.

My stomach growled. I dug through my backpack pulling one of the dozen energy bars out, unwrapped it and chewed while I walked. Out of pure reflex I shoved the wrapper in the side pocket of my pack. My fingers closed over the other things I'd stuffed in there over the course of our hike. I was religious about "carry-in-carry-out" and never left even a single scrap behind when I walked out at the end of a hiking trip.

So I had four days worth of garbage in my backpack. Bears love garbage almost as much as they love honey. That's why they were such a major issue around campsites that didn't have diligent clean up, or kept open garbage sites close to people.

Just maybe I had what I needed to bring that bear where I wanted her.

I emptied my pockets and backpack. I had thirteen energy bars, three vacuum-sealed bags of dried fruit and one of jerky. Alex had a similar stash with him. I had wanted to make sure we would have enough no matter what are circumstances, though for sure I hadn't foreseen *this*.

I hiked on with renewed drive. I had to find that bear.

I knew I wasn't going to live through another night.

Sleep fell away from me slowly. For one brief second before I opened my eyes and tried to move, I thought I was home, in bed. Jason's warm body pressed against mine and I felt a peace I don't think I have ever achieved at any time in my life. I was happy. Up until now I hadn't known what that felt like. I'd been going through life all this time operating on instinct, with no drive beyond my job and solving other people's problems, never solving my own. I had let the dead from my past crowd out unwanted intimacy because it was a hell of a lot easier to pick up some trick at The Vault, fuck him for a few hours then send him on his way, than to face the fact that my life was so fucking empty.

Now I had found someone to fill it, and I had let it slip away because I was afraid. For one hot, delusional second I wanted to believe Jason was here with me so I could tell him that. Admit I was afraid. Just once tell another human being I felt fear. And find out that it wouldn't make me less of a man to him. Because I knew now Jason loved me with or without weaknesses. My flaws meant nothing to him.

The illusion lasted until I tried to roll over and take him in my arms. A bolt of pure agony slammed through me. I bit my tongue as I screamed. It came out as a grunt, and my mouth flooded with hot, metallic blood.

Jason whimpered and I realized it wasn't my lover, but the dog. He had stayed with me through the night. His warm tongue bathed my face, his touch oddly soothing on my fevered skin. My lips were cracked and the blood in my mouth stung them. I was beyond thirst. Not that it would matter much. I'd be dead from the poison in my blood long before dehydration became an issue.

I drifted in and out of awareness. It was easy to welcome the darkness with its lack of pain. Despair ate at me. I fought it with the same savagery I used to bring justice to my dead people.

Wave after wave of pain and heat poured through me.

It would be a lot easier just to stop fighting. Part of me wanted to. I wouldn't see Jason again. He was gone from my life, and maybe he'd be better off for it. I knew he'd survive just fine. My Jason was strong.

Stronger than me. And that was an admission I didn't like one bit. I was supposed to be the unbreakable one. The tough cop who took down killers and rapists and didn't let things like soft emotions interfere with any of that. So why was I lying here in my own piss and blood, dying like a slum dog kicked one too many times?

Speaking of dogs...I reached out to touch the one who had watched over me all night long. The space beside me was empty. He was gone. I guess his protective duties were over. Maybe that should tell me something.

That thought galvanized me. I wasn't going to let a gut shot stop me. Like I told Jason, it was a flesh wound. I refused to admit anything else. I could overcome this if I was strong enough. And if I couldn't do it for myself, I could sure as hell do it for Jason.

In my fevered state, I realized something. I wanted Jason safe above all else. More than my own life. When the hell had that happened? Shaking violently, I pulled myself onto my stomach. If I lay here it would mean I had given up and was waiting to die. And that was so fucking wrong. I had never been a quitter. I wasn't going to start now. My fingers throbbed, the nails torn off earlier. My elbows were raw from scraping across the ground. I ignored the pain that was now so ubiquitous I couldn't remember a time I hadn't been in agony.

I couldn't remember the touch of rain on my face, of sun-warmed air stroking bare skin. The feel of Jason's mouth on me, bringing me more pleasure than any other person had. And what did he ask of me? My possession of him. Totally and without doubt. I was full of doubt. It had poisoned what I had with him. I had no one to blame but myself. Jason had always been there for me, so why couldn't I be there for him?

I would have snorted if the effort wouldn't have cost so much. Fine thing to be thinking about how I had failed Jason, when I was past being able to do anything about it. Would I change that if I could? Don't be a fool, of course I wouldn't. I had too much invested in maintaining my image. I couldn't surrender that for anything.

My lower body was no longer responding to me. On the one hand that meant there was no pain, on the other hand, it meant I couldn't even crawl. I could pull myself along, but with my strength failing fast, I wasn't getting very far.

How many days had it taken us to reach this spot? That was on two legs, with a brain that worked. I'd been slow. I knew it, even though I also knew Jason would never in a million years have told me that. Another thing we didn't share. Jason would walk on fire to keep from bruising my ego. I expected him to take whatever I dished out — bad-temper, work frustrations, my ingrained cynicism — without giving it back in kind. I wouldn't have taken that kind of insubordination, not even from him.

For the very first time in my life I wished there was indeed something after death. I wanted one more chance to get it right with Jason. Maybe if I couldn't do it in life, I could do it in death.

Enough. Stop the fucking pity-fest. Move or die.

I'd like to think I had adjusted to the pain, but who was I kidding? I didn't notice it as much because most of my body was no longer feeling anything.

I dragged myself forward, one inch at a time. I refused to think about how futile it was. I was miles from anything except the men who had tried to kill me. Not exactly people I wanted to interact with.

But I could be stubborn. Jason would have agreed, probably with that smug grin he gave me as though he knew something he wasn't sharing.

The ground sloped down, making it easier to move forward. I knew the sun was on my back, I knew it must be hot, but I didn't feel it. Instead I was wracked with shivers and I have never felt so cold. Then the next minute it was like I was in a sauna with sweat pouring off me, drawing more stinging and sucking insects to my face, tormenting me. They'd be all over my wound too, but mercifully I couldn't feel or see that.

Over my head birds sang and wind soughed through the interlaced branches. All so normal sounding. Somehow I figured things would be darker. After all I lived my life in the dark. It was fitting I die that way. Not in bright sunlight surrounded by some birds singing like they were in a fucking Disney cartoon. Jason would have named all of them and laughed and handed his binoculars to me so I could share his find. I'd look, for his sake, but we both knew I didn't care.

I focused my eyes on a slender twig that still had a few green needles attached to it. That was my goal. I would reach that. An hour later, give or take an hour, I made it. Closing my fist over it, I squeezed it between my bleeding fingers. Breaking needles released a piney smell that reminded me of Christmas. Jason and I had missed last Christmas. We never talked about what we would do for this one. I wasn't much into seasonal cheer, but maybe that would have changed this year. Maybe we could have gone so far as to put a tree up and Jason would cook us a real Christmas dinner. I dropped the broken needles to settle my gaze on a new target that might have been a yard away and crawled toward it.

I was getting nowhere fast. The option was a lot less attractive.

I tried not to notice where the sun was or what darkness would bring.

Tree bark flaked from under my Merrells as I pushed myself onto the next branch. I figured I was high enough here. I stared down at the sleek black form sniffing around the half a granola bar I'd broken up and scattered around the base of a nearby tree. Her cub was nowhere in sight. Probably in the thick brush the sow had come out of ten minutes ago. I was sure she caught my scent, but since I wasn't posing a threat she didn't look for me too hard. The food interested her a lot more.

Over my head a blue jay screamed. Whether at me or the bear, I couldn't tell. We both ignored the irritable bird.

She chuffed and snorted, rooting through debris for more tidbits. When she found nothing, she widened her search. Now and then she would stop and paw through the pine needle covered ground where I knew she would find grubs and other tasty creatures.

But they weren't very satisfying. It took more than a few invertebrates to satisfy a four-hundred pound bear. She swung her broad black head from side to side, testing the air for food or danger. Finding neither, she ambled back into the bush and within minutes the sound of her passing faded.

I waited another ten minutes before climbing down from my perch. Back on the ground I brushed off my jeans. A futile gesture since they were past dirty. I could smell my own sweat and taste a mouth that hadn't seen a toothbrush in days. My hair was matted, alternately clinging to my sweating head or stood up in disarranged clumps I couldn't get my fingers through. Stubble covered my face and itched. Hell, I itched everywhere. It felt like a thousand insects crawled over every inch of my skin and all the scratching in the world wasn't getting rid of them. Not a pleasant experience.

The bears were easy to follow. My biggest worry at this point was getting too close. If the sow sensed I was near, she might backtrack on me. I didn't dare risk that. At the same time I needed to stay in a position where I could lead the bear where I wanted her to be.

I was getting close to the area where Alex and I had stumbled over the grow-op and heard the engine. Preternaturally alert, I picked up my pace. My nerves hummed. I wasn't sure who posed the greater danger to me, the bear or the man with a gun. I didn't dare run into either, yet I had to figure out a way to get the two together.

I knew I was coming up on the marijuana patch when the light grew stronger. The break in the trees allowed sunlight to bathe the plants in the light they needed to grow tall. The brief glimpse I'd had of them when we first found the clear-cut area, left me with the impression of plants that were around four feet tall. While I'd smoked my share of the stuff in my pre-Alex days, I had never seen it in its raw form in the ground, so I had no idea how big they got. A few news broadcasts I'd seen where cops hailed a massive pot farm bust always showed them standing around piles of the stuff, after it had been cut down, readied to be destroyed. But I thought they were tall, taller than what we had seen. If I was right, then what we had seen wasn't ready to harvest. But I'd bet it was close. Did that explain why the man with the gun had been there? Protecting his cash crop?

I smiled grimly. Let him protect it from momma bear. Like I told Alex, no handgun in the world was going to do more than piss off an angry bear.

I pressed on. Growing more attuned to the world around me. Birds chittered and trilled, and the electrical whine of cicadas climbed in volume as the day waxed. I listened for the warning call of a jay ahead of me, knowing it would signal something that alarmed them. Like a bear or a human.

Or me. I had to assume the shooter didn't know what screaming jays meant. The sound shouldn't alert them like it would me.

It didn't stop me from having to be careful. Because it would tell the bear something was near.

I moved silently through the heaviest part of the brush. Fortunately, pine needles make great sound mufflers, so my passage was relatively quiet. If the drug dealer was a trained tracker, I was in shit, even deeper than the stuff I was in already.

For Alex's sake I had to operate on the assumption he wasn't.

Up ahead a jay screamed. I froze, straining to hear what had upset the jay. Nothing but cicadas singing. I kept walking, spotting the odd strands of black hair twined in twigs, claws marks in a rotting stump of a black cottonwood where she had ripped it open for the feast inside. I spotted a couple of squirming grubs she missed.

A hundred feet past the log I found another steaming pile of scat so fresh the flies had barely found it. Using a twig I dug through the reeking mess and was glad to find it was firmer than the last one I'd found. There wasn't any sign the bear had found new meat. I knew I was getting close. I became hyper vigilant.

At first I could barely hear the sound, it blended in with the whining cicadas. Only when it didn't modulate like the singing insects and grew more guttural as it rose to a throaty rumble, I knew what it was. The same engine Alex and I heard earlier, before he was shot.

Then a whisper of voices over the growling engine. One talking in rapid Spanish, the other in broken Spanish, definitely an Anglo. I knew enough of the language to make out that they were talking about clearing out. But first they wanted to find the assholes they shot. They knew we were out there and someone called Dominguez wanted us found. We were unfinished business.

So Alex hadn't been found yet. My heart soared. He was still alive. He had to be. I couldn't think otherwise, not if I wanted to stay sane.

And I had to find him before those two did.

I crouched low, hugging the gnarled side of a pine, the stink of resin filling my nose. My cheek stung as I pressed against the bark, trying to pinpoint the sound more precisely. It was left, north. On the other side of the field of rustling stalks of marijuana.

Trying to figure out how close I was to where I left Alex, I scanned the visible trunks, looking for familiar markers. There, that crooked bough, with the fringe of needles. That was where Alex was hidden. Assuming he was still there.

My nightmare came back to me. The horror of crawling through Alex's blood, the torn earth, the worms. I shuddered and pushed the image away.

Crawling worm-like myself over the rough ground, I ignored needles and sticks digging into my bare hands, working up under my shirt and even into my hair. My muscles cramped up. I had to roll onto my back and dig fingers into my thighs to stop them from knotting up on me completely.

I shut my eyes against the savage pain. I had to bite my lip to keep from crying out. When I opened them again I blinked against the sudden burst of sunlight streaming directly down on me. I'd been in shadow so long it was a shock.

Then I saw the new shadow drift across my vision. I tracked its flight, not sure I wasn't hallucinating. A condor. The one bird on the top of my wish list that I never imagined seeing, though I knew we were in its territory. But there it was, ten foot wingspan unmoving in the rising thermals, looking graceful and ethereal. It banked and circled, moving lower and with an icy certainty I knew what it had come for.

California condors were a magnificent, rare animal, with maybe a hundred and thirty still alive in the wild, but they were essentially giant vultures. They fed on carrion. And they could smell it miles away. What had brought it here? The bodies Alex had literally stumbled over? Or Alex?

I squeezed my eyes shut again, blocking out the sight of the spiraling bird. It was still there when I reopened them, close enough to see the white, covert flight feathers under its broad, unmoving wings and the wing tags, with the tracking number on them. Three-forty. If this had been part of the hike I had wanted to go on with Alex, I would be recording all this and I'd take it home with me to check it against the online Condor Spotter, which would tell me the name, release date and territory of the bird. I could have added my sighting to the growing database charting where the birds were.

But the wonderful hike with my lover had turned into a nightmare I couldn't seem to wake from. Instead of marveling at the sight of this raptor, I feared it. It meant this was a place of death. A charnel site. The bird kept drifting down. I wanted to shout at it to leave. Instead, I bit my lip to keep from making any sound that would give me away.

The sound of the truck engine grew nearer. More Spanish that could barely be heard over the guttural roar of diesel. I backed away from the clearing until I was shielded by clusters of intertwined branches. Movement in the still stalks of marijuana turned out to be a trio of machete wielding Latinos. They were harvesting their crop. Spooked by Alex and me getting away from them? I was glad to see their attention was on getting the harvest out, instead of looking for us.

Then a fourth Latino man stepped into view, passing less than a yard from my hiding place. I swallowed past a sudden rush of fear. A deadly looking Uzi hung around over his chest from a strap over his shoulders. One hand rested comfortably on it, and I knew it would take him less than a half a second to put it to use. He'd cut me in half with the thing if he found me.

I shrank back into my leafy cubbyhole, praying he'd pass me by. His alert eyes scanned everywhere, momentarily looking right at me. My heart was beating so hard I thought for sure he'd hear it. I broke out in a cold sweat that stung my eyes. I couldn't hear anything but the roar of my own blood pounding through me. I stopped breathing. His dark gaze kept moving, then he slowly moved away, circling back to where I suspected the truck was.

How long would it take them to clear this field of their product? They were working in a frenzy, and every so often one of the workers, all young men with faces drawn and ravaged by bad diet and neglect, would look over at the Uzi man. It wasn't my imagination when I saw fear there.

What were they? Illegals forced into servitude because of their status? Hard to complain to the authorities when you weren't supposed to exist. They were all gaunt from malnutrition. Sweat poured off their shaved heads, not even covered with bandannas, soaking their chambray shirts. They were surrounded in clouds of insects that I knew from personal experience were biting and sucking. The torment must have been excruciating, but not one of them even paused to brush away the mosquitoes and biting flies.

Uzi came back, this time in the company of an Anglo, a lanky, tattooed dirty blond-headed man with a mouth barely visible behind a sweeping beard and mustache. No sub-machine gun on this one. He had an old fashioned Beretta. At least that's what I thought it was, having handled a similar handgun when Alex took me shooting. Like his duty weapon.

I wished I could get my hands on one of them now. It might not be much firepower when faced with what an Uzi could do, but it would make me feel a whole lot better. I stayed perfectly still until they passed out of sight again, then I eased backward, keeping the screen of brush between me and the open field. I felt around in the zippered pocket of my safari jacket. Both of them were full of my bars and granola. I wiggled one out and held it in my hand as I moved further and further away from the armed men.

I made my way back to the last bear sign I had passed less than half an hour ago. The scat was now crawling with flies and beetles. I studied the area around it, finally spotting where I thought the bear had gone next. Disturbed ground, bent and broken branches, some still with black hair clinging to them. I had to circle around ahead of them, so I could lay my trail of sweet treasures to lure her closer to the grow-op, and her meeting with the killers.

The jay, or another one, screamed northeast of me. Close. I moved straight north, all the time alert, to not only bear, but for gun-wielding pot growers. The jay grew more raucous and was joined by another one. A mated pair maybe. Which probably meant an occupied nest nearby. Bears loved eggs and young animals, almost as much as they loved honey.

I crept along, staying low, moving slowly, always aware of what was around me on all sides. A flash of blue overhead warned me I was close. If the bird saw me, it ignored me. The bear posed more menace to it than I did.

I saw the cub first. A medium, dog-sized, animal, ten-twelve pounds tops. It was rooting around in the bushes ahead of me, scratching at the pine needle covered ground. Every few seconds it would stuff its nose into the ground and snort and snuffle in its search for food. I knew it would still be nursing, and would keep on doing so for the next year at least, but it wouldn't turn up its nose at something sweet and luscious, like a fat grub. When I knew what direction the pair was heading, I cut in front of them, shredding one bar on the path I wanted to lead them.

The sow would smell me, but she'd be used to the scent of humans. All summer long humans trooped through her woods. She more than likely had been tagged at some point in her life. Maybe the cub had been, too. If she stayed in the park she'd be safe, if she wandered too far hunters might well find her. The same fate might meet her cub if it chose to extend its territory after its mother drove it away when it was time for her to mate again. If either one of them took to hanging out at human campsites, or went on garbage raids they'd be forcibly relocated. Or shot if they didn't stop being a nuisance.

None of that was my concern right now. I had to try to lure this pair close enough to the drug camp to attract attention. I was sure the armed thugs would react badly to a bear showing up in their midst. They'd either flee or shoot at it. I didn't like the latter option, but Alex's life was at stake here, and that overrode my dislike of putting the bear in danger.

I pulled out my half finished bag of trail mix and added some to my lure.

Come on, mama. Come and get it.

I moved between dream and nightmare. It was impossible to know when I was conscious. I knew I was dying, that was no longer a vague concept, but a hardcore fact. The rare time I was awake enough to know it, the pain was overpowering. It was easier to welcome the twilight world of my hallucinating mind.

But I couldn't ignore the cold, wet nose that snuffled loudly over my ear and cheek, followed by warm doggy breath and a wet tongue.

Normally, the gesture would have disgusted me. But now, dying, it became a welcome release from the overwhelming feeling of loss I had dying alone. Funny how being alone for years had never bothered me, until Jason came along. Then I found out how empty my life had become. I had thought those days gone. Now mine had come full circle and I was going to meet the end alone. The dog whined softly, then stretched out beside me, pressing firmly against my side, stilling the tremors that had become a constant. Pain lessened and some of my lucidity returned. Enough to know the dog wasn't the only thing that had returned.

There was more light around me. I must be in or near the opening the pot farmers had carved out of the forest for their plants. Wanting to feel the sun on my face one more time I rolled over, clenching my teeth together at the rush of pain that subsided slowly when I stopped moving. But it was there. Sun. Warmth and the gentle caress of sun-warmed air on my sweating, fevered face. I took as deep a breath as the pain in my side allowed, no longer caring about inhaling bugs. The air no longer smelled funny. Now it was the sweetest thing I'd ever drawn into my lungs. Jason would be happy. He had wanted me to like this week so badly. Too bad I wouldn't be able to tell him that I was all set to do just that.

Something big flew overhead. At first I thought it might be a plane, flying low, until I saw the wings were too wide and rough-edged to be a man-made object. It had to be a bird. I couldn't tell what kind or even how big it was. It must be very close, nothing was that big right? It seemed to be circling.

Finally I did recognize it. I'd seen enough old Westerns to know a buzzard when I saw one. All the old jokes about buzzards hanging around, waiting for something to die came back. But did they always wait? Maybe some of them were willing to come in early to the feast. Or speed death along.

I shut my eyes, not wanting to see it if it came closer. Hoping it would wait.

God, I didn't want to die. Was that so much to ask? To live a while longer? Jason and I hadn't had enough time. Both of us came to love late. It wasn't fair we lost now what we had found.

The dog nuzzled me again, pulling me out of my pity-fest. Don't be a fucking pathetic fool. I opened my eyes again and rolled back over onto my stomach. I'll keep dragging myself if that's all I'm capable of doing. But I wasn't going to lie here and be some fat bird's smörgåsbord. Not going to happen, now or ever. They could do whatever the hell they wanted, but they were going to have to wait until I was gone.

I dragged myself forward, one inch at a time. At first the dog stayed beside me, but maybe my pace was too slow, eventually he started leaving me, sometimes ahead of me, sometimes going out of my sight. I couldn't pay attention. If he left, he left. Finally, he didn't come back. So that was that.

I thought of nothing then but pulling myself across the ground. As sorry-assed as the effort was, at least I was doing something.

The voices grew louder. Was that what had driven the dog away? Couldn't blame him for protecting his butt. He'd probably seen his master die, and been shot at himself. Hard not to get skittish when that happens. The Anglo guy was talking.

"Swear I saw that damned dog. How's he keep getting away?"

"*¡No manches, cabrón!*" the Latino growled. "*Estás chingado, guey.*"

"Fuck you, *menso*. I know what I seen."

More muttered Spanish, then booted feet thudded over the ground near my head. I knew the minute they saw me. "¡*Diablos*!"

"What the fuck? You think he's dead?"

A booted foot prodded my shoulder. In response I rolled away from it, onto my uninjured side. A pair of scruffy faces stared down at me. One white as paper, the other older and Latino. The white one looked like he was going to be sick.

"*Sabe... esta jodido!*"

"He's gotta be. Shit, look at that." The boot touched me again, near where the bullet had grazed me. Pain unlike anything I had ever felt before shot through me, switching every nerve in my body on as though electrodes had been rammed into me. I screamed, but my throat was so dry and my lungs airless and all that came out was a weak grunt.

"Hey, it's alive. He the guy we shot? Told you we hit his sorry ass."

"*Se muere.*"

"Course he's dying. Shit, look at him."

Our eyes met, the Anglo smirked. He had his Beretta tucked into his waistband. His buddy came more heavily armed. An Uzi, with the sheen of long use, hanging over his chest. He couldn't seem to keep his hands off it. His eyes never left mine. Calculating whether it was worth the effort to waste bullets?

"*Mátelo.*"

Anglo's smirk grew broader. He was enjoying the prospect. He fingered his gun.

"You don't look so hot." The Anglo broke into a grin. "How'd you get hurt, mister? Run into a bullet someplace?"

"You really want to kill a cop?" I stuttered through my shivering, knowing the answer already. But thinking maybe I could slow them down. For what I didn't know. But I wasn't going to walk into death without kicking and biting all the way.

"*¿Policia? ¿Usted policía?*"

"Santa Barbara PD," I gasped out my credential, knowing it wasn't going to make any difference to this pair. They'd crossed the line so far and so long ago, one more death wasn't going to faze them. Still, I tried, though my voice was barely above a pain-filled whisper. I infused it with as much strength as I could. "Detective Alexander Spider."

"*¡Es tira!*" One of them had brains enough to understand the mess they had just stepped into. Not so his partner.

"So, he's a cop? You think he's gonna arrest us, *idiota*? He's already dead, look at him. I ain't never seen a more fucked up dude. We're just doing him a favor. Putting him out of his misery, as it were."

"*Si. ¿Somos filántropos, derecho?*"

"Right, Juan. That's what it is." The Anglo seemed to be enjoying himself. "We're just putting him out of his misery. Cutting short his poor, miserable existence. Horse breaks his leg, you shoot him, right? Only thing to do."

Anglo pulled out his Beretta. He made an elaborate show of checking his magazine, making sure he had a round in the chamber. His grin showed tweaker teeth that desperately needed a dentist. Casually, his eyes locked on mine, he leaned over and spit. It might have hit me, I couldn't tell. I didn't really care.

I braced, staring at him as he took aim, refusing to shut my eyes. I wish I could have seen Jason one more time. But there was more comfort in knowing he was safely away from here. Probably down the mountain by now. Whether he got anyone to come back was moot. If they came fast enough, maybe they'd catch these clowns. I'd like to think so.

A scream rent the air.

Anglo jerked as though the sound had shot electricity through him. The barrel of the gun swung away from me. "What the—"

"*¡Estupido!*"

Before anyone could do more, a shot followed the scream.

Before I could blink, both of them were gone. There were several more shots and panic stricken screams that mounted in terror. I heard the armed pair crashing through the underbrush, cursing in Spanish and English. Another scream. What the hell was going on? Had the police arrived? Had they been that quick?

That had to mean Jason was safe, didn't it? If someone was making them scream like that, something bad was going on. Jason must have brought help.

The cub was the first one to find my treat. It vacuumed up the crumbs I laid out and snuffled along the trail searching for more. When it found the rest, it followed eagerly. It wasn't long before the sow came to find out where her cub had gone. Now I had them both moving toward the drug camp.

But did I have enough of the bait to keep them coming?

I doled it out, hoping they wouldn't come across something more enticing. We didn't have far to go, maybe a couple of hundred yards. But a couple of hundred yards where I had to avoid being noticed by the bears and the drug dealers.

The determined pair of jays followed the bears, and maybe that had something to do with their willingness to move away. As Alex had found out, even three ounces of bird could be annoying to something a thousand times bigger than they were.

The roar of the truck engine grew louder. I was getting closer. Close enough to hear the thwack-thwack of the machetes slicing through plant stalks. I swore I could smell the diesel, but that was probably my own stink. I've heard some hunters don't bathe before a hunt, on the principle that their fresh washed scent will spook the prey more. Me, I think they can smell me from further away. But what do I know? Except for the birds I try to find, I don't hunt.

I almost stumbled and fell at the feet of the nearest cutter. He jumped back with a Spanish oath and stared at me wild-eyed like I was an apparition. I probably was a sight to see. I hadn't shaved in days, my hair stood up in tangles of hair and forest debris.

"*Madre.*" The Latino, an older guy with streaks of white in his hair crossed himself and nearly dropped his machete. We stared at each other across a space of less than a yard. I knew I had landed in some shit when the second Latino appeared clutching his machete in both hands, face grim with anger.

The older guy grabbed his weapon and took a menacing step toward me and I scrambled to my feet, ready to bolt. But they were too close. I'd fucked up good this time.

"*Pendejo*!

I barely saw the machete swing toward me when a bolt of tan and black shot by me with a snarl. The Spanish curses turned to shouts of dismay and fear. I ducked and twisted, watching in amazement as the dog grabbed the bare arm of the nearest man. A scream ripped the air and man and dog both went down.

I almost didn't see the bear cub lumber toward me, head down as it concentrated on the granola I had put down. So intent on the treat it didn't see me until it was almost at my feet. It grabbed the remaining trail mix and scrambled away.

Dog and man were still rolling on torn up earth, neither one noticing the latest arrival. Then it all fell away as the sow arrived. She was not happy. I don't know if her annoyance was at her cub getting ahead of her, or because unlike it, she sensed trouble. But when she burst on the scene I made sure I wasn't the first thing she saw. That fell to the second, younger Latino who had dropped his machete and pulled out a handgun, which he was waving around, his face suffused with fury. He fired. I'm not sure if he was aiming for the dog or me, but the effect was instantaneous.

The sow reared up on her hind legs, trying to make herself look bigger and scarier. I could have told her she was the scariest thing there, but it wasn't my reaction I cared about. It was the three drug dealers I wanted scared. She roared. This time there was no doubt who the gunman was aiming at. Bullets smacked into the ground around her feet and into the brush behind her. If any of them hit, she didn't show it.

Instead, she dropped to all fours and charged. Bears aren't the fastest land animal, they tend to be clumsy, but they can move fast enough when the need strikes them. And this was one bear that felt the need. Opening her mouth in a toothsome snarl she covered the distance to the shooter in maybe five seconds. He screamed and shot again.

Then I don't know if his gun jammed or his panic messed him up. By the time he realized his problem, he spun around and tried to flee, too late. She hooked up his shooting arm and spun him around into his partner. With a muffled shout they both ended up piled in the dirt. The dog was nowhere to be seen.

The bear roared again and thwacked the nearest man's knee, tearing denim and exposing skin, which immediately started bleeding. Several yards away the cub was scrambling up a nearby tree like its mother would have taught it to when threatened. The gun went off again, but this time I knew it wasn't deliberate. The gun's owner was screaming and trying to drag himself away, while the bear bit and tore at his lower legs. Blood stained the torn denim. His partner was long gone. Once the dog had released him he had fled, leaving his machete behind, making smoke as he bolted towards where I suspected the truck I had heard earlier was. Saving his own ass, I guess.

A new voice shouted harsh Spanish as two more men, one Latino, one Anglo ran toward us. My heart slammed into my chest when I saw the Uzi. That was going to do some serious damage to all of us.

Then I heard the sweetest sound ever. I looked up. This time, instead of the circling condor a forest services' helicopter roared overhead, so close the wind from its rotors made the tree tops shiver. The aircraft circled, dipping lower then rising, but always coming back. It was obvious they had seen us.

Uzi knew it, too. He swung the nose of his weapon up and opened fire, strafing the treetops. The assault of noises from everywhere spooked the bear and she fled, crashing through the bushes, her cub squealing after her.

The mauled dealer writhed on the ground, his clothes and the surrounding forest floor saturated with blood. His partner was gone. Uzi and the Anglo chased after him. I didn't care anymore. I broke away and began a frantic search for Alex. He couldn't have gone far.

I found the bower where I had been forced to leave him on his orders. The ground still held a depression of his body. I was dismayed to see blood there, too. But not a lot. Not enough to signal he had bled out, right? I had to cling to that belief as I quartered the ground, first east, then south, then swinging north.

God, how far could he have gone? I knew none of the pot farmers had found Alex. They'd still been looking for him when we'd stumbled across each other. I don't know when I first noticed it, in the beginning it was so low and unfamiliar to register. It had seemed like forever since I'd heard the familiar sounds of the city, and Goleta wasn't exactly a hot crime zone. We could go days without hearing sirens. But eventually I realized what I heard was the wail of fast approaching emergency vehicles. Cops? EMTs?

Who cared? It meant rescue.

First I had to find Alex. I wanted to stand up and scream his name, hoping he'd hear me and answer. But I didn't know for sure that those men were gone. They might circle back and shoot anyone who moved. For that matter, the cops themselves might be trigger happy.

Fighting every instinct to hurry, I crept through the dense brush and around shadowed tree trunks, looking for any sign that Alex had been this way. How far could he get? He'd been injured, but I had never been able to assess how bad his wound was. It hadn't been bleeding enough to cause worry, but there were worse things than blood loss. I'd cleaned it as best I could... so why was I still worried? It had been days since he had ordered me away. Days for infection to set in and do considerable damage. As part of becoming an Able Bodied Seaman I had taken first aid and knew how to handle myself in a crisis. But it was one thing to know the mechanics and practice on dummies or volunteers, another altogether to use it on your lover.

I thrashed through a heavy section of bush, swatting flying things away from my face, sweat stung my fresh scratches.

The nearest siren wound down before growling to a stop. They had arrived. Distant voices rose in command. A rattling series of gunfire was met with return fire, then silence. The helicopter flew overhead again. For several seconds, the dull thwack-thwack of the rotary blades were all I could hear. When it moved off and silence flowed back in, I thought I heard something. Was it a cry? I knew it wasn't birds, they would be in hiding from all the harsh noises and unusual activity in their normally quiet environment.

But right now silence covered everything with a blanket of peace.

I heard the noise again. A low whine. Animal. I was sure the bears had fled in the other direction, probably halfway to Sespes by now. The dog? Had he been shot in the melee?

I didn't have time to find a wounded dog. Not with Alex out there in God knows what shape. He was the one I had to concentrate on finding. Before it was too late.

The somnolent buzz of flies sent chills racing along my already ragged nerve endings. It reminded me too damn much of when Alex and I had stumbled on the body. I might have been something else, flies on a new pile of animal scat but somehow I knew it wasn't. I crept through the bush, pain forgotten. The buzz grew louder.

"Alex?" It was a whisper at first. I cleared my throat and tried again. "Alex, please..."

A soft sound. Oh, my God, it was Alex—

"Alex!"

I forgot to keep silent. I forgot being careful. I tore through the brush. I was desperate, beyond thinking. He was here, I had to find him. I had to make him safe.

"Oh, God, Alex, where are you?"

"J-Jason?"

I saw a foot. The Merrills I had bought Alex for this trip. The ones like mine that we had tried on to have some of the hottest sex we'd had in weeks. Alex had truly been inspired that night. I was weeping as I crawled across the forest floor. There was no movement and no further sound. There were the relentless flies that ignored me as I crab-crawled up alongside the too still body. I scrambled around him, furiously chasing the insects off.

He was lying on his side, his back to me as I reached up

to touch his shoulder. "Alex please, talk to me." I stroked his neck, red and rough from sunburn. No response. "I need you, Alex. Don't leave me." I crawled around him, needing to see his face. His eyes were closed, his face so pale his freckles stood out in sharp relief. He had lost his glasses. How could he see anything? How could he see me? Maybe he didn't know I was here – frantically I looked around for his glasses. He needed them, didn't he? He—

I realized I was acting crazy. Alex didn't need his fucking glasses. He needed to get to a hospital. Was I fucking nuts? I scrambled back to Alex. I knelt beside him and gently eased him over onto his back. Taking him in my arms, I begged him to stay with me. He looked so white. Dead. I was so sure he was dead. My tears left streaks of clean flesh on his pale face. Only when his eyes fluttered open and I saw his chest move did I know he was alive. His eyelids fluttered again and a soft groan cheered me as I'd never thought the sound would. He was in pain. But he was alive.

Then I saw his side and nearly passed out. His shirt was in shreds, torn by God knows what. The wound I had tended so carefully only a few days ago was a writhing mass of white, squirming maggots. I bit my tongue to try and stop myself from gagging, but it had been so long since I'd eaten anything that nothing came up except bitter bile.

"Oh, God, Alex. Oh baby...I should never have left you. I won't ever again. I'll never let you make me do that again."

I wanted to sweep the loathsome things off him, but I was terrified I'd hurt him more. There were shouts in the direction of where the sirens had come from. No more gunfire, only staccato orders shouting out commands. The cops? Had to be. The drug dealers wouldn't be making that kind of noise with the cops nearby, and the cops wouldn't be announcing their presence if the dealers hadn't been caught. I straightened and started screaming.

"We're here. Help! Over here." Then I thought of the one thing that would bring them fast. "Officer down. For God's sake, there's a cop here and he's been shot! Help!"

A heartbeat filled with silence then the voices drew nearer. Bushes crashed and more voices shouting orders. Then I heard the welcome crackle of radio calls. They were putting out the call for help.

When the first uniformed officer, a thin Anglo forest service guy, broke through I wanted to cry, but I couldn't give in to weakness now. Alex needed help. Fear would just have to wait.

"He's been shot. He needs a doctor, now!"

"Easy, mister, help's coming. Who are you? Who is he?"

"Detective Alexander Spider, Santa Barbara PD. He's been shot. Days ago."

The cop that followed him had his hand on the butt of his gun when he came into view. "Step away from him. Keep your hands in plain sight."

I wanted to scream at him that I wasn't armed but I knew that would only raise his hackles and turn this whole thing into a macho farce. I scrambled back then stood slowly, hands out at my side, making it obvious I had no weapons. Not satisfied, he approached me, one hand on his gun, the other thumbing open his radio.

"One man down, unknown injuries. We have a male Caucasian in our custody." Without a word to me he whisked my arms behind my back and cuffed me. Any other time that would have sent me off, but now all I cared about was getting the help Alex needed. I could stay calm for him.

"He needs help," my voice was shaky, but I managed to keep my hysteria at bay. "Will you do something for him?"

"Help's here." The officer pulled me away from the scene, toward where the sirens had come from. "You can start by telling me who you are and what you're doing up here."

"We're hikers. We came up here a week ago." I tried to ignore the heat flowing down my arms from being pinned behind my back. "He's a cop, for God's sake. We came up here together. We stumbled across them and they shot at us."

"Who is them?"

"Whoever those guys were. The pot growers. We found their plants. They were trying to kill us. They killed those other poor hikers. Did you catch them? There were at least four of them. Maybe more—"

"We have the men in custody. One of them was severely injured. Did you do that? What did you use? A knife? One of those machetes we found?"

I knew they wouldn't believe me, not right now at least. Still, I had to try.

"It wasn't me. It was a bear."

He stopped and swung me around to face him. His face was torn between confusion and anger. "You trying to tell me a fucking bear did that?"

"Believe me or not, but yes, it was a bear. He shot at her and she attacked him."

He scanned my face and I didn't know what he was looking for, or even what he saw. I knew I must look a mess, bloody and beaten from the last few days. My clothes filthy and not in much better shape than Alex's. I imagined I must have looked half mad. Maybe I was.

"Please, forget about me, just get Alex out of here. He's in bad shape. Take me in, I don't care, but get him to a hospital right now."

"He'll be taken care of. You're coming with me." He started me moving again and within minute we entered a clearing filled with Forest Services' vehicles and Sheriff's cars, lights flashing and one blessed ambulance standing on the sidelines, two EMTs standing at the open rear door clearly waiting for Alex to be brought out. As I was stuffed into the back seat of the nearest Sheriff's black and white, two other EMTs emerged from the trees with a stretcher between them and Alex laid out on it, covered with a sheet. Seconds before the ambulance doors closed I saw three of them working around him, slapping blood pressure cuffs on him and getting an IV ready.

I sighed and lay my head back on the hard headrest, and for the first time in days allowed myself to fully relax. He was safe. My Alex was safe now.

I shut my eyes and slept or passed out for my trip down the mountain to safety. I wasn't even really awake when they took me to emergency services to have my own injuries looked at, and tried to figure out what to do with me.

Thankfully they called Alex's boss and she was able to come down and tell them who I was. Still, I spent the night in the same hospital as Alex, released the next day only to find they weren't telling me anything about Alex or letting me see him.

Nancy left me once she knew I was safe. The screaming fit I threw brought her back.

She found me in the lobby of the hospital threatening bodily harm to the next person who tried to throw me out on the street. Unlike anyone else present she wasn't afraid to approach me. She was in my face and took an iron hold on my shoulders.

"Jason! Settle down. Alex is okay, got it? He's being taken care of, but no one can see him right now. Not you, not me. Not anybody."

"I'm not leaving until I see him."

"Then you're going to have to settle down and stop acting like a madman. You keep this up and they'll toss you in the can. You don't want that, do you?"

This was the first thing that actually penetrated my rage. Like a slap of ice water, I blinked and stared at her. "All I want is to know he's going to be okay," I whispered.

"I know. I want that, too. We all do. But you aren't helping anyone by being hysterical. He's in good hands and right now we have to let them do their job."

"What am I going to do?" I realized how plaintive and weak that sounded but I couldn't help it anymore. I was tired of being strong. I wanted Alex in charge again. He was my real strength. "I'm so tired."

She guided me over to a row of hard orange chairs and forced me to sit. "You've been through a lot in the last few days. We need you to tell us about that, Jason. Tell us exactly what happened up there. Can you do that?"

"I...I don't know."

"Do it for Alex, okay?"

"I...okay." I took a deep, shuddering breath. "Now?"

"Yes. Then you can rest, I promise. And I'll make sure someone tells you as soon as Alex is able to see you."

"Where is he?"

"He's in surgery. He'll be in there for hours. But the doctor's told me it looks good. He was brought in, in time. You did a good thing, Jason. You saved his life."

I shook my head, feeling my filthy hair flop over my forehead, almost reaching my eyes. "My fault. I made him leave his gun at home. If I hadn't he wouldn't have been hurt. My fault—"

"No, Jason." She shook me again. "Not your fault. None of this is your fault."

I buried my head in my hands. She patted my shoulder awkwardly.

"He's going to be okay. He needs you to believe that."

Finally, I raised my head to meet her gaze. "He is?"

"Yes, he is. Now go, get some rest. Come back in the morning."

After I answered all their questions, I let a uniformed cop take me out of the hospital to a nearby motel where he booked a room for me. I think I remember entering the room. I thought about taking a shower but never made it that far. I didn't even take off my Merrills when I fell across the bed and passed out.

The next day one of the Sheriff's deputies drove me up the mountain to get Alex's pickup and get a more detailed report of what we had seen on our hike. Now that I was no longer under their suspicion radar I felt free to talk to them. They already had statements from all the people we had encountered on our hike, and the Sheriff gave me the impression they had also recovered the bodies of the dead hikers, including, sadly, the two women we had seen with the young man.

I had been about to drive off when I caught movement in the distance. I paused, wondering if it was more hikers, and was startled when the Shepherd crept out. He looked terrible, fur matted and burr covered, his paws lacerated from too many days running over rough ground. I didn't think twice. I called him over and when he shoved his nose into my hand and whined I opened the truck door and signaled him to jump in. I swear he sighed when he settled on the passenger's seat, spilling over the sides he was so big.

The Sheriff watched this, a bemused expression on his face. "He yours?"

"No, but we've got some shared history. I can't leave him up here."

He shrugged. "Well, you take care, sir."

"Thanks." I shut the door and fired up the truck. All the way down I struggled over what I was going to do with the dog. His owner was dead, I had no way of knowing if there was anyone else who might want him and I sure as hell wasn't going to dump him in some pound awaiting God knows what fate.

In the end, I found a kennel willing to take him until I decided what I would do. Knowing the choice wasn't really going to be in my hands. Only Alex could make that kind of decision.

I patted the dog one more time on the head before the kennel girl led him away, then headed back to the hospital where I planned to stay until I knew Alex was safe.

I blinked. Blinked again. Then I shut my eyes against the glare and realized the pain was gone. Did that mean I had died, and there really was an afterlife? Wouldn't that be a fucking bitch? Without opening my eyes again I took a deep, lung-purifying breath. No, this can't be heaven or hell. Unless one of them smells like antiseptic and starch. My awareness came back in slow increments. I was lying on my back, underneath stiff, but clean, sheets. I wiggled the toes of my left foot. They scraped across the sheet that covered them. A rush of joy filled me. I wasn't paralyzed. I wriggled my right foot and felt the same satisfaction when it moved, too.

Then I began a closer examination of the rest of my body, one part at a time. My side felt stiff, but the sheer agony that had existed before I had passed out for good was gone. In its place, a numbness I suspected was morphine or Demerol induced.

Voices still filled my head but they were gentle, civilized ones. They were real. Wheels squeaked and rattled over hard floors. Metal banged and music played something soft and classical. Something else beeped beside me and I was vaguely aware of a needle in my arm, tape tugging at my skin. I suspected it was an IV. How long had I been here? Hell, where was *here*? Was I in Santa Barbara or L.A.? How bad was I? My memories were flaky at best, but I knew I had been dying. That memory was too solid to be a dream or a hallucination.

I suspect I came damn close to taking the big sleep.

I was fuzzy on all of it. Who had found me? Who had brought me out? Jason—

Jason! I surged up, adrenaline pumping through me. My eyes flew open. I looked around frantically, ignoring the hands that tried to hold me down. The face peering down at me was a stranger. Dark skinned, gray-streaked beard. He had sharp, brown eyes hiding behind thick glasses.

I tried to shove his hands away but didn't have the strength to lift paper. I was pitifully exhausted when I sank back into the bed. I blinked up at him, but no matter how hard I tried I couldn't bring him into focus. Then I realized I wasn't wearing my glasses. When had I lost them?

"Take it easy, Mr. Spider. You're in Cottage Hospital. You've been through a rough spot, but I assure you that you're going to be okay."

I tried to remember where Cottage Hospital was. Santa Barbara. That didn't answer my main question. Where was Jason—?

Then he came into view. He looked like shit. I tried to smile at him, but from the look on his face I knew the effort failed miserably. His attempt was equally disastrous. His eyes were full of pain and exhaustion, and something I didn't want to identify. But I knew what it was. Fear. When I raised my hand to touch him, the IV in my arm jerked. Jason grabbed my wrist and leaned in, his face inches from mine. So close I could smell his sweat and fear. Sweat dotted his forehead and deep pouches of darkness under his eyes made him look like a cadaver.

"Don't, Alex. Don't move."

"I want..." I was appalled at how weak I sounded. I cleared my throat and tried again. "Want to touch you."

He leaned down and touched his lips to mine. His hand stroked my cheek and I closed my eyes again, savoring the feel.

"I love you, Alex. Now I want you to stop fighting and rest."

"How...long?"

I saw him look over me at the man on the other side of the bed. My doctor, I assumed. He nodded but it was Jason who spoke.

"Ten days. You've were in surgery for six hours and they moved you from ICU to here four days ago."

Ten days? Ten days gone who knew where. I didn't need Jason telling me to know that a lot of those ten days had been spent keeping me alive. A chill sent shivers down my limbs and I realized to my horror that I was shaking.

My distress upset Jason. He sat on the bed facing me. Holding my shoulders in both hands he leaned down and whispered for my ears only. "You're going to be okay, Alex. But you have to rest. I won't leave you. I'll be here forever. No matter what, I'm never leaving you again."

I had to say it, because if I didn't, maybe I'd never be able to again. From the looks everyone was giving me, I knew I wasn't in the clear yet.

"I love you, Jason. Always. Never forget."

"I know, hon." And his lips brushed mine. "I love you. More than you will ever know."

Relief washed over me, along with a smile.

"I need my glasses," I finally whispered. "I can't really see you without them."

"Right now that's probably a good thing. Don't worry, I'll have some new ones brought to you. Now you have to rest. And that's an order from your doctor, not me."

"Good. I don't want you forgetting your place, do I?"

"Never. I know where it is. Right beside you."

Still smiling, I let sleep claim me again.

The minute I knew Alex was no longer conscious I got up off the bed and started pacing. I was torn between wanting to scream or fall on my knees and beg Doctor Abena to make it right. He watched me, silently. The gibbering horror I felt when I had stumbled onto Alex after I drew the two shooters away to their encounter with my bear, still hovered in the back of my mind. It was too ready to unleash again if I didn't keep rigid control. I'd asked about the men the police had arrested. Last I heard one of them was in another hospital, they were all under federal indictment for drugs and interstate commerce or some such bullshit. I didn't care. All I could remember was the first sight of Alex. Sprawled on his side like a discarded sack of potatoes. His hands had been bloody, his fingernails torn off, his face scratched and covered in pine needles and dirt. Flies buzzed around him, landing on his lips and crawling over his half-shut eyes. Crawling and buzzing everywhere, including his still open wound.

I had dressed that wound maybe five days before. Cleaned it with antiseptic and bandaged it. Crudely, yes, but it had been *clean*. When he forced me to leave him, the bullet wound had been a slice across his side, opening up a six-inch gash that had still been leaking blood.

This time it was crawling with maggots. Small, white things writhed in Alex's flesh. In my more frequent hikes, when I was younger, I had come across my share of carcasses, from fresh to reeking piles of maggots and beetles.

But this was Alex, and he wasn't dead.

I don't know what I would have done if the sheriffs and the rangers hadn't arrived then. They had come, not only responding to my call, but to the two bikers who had reported gunshots and subsequent calls that Danny and Niko made after I left them.

It had taken them hours to get Alex off the mountain to Santa Barbara and the hospital. Hours that had shaved a decade off my life. They had taken him straight to the OR and six hours later had put him in ICU. I had thought it was over then, but now this Dr. Abena told me Alex had to have more surgeries. That he wasn't out of the woods yet.

I stopped pacing and faced him. If he saw my rage he didn't react to it.

"Are you still saying he needs more operations?"

"At least one," Abena said. "His body has been through tremendous trauma. The maggots were a great aid in keeping infection at bay, without them I'm not sure he would have survived. But even with their presence, there is still considerable organ damage."

I had been horrified when I found his wound infested with fly maggots. But according to this doctor, if left, the wound would have become necrotic and would have poisoned Alex's blood. It would have killed him long before I found him. The maggots had consumed the dead flesh, keeping it from poisoning him. It was humbling to think we owed Alex's life to a disgusting grub.

"I've scheduled the first of them for tomorrow. Following that, I will assess him again, then we can talk about the next, and hopefully last, operation."

I stared helplessly over at Alex. I wished he had stayed awake, even though I was glad he was resting, getting stronger. I wanted his strength. But I also hated having this decision put in my hands. But Alex had no family beyond his ex-wife and she was hardly one I could approach about what to do. I was his registered partner, so the whole thing was square on my shoulders, where I didn't want it. Alex was the one who was supposed to be in charge. He should be making these decisions.

Only he couldn't, could he?

I had his life in my unqualified hands again. And the responsibility terrified me.

I took a deep breath and without taking my eyes off Alex, I nodded. "Then schedule it. Do whatever you have to do to make him well."

"I'll see it through myself."

He left soon after, leaving me alone with my lover and my dark, empty thoughts.

I barely left Alex's side. Every night someone would come in and send me home. Only there was no way I was driving all the way to Goleta every night, so I kept the motel near the hospital. I would eat breakfast on the way in, barely stop for lunch, which usually consisted of coffee and a sugar fix that I paid for later in the day. Dinner was barely much more.

I was losing weight. I didn't notice or pay any attention until Nancy came by to see how he was doing. Since she had stopped my rage-filled rampage the day they wouldn't let me see Alex, I hadn't seen her. The day after Alex's second surgery she was in the room with a young Latino man. She took one look at me and dragged me out into the hallway.

"What the hell do you think you're doing, Jason?"

"What do you mean?" I wanted to pull away from her. I needed to be in there with Alex, not out here with this woman.

"Christ, man, have you looked in a fucking mirror lately? Do you shave on autopilot? Have you eaten anything today?"

I wanted to tell her to go away, but she had been part of Alex's life a lot longer than I had. She had been there, right from the day he and I met. Before I could snap a retort at her, she took my chin in her hand and forced me to look at her.

"Go home, Jason. For Alex's sake if not your own. You're not going to do jack shit for him if you collapse and end up in the bed next to him."

I wanted to jerk away from her, but her look was so worried I caved. I took her hand and squeezed it hard enough to leave my knuckles white. I could tell her one thing I would never have admitted to anyone, even Alex.

"I'm scared."

"What does the doctor say?" she asked, gently.

"He says he'll be okay, but what if he's wrong? God, you

didn't see him up there. You don't know what he looked like. I thought he was dead." I knew my voice was rising, I was edging into hysteria. Maybe it was exhaustion. Maybe it was just the whole thing finally crashing down on me. What I might lose. What I still could lose. "What would I do without him?"

"Don't think like that," she said fiercely. "Alex sure as hell wouldn't give up on himself. He got this far by fighting. He's still fighting."

I was barely aware of the Latino man who had come with Nancy joining us. Nancy took advantage of his arrival to pull away from me. She indicated the other man.

"This is Detective Miguel Dominguez, Alex's partner. Miguel, this is Jason Zachary."

Alex didn't talk a lot about his job. I knew when things were going well for him, and I knew when he'd had a bad day. I tried to make our home a sanctuary for him so he could leave the ugliness of his world behind him. I knew Nancy had succeeded Alex's old boss, going from being his partner to being his boss. A lot of men would not have taken that well, but Alex seemed to have nothing but good things to say about this new boss. But he never mentioned his new partner. Was that a good sign, or a bad one?

I kept my questions to myself and extended my hand, which Miguel took gingerly. Only then did I notice the cross on a chain around his neck. So his next words didn't really surprise me.

"I've prayed for Alexander. God will be with him in his hour of need."

I didn't know what to say to that. Neither Alex or I were very religious. My life hadn't lent itself to having much faith in an outside deity and Alex never talked about it. It just wasn't part of our life. I had to say something, though. I nodded stiffly.

"Thank you."

"Have you eaten anything today?" Nancy demanded.

Reluctantly I shook my head. "Breakfast—"

"That's what I thought." She took my arm and I wasn't

surprised when she said, "You're coming with us then. I'm going to see that you at least have one solid meal. From the looks of it, it will be the first in a while."

I bristled, but in the end, didn't have the energy to argue. We ended up at a nearby Denny's. I ordered coffee, not sure my stomach could take much food. The last couple of days my appetite had been non-existent. I got queasy every time I thought about what Alex faced. I was sure if I tried eating I would only be sick. I didn't need that right now.

But Alex's boss wasn't listening to my stomach or my protests. She ordered herself steak and insisted I at least get a salad. I said Caesar, she made them add chicken to it. I resigned myself to eating, figuring I could get some of it down. When the food was delivered, Miguel bowed his head and said a silent prayer. He caught me off guard so I didn't have time to do more than dip my chin down on my chest before he muttered "Amen" and picked up his napkin. I traded glances with Nancy but she remained impassive. Instead, her laser gaze settled on my salad, making it clear what she expected.

I had an easier time going through maybe a gallon of coffee, though from the looks Nancy kept throwing me she wasn't impressed. In the end, I shoveled food into my mouth, barely tasting it, but apparently it satisfied Nancy. At least I kept it down.

I finished long before either of them and spent the time waiting staring out the window beside me at street outside. A steady stream of vehicles passed, and I checked each one out. I watched the movement, not really seeing anyone. Finally, Nancy signaled for the check after telling me it was a department business expense, so it was on her. Not that I cared whether she got it past accounting or not.

All I wanted to do was get back to Alex.

Nancy had other plans. We were in the parking lot of my motel before I realized what she was doing. She jerked my door open and stood there until I climbed out.

"You are going to go in there, and you are going to stay

here until either I or one of my men comes back for you. I can guarantee that won't be for at least six hours. I don't care if you don't sleep. I don't care if you stand on your head for six hours, but you are not going near that hospital until I say you can. You get sick on my watch, and we both know Alex will have my head."

I opened my mouth to protest but the look on her face stopped me. I could see why she became Lieutenant and why Alex accepted her as his boss. She was a strong woman. And she was right. Alex would be pissed. The last thing I wanted to do was aggravate a sick man.

I nodded at her, feeling grumpy, but I pulled my keys out and headed for my room. I didn't need to look back to know Nancy and Miguel were still there when I shut and locked the door.

The room was dim and cool. I turned the TV on and mindlessly flipped through the dozen channels available, ignoring the posted sign that enticed me to watch hours of XXX videos. I stopped at CNN and let it play in the background. There were no more stories of the huge pot bust the Sheriffs and Forest Service claimed had netted them something like ten thousand plants worth twenty million on the streets. Alex had been briefly mentioned in the first reports, but when he survived and was just a guy in the hospital he became yesterday's news fast. Not that I minded. The last thing either Alex or I wanted was being hounded by two legged vultures out for a sound bite.

I lay down on top of the bed, knowing Nancy had been right. I needed to rest. The Denny's lunch sat heavy in my gut. The coffee left my nerves jangled and I doubted I'd sleep, no matter how much I might need it.

I shut my eyes, expecting my mind to start racing again like it did every time I tried to rest. Memories of Alex when he sent me away. Sent me off, knowing he was going to die. He wanted me safe and that enraged me, even as it only deepened my love for him. Who makes that kind of sacrifice for another person? I always knew I would die for him, but to know he would do the same for me was numbing. How could I ever be enough for this man?

I blinked and rolled over on the scratchy bed cover. I blinked again. It was dark. Night pressed against the barred window that looked out on the parking lot. A splash of light from a car entering the lot must have been what had awakened me. I had slept after all.

I squinted at my Timex. Jesus, I'd been asleep for hours. It was dinner time at the hospital. Alex wouldn't be eating tonight, not with surgery tomorrow. But with luck he would be up. I had to get there before visiting hours ended.

Shit, my car was still at the hospital. I'd have to call a cab. I had to take a shower. Shave. Get dressed. I'd lost the new iPhone in the forest, but I'd still had my old one at home, but I hadn't been back home to pick it up. I'd have to use the motel phone.

Before I could find the number for a cab there was a knock. Without thinking, I threw the door open to find Miguel standing there looking uncomfortable.

"Are you here to take me to the hospital? Where's Lieutenant Pickard?"

"She's at the station," he said stiffly. "She asked me to take you back to the hospital."

"I'm not quite ready. Can you give me five?"

The shave would have to wait. The shower was nothing more than a quick wash down with a wet cloth and some deodorant under my arms. Throw on a pair of jeans and T-shirt and I hurried out. I slid into the minivan and without a word, Miguel rolled.

I tried for small talk during the ten-minute drive.

"How long have you and Alex been partners?"

"Five months. Since the Lieutenant became squad commander."

I wanted to ask him how that was working for him, but decided that sounded too flippant and I wasn't feeling all that flippant at the moment. I watched the passing scenery. Lights were going on all over as dusk deepened. The sky to the west was stained blood red as the sun sank into the Pacific.

I kept talking. "How long have you been a police officer?"

"Nine years."

Short answers. The guy wasn't a talker, that was for sure. Maybe he didn't like talking about his work with an outsider. So ask him something else. "You married?"

"Yes. Ten years."

Ah, two whole sentences. I was on to something. "Any children?"

When his face lit up I knew I'd hit the spot.

"We have three. Two sons and Maria, my little girl. She is five and the sweetest angel ever."

Not having spent any time around kids I took his word for it. "What are your sons' names?"

Now he puffed up like a pouter pigeon. "Ramon and Miguel Estefan, my oldest."

The hospital was just ahead of us. "How old are they? Are they in school?"

"Miguel is eight and Ramon is two. Miguel goes to Our Lady of Mount Carmel. He is an honors student." He surprised me by smiling. "He's smarter than his old man."

"Most kids are," I murmured, remembering how it had been with my dad when I was that age. We had been very close until I stormed into my teen years and got racked up with accusations of fooling around with a neighbor boy. After that, no one in my family talked to me for years. But before that had happened, my dad thought I was smart, too. Both he and my mother plotted out my whole life, through university to something big. A doctor. CEO. Somebody important.

Well, destiny delayed didn't have to be destiny denied. I had come a long way from the self-destructive jerk Detective Spider had arrested less than a year ago. Part of that was because of Alex, but part of it was my own success. I had changed my path. When Alex came back to claim me, I had been on my way already. He had supported me in everything I had wanted to do. Had been there for me a hundred percent and given me a reason to be the best. For him.

And for me.

I understood that now. It wasn't enough to hand myself over to anyone, even Alex. I had to keep a part of my soul. My core.

And be the man *I* wanted to be. For me. Not for anyone else.

I was surprised when Miguel followed me in to Alex's room. I guess I thought he'd been by to check on him before he came out to get me. Had Nancy told him to keep an eye on me?

But I forgot all that when I walked through the door and found Alex awake and propped up in bed. A white bandage covered his abdomen and his face was unshaved, but I had never seen a more beautiful sight in my life.

His face lit up when he saw me. We both ignored Miguel who hovered in the doorway, not coming or going.

I sat on the bed facing him, touching his rough face. He smiled against my hand. "You're awake," I said, grinning inanely. "How are you feeling?"

"Good. Considering."

"Considering what?"

"The alternative."

That threw a dash of ice water on my humor, deflating it. He read my fear and took my hand in his. "Hey, I'm really all right. Even the doctor agrees."

Maybe he just realized Miguel was there. He didn't let go of my hand but he did direct his focus on his partner.

"Miguel."

"Detective Spider. Lieutenant Pickard wanted me to bring your, ah, friend to visit. He left his vehicle here today and needed a lift."

"Why'd you leave the car?" Alex met my eyes, looking puzzled.

I shrugged and threw a scowl toward Miguel. "Your boss took it in her hands to send me away to rest."

"She took you back to Goleta?"

"No," I admitted. "A motel."

"And did you?"

"Did I what?"

"Rest?"

"Yes."

Alex looked over my head. "Was there something else, officer?"

"The Lieutenant wanted me to tell you she has a deposition tomorrow so will not be available and that if you wanted anything, I was to be at your disposal after my watch."

"Thanks, Miguel." Alex squeezed my hand. "I think we'll be okay, won't we?"

"Yes, we'll be just fine."

Alex let his head fall back on the pillow as soon as Miguel was out the door. In alarm I leaned over him.

"Are you really okay?"

At first, I thought he was going to brush off my concern with his usual brusque yes, he was fine in that voice that brooked no argument. Then he stopped what he was going to say and a look of pain crossed his face.

"No," he said softly. "I'm not."

I didn't know what to say. Not once in all the time I had known him had I ever heard Alex admit a single weakness.

"He wants me under the knife again tomorrow. And probably another one after that. He won't say when, says it depends on how tomorrow goes."

"Alex..."

"I'll probably lose a kidney. Maybe my spleen, but that's not as big a deal. And I still have one kidney, right? For now. What if it doesn't go well? What if he wants to put a God damn bag on me?"

"You know I'll always be here for you, no matter what."

"Here to what? Look after a fucking cripple?"

"That doesn't make you a cripple!"

"No?" he snarled and jerked his hand out of mine. "Then what do you call it?"

"It's not going to happen."

"You don't know that."

"I don't fucking care!" I was yelling now, furious at him for suggesting I would leave him. For thinking I would be that weak. For admitting he was. I didn't want Alex to be scared. I was scared enough for both of us.

Footsteps behind me warned me we'd attracted attention with our outburst. I turned to find a frowning nurse barreling down on us.

"I'm going to have to ask you to leave. I can't have you upsetting a patient the day before surgery."

"Jason—"

I released his hand and stood up. "She's right, you need to rest. I'll be by first thing in the morning."

From the stubborn set of his shoulders I knew he was going to order me to stay. I closed my eyes and shook my head.

"No, Alex. I'm going."

I kept my word, though every breath I took on my way out of the room and down the hall to the elevators was drawn through a chest so tight it's a wonder I could breath at all. Outside, it was full dark and a waning moon cast a wan light down on me as I made my way to the truck. I had left my Honda in Goleta when we went into the mountains and hadn't bothered to go back since. I was going to have to make a trip home soon, to check the house and make sure the bills were paid. The last thing I wanted Alex to face when he came home was a mess of bills and mail to sort through.

I also had to check on the dog. He was still in the boarding kennel until I could figure out what to do with him. I hadn't yet mentioned the dog to Alex. I knew what I wanted to do, but that was a choice Alex had to be involved in. I knew he wasn't a dog person. I didn't know if what had happened would change that. I couldn't worry about it right now. I would make sure the dog was safe. His future was still up in the air, though.

All my energies had to go into worrying about Alex. And I was worried. I'd never let Alex know that, but the doctor had told me enough to let me know success tomorrow wasn't a given. Alex's fears might be realized. What I couldn't convince him of was that I truly didn't care. However this turned out, I was going to be there and nothing Alex or anyone else said was going to drive me away.

I just wished 'this' was over.

I hated this waiting more than anything.

I was glad to find I was alone when I woke from an unrestful sleep infused with nightmares. Nightmares where I was back in the forest, on my belly on the ground, helpless, unable to move or even breath. Something pressed down on my back. Liquid fire licked my side where I could feel my flesh being consumed. I knew someone stood over me. Opening my eyes I saw Jason's boots less than a foot from my nose. I tried to call him, but my mouth filled with dirt and metallic liquid I knew was blood. I struggled to spit it out, to call out to him, but no sound emerged. The weight on my back grew, pressing down on me, sinking a thousand teeth and claws into me. White-hot agony slashed through me. I tried to scream but couldn't even breath. A spreading darkness dragged me down a long tunnel and I was helpless to stop the fall.

I woke with a jolt that sent a wave of pain through my jaw. I had bitten my tongue. Before I could cry out a nurse was beside me, her soothing hand on my brow, a comforting smile on her lips.

"The doctor will be along soon, Alex. He'll want to talk to you about the upcoming surgery."

I wasn't thinking about that. My only thought was Jason. I pressed my tongue against the back of my teeth, trying to see how bad it was. It had stopped bleeding, leaving behind the foul taste of blood.

"Jason?"

Before she could respond a second figure was beside her. Jason. Relief washed over me, leaving me weak and disoriented. I smiled, though from the look on his face, the gesture was not reassuring.

Jason's face had always been a mirror. All too often I could see my own thoughts reflected back on me. This time he radiated fear.

Was that what I felt? Fear? I shook my head, a new wave of dizziness leaving me weak and shaking. Alexander Spider didn't fear anything. Didn't Jason know that? I opened my mouth to tell him so, when he pressed his finger to my lips.

"Shh, the doctor's coming. Let's wait till he gets here."

I dropped my head back on the thin pillow that smelled of my own sweat with an underlying scent of bleach. My eyes slid shut, blocking out the knowing look Jason gave me.

I kept them closed even when a third person entered the room. Opening them, I found the doctor frowning over my chart.

"How is he, doctor? Is he strong enough for the surgery?" Jason asked. His gaze kept flickering back to mine, then he'd stare at the green garbed doctor.

"Yes," the doctor said. He glanced at his watch. "He's doing quite well. I have him slotted for ten o'clock in the OR. I expect the procedure will take two hours."

"Can I be with him?"

"You can stay until we take him to be prepped. Remember, both of you, no food or drink until told otherwise."

"Of course, doctor," Jason murmured, reaching down to take hold of my hand. "I'll sit with him until then."

"Good, good. Just remember, no ingested substances at all."

I ignored the doctor after that. All my attention was focused on Jason. His thumb stroked the back of my hand absently, like he was barely aware of doing it. When our eyes met, he smiled, though the tension around his mouth and the shadows under his eyes told me the real story.

"Hey, we've come this far, right? Let's finish things."

He flushed and ducked his head. I brought his hand up and lay his palm across my cheek. When he raised his head, our eyes met.

"I'm going to be okay, Jason. Do you believe me?"

"Yes, Sir."

I kissed the palm of his hand. "Good. When I go into surgery, go back to the motel. You will stay there until you are called. Do you understand?"

"Yes, Sir, but—"

"No buts," I said sternly. "You've disobeyed me too many times lately. You know I don't accept that."

"Yes, Sir," he whispered. "I love you, Sir."

I closed my eyes and kissed his palm. "I know."

They came for me an hour later and with one last, reluctant look, Jason slipped out of the room. I knew he would obey me. I just hoped I wasn't seeing him for the last time.

Shortly after, I was rolled down to surgery and slid into a gentle, dream-free sleep as the anesthetic carried me down into oblivion.

I followed the gurney as far as they would let me go. Only when the doors to the surgical ward close behind it did I retreat to the nearest waiting room. At first I sat, flipping through a six-month old copy of People, trying to read the articles on skinny actresses, on fat actresses and heroes plucked from obscurity by some plight that had befallen them. I registered none of it. I didn't care about the latest goings on about Johnny or Brittany or Oprah. Their lives meant nothing to me. The only thing I cared about at this moment was what was going on behind those doors. What were they doing to the man I loved? At one point, when I looked at the wall clock and saw only ten minutes had passed, I squeezed my hands into fists and didn't realize I had crushed the magazine I currently held. Pissed at my own anxiety, I threw the mangled glossy paper down on the low table between rows of chairs and jumped to my feet. My nerves were humming and I couldn't sit still. I started pacing. There were a few other people in the room, and it didn't take long to realize they were watching me with alarm.

I realized I must look a mess. I hadn't been to the motel in hours. Hadn't had a decent shave in longer. My face was covered with dark stubble and I knew I still showed signs of my own ordeal on the mountain. Losing weight left my face cadaverous, my eyes sunken and my hair shaggy and uncombed. I must look like a madman to them. When I saw one woman draw her young daughter into her arms and obviously try to shield her from me, I knew I had to get out of there. I hurried out of the room, my face flushed and my breathing coming in shallow gasps.

Outside, I almost slammed into Nancy, who stopped me with a hand on my chest and a startled "Whoa there, Jason. Slow down." She studied my face and clearly didn't like what she saw. "He's in surgery, isn't he? Has anyone told you anything?"

"No, they haven't. He's been in there for at least an hour."

"He'll be fine, Jason. Come on, let's go get some coffee."

She led me down to the cafeteria where I ordered an extra large brew and followed Nancy to a seat in the corner by ourselves.

"You realize he's going to be in therapy for a while. He needs to build up his strength to overcome this. He's going to need you."

I bristled. Did she think I didn't know that? "I'll be there for him the whole way. I don't care what it takes."

"That's good." She stirred a pack of sweetener into her coffee. "He's a tough bastard, but even tough bastards need help sometimes. Not that Detective Spider would ever admitted that. You might be about the only person he'd ever take it from."

"You think?"

"I know. You get him through this, Jason, and you'll be saving more than his life. He's a damn fine cop and I want him to come back. But he has to come back all the way to do that. You're the only one who can help him do that."

I ducked my head, swallowing a massive gulp of overheated coffee. "You know I will."

"Yes. I do."

She left soon after, and I forced myself to finish the coffee before I returned to the waiting room, and a few more hours of waiting. God, I was so tired of waiting.

I half expected Nancy to return, instead Alex's partner, Miguel, came. He nodded at me when he came through the door.

"Have you heard anything?"

"No," I said gruffly, then took a deep breath. The guy obviously cared or he wouldn't be here. "He went in about three hours ago. I expect to hear from the doctor soon."

"I've prayed for him."

"Thanks, we both appreciate it." I still didn't know what to say to that, but I wasn't going to turn down any well wishes or intervention if it would keep Alex safe. "How are your children?"

"They are fine. My youngest is at home today with an ear infection." He grimaced. "He kept my wife up all night with his pain."

"I'm sorry to hear that. I hope he' s well soon." I took a deep breath. "I'll pray for him, too."

"*Gracias.*"

Miguel sat. He planned to stay, I guess. That meant I had to make small talk. Might as well stick to the one thing we shared.

"Do you like working with Alex?"

Miguel didn't answer right away. I wondered if he wanted to find the right words or if he was just a cautious man who never spoke quickly.

"He is an excellent officer."

I could almost hear the but there. I nodded, smiling. "Nancy – Lieutenant Pickard seems to think so. I know he works very hard to be a good cop."

"I admire him," he said stiffly.

Despite the fact he's gay? I didn't say that out loud. The poor guy was obviously sincere, and didn't deserve some snarky remark from me.

"He thinks you're a fine cop, too." Miguel brightened, so I added, "He was really satisfied to solve that last murder you cleared. I hear it was a fine piece of work."

"That was a good collar. A lot of bad men will go to jail for a long time for that."

"Maybe save a few lives. I know Alex would like that. He really cares about his victims and getting them justice."

We spent the next half hour nattering away, and for the first time since Alex had gone under the knife, I wasn't crawling walls. I was startled to look up and find Dr. Abena standing over me, a satisfied smile on his face.

"The surgery went well. Alexander is in excellent shape, and if his recovery is as smooth, I foresee no more surgeries being needed."

I surged out of my chair, Miguel forgotten. "When can I see him?"

"He's in ICU right now. I suspect they will keep him overnight. I might allow a ten minute visit later on this evening, but that will be all until he's moved onto the ward."

I wanted to wring the guy's hands and thank him, but I felt too close to tears to do anything but nod my head and watch him walk away. I turned glowing eyes on Miguel, no longer caring who or what he was. Right now he was just a man I could share my joy with.

"He's going to be okay."

"God be praised."

"Amen," I whispered, then rushed into the bathroom where I vomited into the toilet. I leaned over the porcelain bowl, shaking so hard my vision blurred. I realized I was hyperventilating when I nearly passed out. "If You really are up there, then thank You. Thank You for giving me Alex back."

I splashed water on my face before I returned to the waiting room to find Miguel still there.

"I have to go tell the Lieutenant the news. Perhaps one of us will be by when Detective Spider is moved to a room and can have visitors."

"Tell her thank you from both of us."

He left and I was alone. But now my thoughts were not dark ones, but were filled with renewed hope. Maybe this really was it. Did that mean Alex would be coming home soon? I remembered Nancy saying he would need therapy. Could he do that at home, or would he need to stay in the hospital longer? I wanted him home. I'd take time off school and be there twenty-four/seven if they'd only let me take him home. We could both rest a lot better there, under a familiar roof.

Face it, I just wanted him home.

It soon looked like that was going to happen a lot sooner than later. Dr Abena approached me once I was alone, and wanted a little heart to heart.

"You realize that his recovery is only beginning," he said as an ice-breaker. I nodded. "He will be weak for several days, possibly even weeks. In that time you both must be careful of what you do. He has to avoid all strenuous activity."

I nodded, figuring I knew where he was going. I was right.

"That includes all sexual activity." He paused. Waiting to see if I was going to object? That was okay, I might not like it, but I'd give up sex with Alex forever if it meant he was with me. I might not like it, but I would abide by it. I nodded firmly, letting him know I was onboard. "Good."

"Have you talked to Alex yet?"

"We touched on it. Perhaps I'll wait until you are together to talk of it more. Don't worry, Jason," he said dryly. "It won't be forever. It's just that his abdominal injuries were severe and a small section of his bowel was removed. As long as the sutures hold this should cause minimal issues and will heal over time. He needs a special diet, too. Only soft foods. We usually recommend baby foods as being the easiest to digest. Some diet supplement like Ensure as well."

"I understand. I'll buy some before he comes home."

"Good. Now let me return to my patient. You should be able to visit him within an hour."

I brightened. "I'm going to go to my motel and shower. You've got the number there if anything comes up, right?"

"We do. He's going to be okay, Jason."

This time I believed him.

I called Nancy from the hospital lobby before I headed back to the motel. Before I got there, I stopped on State Street and picked up a pair of jeans for both of us and new shirts to replace what had been ruined on our ordeal. Then I stopped at a barber and had my mess of hair tamed. I wanted to look my best when I visited, and I knew Alex would want something decent to put on when he was discharged.

By the time I had showered and shaved I felt a thousand percent better than I had in days. I'm sure it showed in my step and on my face when I bounced into ICU later that evening.

I was still feeling groggy when Jason came into the ICU. It didn't stop my heart from giving a lurch in my chest. God, he looked delicious. His eyes still held a haunted look, but he looked fresher than he had in days and he had clearly gone all out to fix himself up for his visit. I'd have loved to see him in his skintight leathers and mesh shirt, but the doctor had warned me about that. I could look, but for now I couldn't touch. And I was supposed to curb my sexual arousal. Good luck with that.

Still, I refrained from hauling him into bed with me when he leaned over and pecked me on the mouth. He even smelled good. A wave of dizziness rolled over me. I shut my eyes and savored it. Maybe I couldn't fuck him, but I could enjoy his aura.

"How do you feel?" he asked softly, as though afraid of speaking too loudly.

"A lot better." I stroked his cheek, loving the smooth feel of his newly shaved cheek. He put his hand over mine and our fingers entwined. I cupped his chin and made him look at me. "They say the worst is over. I'll be coming home soon."

A few more shadows fell away from his face. He sat down on the edge of the bed, careful not to jar any part of me or the tubes that ran out of various parts of my body. After a few brief words about innocuous things like the weather and local news, Jason got a distant look on his face.

"You remember that dog we saw with those three hikers, the girl who said they were from Portland? The one we heard a couple of days later?"

I didn't want to talk about that just yet. But I had to respond to him. "Yes. The second body I found was the boy's."

"I figured that. Sheriff told me they found the two girls, too. They killed them all."

"Except the dog," I said, wondering where he was going with this.

"Except him. He followed me down the mountain and was following me back up. He attacked that one guy who was going to shoot me."

My grip on his hand tightened. This was the first I'd heard of Jason being endangered and I didn't like it one bit. But something puzzled me. "He followed you? But he came to me. He stayed with me one night, when my fever started getting bad. Half the time I thought he was a hallucination." I hadn't spoken about those things to anyone. I didn't like the idea that my mind had been so frail and I had lost it so easily. But I could joke about it. "He was a nice figment. Why do you bring him up? He disappeared before you found me."

"But he didn't, really. He was still around. He came back down when everybody left." He dropped his gaze and stared at our intertwined hands. "He was there when I went back for your truck. I brought him into town."

I frowned. "Where is he now?"

"In a kennel." He flushed and kept avoiding my eyes. "Camp Canine. I couldn't just dump him at the pound. He has no one left."

I dislodged his hand and reached up to take his chin in my hand. I forced him to look at me. "What do you want to do, Jason? You can tell me, you know."

He took a deep breath. "I want to keep him."

I didn't speak. I studied his face, his cheeks still flushed, his eyes full of both pain and yearning. I knew if I said no, he would take the dog to the pound and would never talk about it again. But he would never forget him.

It was funny, but I knew in that instant that I would, too. Somehow the dog had made a separate connection to both of us. I could deny it all I wanted, but it didn't change facts. He had kept me from feeling alone at my lowest moment, a moment I would never share with anyone, not even Jason. He'd certainly crawled under Jason's skin. So, could I tell Jason to forget it? Get rid of the dog? We didn't need it or want it.

I tried to look fierce, knowing I was probably too sickly looking to pull it off. "Is he well behaved?"

"Very. Probably better than me." He grinned. "A lot better. Though he doesn't do the dishes very well."

"Hmm, neither do I." Which was true. Jason was a far better housekeeper than I was. I cupped my hand over the back of his neck and drew him down until his face was inches from mine. "Okay, go and pick him up. Take him home, and we'll see how it works out."

His face alight, he closed the gap between us pressing his mouth over mine. Our tongues tangled. When we broke apart, he was flushed and breathing hard. My heart was thudding in my chest.

"We shouldn't..."

"We're not going to fuck, though I want to. But that doesn't mean we can't touch each other."

"I guess," he murmured. A smile lit up his face, making him even more beautiful. "God, I hope so."

"We can."

His smile faltered. "I can't stay. I can come back once they move you out of here, but I have to leave now."

"Yes, you have to go. Come back tomorrow after six. Bring some clothes with you, and a razor and deodorant. I can't shower yet, but I get sponge baths. Better than nothing."

"I've already told you I like the way you smell."

"Which is a good thing. Now go home, Jason. Get your dog and take him home. Get him settled in – don't even think about letting him in our bedroom. He's most definitely not welcomed there. You'll have to get him a bed."

"Yes, Sir."

"And food, I guess. That's all in your hands. I expect you to tend to everything."

"Yes, Sir. Everything will be ready for you when you come home."

I dropped my head back into the stiff pillow. "Bring me a robe too, and something comfortable to sleep in. These things," I indicated the hospital gown with distaste, "aren't fit for anyone."

"I'll put everything together and bring it tomorrow. After six."

"Good boy. I need to rest, now."

"Goodnight, Sir." He leaned down and brushed my lips again. Then he was gone and I was left missing him. It wasn't long before a nurse came in and took care of the evening duties, tucking me in and giving me my pain medication. I hadn't intended to tell Jason, but all the while he had been here I had been in near constant agony. I wouldn't even let this nurse know.

The next morning, the doctor checked in on me. He looked over the incisions and all my vitals. "Everything is looking very promising. I don't foresee any complications."

"Good. When can I go home?"

"A couple of more days. We'll see then."

I nodded tersely. I'm going to make sure that happens. I was tired of this hospital and this doctor. I wanted my own bed and pillows. I wanted Jason.

He came every night and stayed as long as I would let him. Which was never as long as I wanted, but I had to maintain some semblance of control, and that was damn hard to do from a hospital bed with tubes coming out of my dick.

On the third day, Dr. Abena told me all their final tests showed the incisions were holding well and there was no leakage. He was releasing me. He had already called Jason who arrived less than half an hour after Abena signed me out. Getting dressed in street clothes was a nightmare. I was glad the only person who witnessed it was Jason. After that, I suffered the indignity of having to sit in a wheelchair and be rolled out to my Toyota.

But finally it was just Jason and me. I leaned my head back

against the truck seat and took a deep breath. Jason drove carefully. We wound through the streets of Santa Barbara to the 101 and before long we pulled into our driveway, behind Jason's Honda. I studied the ancient vehicle critically. When Jason came around to my side to help me out, I shook his hand off.

"I'm not crippled. When I need help, I'll ask for it." He stepped back and shoved his hands in his jean pockets. I walked steadily, taking care not to take long strides that would stretch my side muscles. I ran my hand along the trunk of his car. "I need to buy you a decent car. What do you think you might like?"

"I never thought..." He stood staring at his car. "Something like this, I guess. Can we afford a hybrid?" His hands followed mine, coming to rest on top. His warmth gave me the familiar kick in the gut. I realized this was going to be more of a trial than I expected. Being in the same house, hell, the same bed with this man was going to be torture if I couldn't touch him.

"We can afford anything you want." I ran my thumb over the back of his hand.

He startled me that night by bringing a blanket and pillow out into the living room when the credits rolled on our evening movie, *Sunset Boulevard*. First he handed me my nightly meds and a glass of juice, then he tossed the bedclothes onto the couch beside me.

"What are you doing?"

The dog he had called Buddy, followed him and came to sit beside me, close enough for me to touch, but not demanding attention. Jason was right, he was well behaved. So far, a pleasure to have around. I didn't regret giving Jason permission to keep him.

"You need to rest. You heard the doctor. We can't fuck."

"We don't have to fuck. You think you're sleeping out here?"

"Just for a few days—"

"Forget it. Put those away," I said sternly. I popped the meds in my mouth, chasing them with the OJ. "I'm not putting up with this."

He clutched the pillow to his chest. "I don't want to hurt you."

I took it away from him and pulled him into my arms. "You won't. There are still things we can do." I planted my mouth on his neck and tasted him, feeling his pulse jump under my lips. I cupped his swelling cock in my hand. "We can still do this," I whispered.

He gasped and closed his eyes. "Oh, sweet Jesus."

I opened his fly and shoved his new jeans down around his ankles. Then I wrapped my fist around him and pumped hard. He moaned and thrust his cock into my hand, crying out when he came.

I found his mouth and pushed my tongue down his throat. I broke away and gripped his shoulders, forcing him to look at me. "Now, no more talk about sleeping on the couch. Not now, not ever again. Trust me, Jason. The good stuff will come soon enough."

He smiled his adoration. "Yes, Sir."

He followed me into our bedroom. We went to bed and held each other all night. I don't know about Jason, but I had no more bad dreams.

Dianne, my sister came to visit us four months after Alex came home from the hospital. She was our first visitor in all that time, except for our closest neighbors who had heard about our ordeal, and Nancy and her husband visited once. Dianne was the most welcome one. Thanksgiving was next week and my whole family would be in town. The prospect scared me as much as it excited me. It would be the first time my father and Alex met. It was the first time my father would come face to face with who his son really was.

It had been Dianne's doing. She had initiated this dinner. Alex had been all for it, which surprised me at the time. But like he told me earlier today over breakfast, "I want to know your family. I don't have one. Besides," he said softly, brushing the hair off my face, "I know how much you've missed them."

I swelled with pride when I thought of his words. Sometimes I think Alex knows me better than I know myself. It didn't make me any less nervous, but it did make me love him all the more.

This weekend though, a late November day that had started out hot, but mellowed at the end into a beautiful evening, was for my sister. Next week we would all get together, a real family for the first time in years.

I cooked up a sumptuous roast pork dinner with garlic mashed potatoes and green beans. Alex had worked hard to turn me into a gourmet cook. Me, who barely boiled water before I met him. Now I had a chance to show off my new skills to someone besides my appreciative lover.

Dianne came bearing gifts and a multitude of stories from her world travels. An exquisite crystal Limoges from Italy, and a striking red and yellow *Phalaenopsis* orchid my father, who had recently taken up cultivating the exotic plants, sent from Petaluma – Dianne was very careful to pronounce the species name correctly. Dad would bite both our heads off if we got *that* wrong. I had arranged everything as a centerpiece, throwing in a trio of tapered yellow candles to match the flowers that cast a soft glow over our table.

We had a pleasant dinner, which Dianne praised so effusively I blushed and couldn't meet anyone's eyes. Alex lifted my chin and smiled.

"Hey, she's right, you know," he said. "You're an incredible cook. If you ever want to open your own restaurant, I'll back you. Even if the science world would lose a brilliant mind."

Now he really had me flushing hot. To cover my embarrassment I took a gulp of wine, then choked until Alex pounded on my back and I hiccupped into silence.

"Thanks," I managed.

"Let's finish dinner." Alex refilled my wine glass. "Dessert awaits."

Since I knew I hadn't made any dessert, on his orders, I was puzzled. Then Alex left the table and returned with our absinthe. I was more than a little surprised – the absinthe ritual was one we normally reserved for private moments, but he left the room with a smile and wink towards me and returned moments later with the tools – spoon, bowl of sugar cubes and the ice water. As always I performed the louching – pouring the icy water over the absinthe and sugar cube in the small crystal glass, turning the clear, thick liqueur milky. I handed the first glass to Dianne who eyed it apprehensively before sipping it. When she made a face, we both laughed. I remembered my first encounter with the stuff.

"It's the wormwood that's so bitter," I said. "But it's worth it."

"You say so." She didn't sound convinced. She flipped her shoulder-length flame-colored hair, that I have always envied, off her forehead. Gamely she finished the shot. I served Alex next. Finally I poured my own. Our eyes met as I poured the concoction down my throat, waiting for the warmth to spread, knowing what was going to follow, though we'd have to wait for Dianne to leave. Already my body hardened in anticipation, my cock pressing against my linen pants. I remembered other times when he poured the liquid over my body and lapped it up, leaving me helplessly writhing in my restraints until he would finally bring me to climax in his mouth. The familiar jolt of desire that happened whenever I'm in the same room as Alex swept through me. I only had to smell him and I grew aroused. Even after the months we'd been together. I'm thankful the tablecloth concealed my erection. I'd really be flushing if my sister got an eyeful of that.

Finally, after coffee and more small talk about her latest adventures in Nepal, India and Sri Lanka where she worked on setting up micro-loans for small business ventures, she took her leave. We knew we'd be together soon. I was still a little apprehensive and giddy about the prospect of my father meeting Alex next week. What if Dad didn't like him? What if Alex didn't like Dad? She must have seen that.

I followed her to the front door and we hugged. She whispered for my ears only, "I like your man, little brother. So will Dad. Trust me. Be good to him."

"I will."

Alex slipped his arm around me and we stood in the opened doorway, listening to the night music from the fields around our tiny bungalow below Los Padres National Forest. Spread out below us, the lights of Goleta glittered in the late November night. I smiled at her, then looked up at him, knowing my adoration would be all over my face. I used to hide it from the world a long time ago. Not anymore. It had taken him longer, but he was no longer a cool stranger when others were around. The look on his face was so full of wonder it made my knees weak. Nearly losing each other had taught us that our time together was something to be savored, enjoyed and explored whenever possible. "I will," I said again, as much for him as for my sister.

Buddy, the shepherd, stepped between us. I let my hand drop to his head, rubbing his ears. Alex's hand moved over mine and we both stroked the dog. The dog we acknowledged helped keep both of us alive in our wilderness ordeal. Dianne, who knew the story well, knelt down and gave him a hug.

Then my sister left and I leaned back into Alex. We stood hip to groin in the doorway. His erection pressed into my pelvis. All around us the songs of the night cascaded over us. He tightened his grip on me. At my feet, a cricket chirped. Then another and another filled the night with their music. I peered into the shadows thrown by the hall light but there was no sight of anything living. They remained hidden, singing to us. After my sister's BMW vanished around the curve on her way back to the freeway and home, I sidestepped Alex to go back into the house. Laughing, Alex captured my hand and dragged me inside. The dog followed, then at Alex's command went to his bed in the back of the house. Alex led me into the bathroom and on his orders I stripped. While he readied his razor I showered, cleaning every orifice in anticipation. He vibrated with tension while he removed what little hair covered me and I didn't need to look at his swollen crotch to know he was rock hard and ready for me.

After our return from Los Padres and his lengthy convalescence from his massive blood infection and the two harrowing surgeries that followed – where I enjoyed tending to him in more ways than one – Alex had grown serious about his fitness and embarked on a structured exercise program. The results had been on the far side of incredible. He had gone beyond the sexy, virile man I had met over a year ago. Along with an incredibly hot body he now had the stamina of a twenty-five-year-old. And the sex drive of an eighteen-year-old.

"She likes you, you know," I told him, my voice shaking from my rising desire. I discarded the towel I had used to dry myself, folding it neatly over the rack. Then I followed him into our bedroom and stood in front of him. My thick, red dick glistened with precum and jutted out of my hairless crotch. My hands trembled when I reached for him.

"Does she?" He smiled, stroking my cheek with the back of his hand. I caught his thumb between my lips and sucked gently, never taking my eyes of his. His pupils widened. He sucked in air but managed to say, "What's not to like?"

He slipped on the ankle restraints, then bound my wrists to

form an X in the middle of our bedroom and rose to meet my feverish gaze, pausing on the way to kiss the tip of my leaking, tattooed cock. I sighed and bucked my hips toward him.

"She doesn't know what you do to me in here when we're alone."

He stroked my cheek again before slipping the gauzy blindfold over my face.

"Probably a good thing, don't you think?"

The darkness that fell wasn't total. I saw a film of red through the diaphanous material covering my eyes. He moved behind me, his hands stroking my hips, fingers feathering over my shivering skin. His breath was heat and flameless fire on the back of my neck.

"A very good thing," he whispered. "She might not understand." Then he was gone again. I was always so preternaturally attuned to him, I heard him in the other room, then in the kitchen. Finally he was back. The anticipation sent desire pulsing through every nerve in my body, all culminating in the base of my dick, which throbbed in mounting anticipation.

The hand that stroked my flank was oiled and scented. He dipped his thumb into my mouth. I tasted honey and mint. His lips brushed my ear lobe, electricity jolted into my dick. He repeated the gesture; I moaned.

"I made this for you," he said.

"What is it?" I gently sucked his thumb, hearing his sharp intake of breath. What flashed between us was pure electric lust.

"Oil and honey." He licked my throat, the rough heat sent bolts of raw need straight into my cock. His oil covered fist wrapped around me and his mouth worked my throat, lips and tongue and teeth, tasting me, growling his need. "And some of your garden mint."

Sudden sharp pain in my nipples, the weights he clamped on pulled them down. I groaned behind the gauzy mask, thrusting my hips out in blind need. I whimpered. His response was to jerk on the chains attached to my nipples. His warm breath, redolent of the honey and mint he had covered me with, caressed me.

A delicate dance of slick, liquid heat poured down my spine and over my hips through every nerve in my body. His lips traced a path down over the curve of my ass, stiff fingers slid between my cheeks, parting them. He crouched behind me. I shivered and whispered his name, "Alex."

His stiff tongue dipped into my crack, digging open my hole. I moaned again. The scarf doesn't blind me, instead it lent a rosy glow to everything. I couldn't see him; he knelt behind me, but I was all too aware of him, his smell, his presence that ruled my life so completely. His fingers feathered over my skin, pinning me in place with the lightest of touches, barely touching me at all. I twisted in my bonds, legs and arms extended in an X, forced to balance on my toes. I threw my head back, shouted and arched my spine, wanting more than his tongue in my ass. He must have felt my need. My entire body shivered with it.

His tongue delved deeper. My dick thrust out of my newly shaved pubes, but he refused to touch me. I needed him to touch me. Writhing helplessly, I sought a release he wouldn't give me.

Darkness embraced my world. Smells I would normally never have noticed enticed and aroused me with their promise. The animal smell of his musky need, the oil he used to coat my hairless body, the spicy, familiar aftershave that made me ache, my own desire, rich and pungent, like fresh blood. My hoarse breathing roared in my ears, his breathing was more controlled, he hadn't yet reached his peak and I was damn close.

I groaned when the twisted strands of his suede flogger lightly brushed my straining dick, the sharper lash when he stroked my back and butt with it, sending the ends singing across my flesh. I could hear the plink, plink of water in the shower. I swear I could hear the heartbeats of the doves that nested in the eaves outside our bedroom. The sharp creak of the leather bonds that held my wrists over my head, the crackle of the soft padding under my toes. All musical interludes to the sounds of his presence.

He circled me, the whisper of air marking his passage in the darkness. A match hissed and the rich stench of sulfur filled my nostrils, followed by the odor of hot wax. I shivered in anticipation as he moved closer, his leather boots thudding on the soft matting that he had rolled out to cover our bedroom floor. I strained to turn toward the sound, but he kept circling, touching me lightly with the butt of his flogger, his fingertips, his knuckles and finally the hot splash of body wax on my chest. I hissed and arched toward the source of the heat and pain, the electric charge of pure desire that erupted from the base of my dick embedding itself in my spine.

"Alex," I moaned. He leaned over me, his voice purring as he whispered. His breath warmed my ear.

"You will know such pain," he said. "Such infinite pleasure. All from me. Only from me."

He tugged at my leashed collar that he had slipped on after the shower. I rocked forward, stopped only by the leather restraints around my arms and the strap around my throat. I tugged at them, testing them. Wanting to get closer to him. The whistle of the suede flogger came seconds before the first lash struck my back. I writhed, crying out at the sharp burst of pain. He stroked me with brilliant flashes of pain that quickly became raw pleasure embedded in my cock. The heat in my back flared, spreading and encompassing me.

Finally denim rustled. He adjusted the restraints, lowering me until I knelt in front of him. A metal zipper slid down and the musky tip of his cock slid past my open lips. Without touching me with any other part of his body he thrust into me, burying himself down my throat, rocking into me until his balls brushed my chin. I swirled his thick staff with my tongue, nibbled on his fat head and licked his piss slit clean of spunk. I tasted his precum and the hot odors from his groin. He moaned and thrust blindly, brushing my chin with his stiff pubic hair. Fire poured down my back as he dripped more hot wax on me. I groaned and sucked harder. Before he could come, his dick slid out of my disappointed mouth. He stepped away from me, taking his pain and his pleasure with him.

Until I felt the head of his cock slide up my hole. He grasped my painfully hard dick in one hand while he worked his thick piece in and out, scraping over my prostate, reaching up inside me to touch my gut. His fist grew rougher, pounding my meat, tugging at my balls, urging me on with hot words.

"I love you in ways you will never know," he whispered.

He was wrong. I did know. Just as I knew how deep and unending my love was for him. He pulled on the leather around my neck, bowing my body to his need. My mouth opened but I still couldn't breathe. I squeezed my eyes shut and released myself totally to him. My lord. My Master. My love. There will never be another like him.

My cum blasted all over his hand, splattering my chin where I licked it off and savored the taste of myself. Only when my dick shrank against my flaccid balls did he let loose, slamming into me again and again. His movements grew frenzied and uncontrolled. He unloaded inside me with a deep, guttural groan. Finally, slowly, he withdrew and pulled the gauze off my head with shaking hands.

I blinked against what appeared to be a dazzling light, though I knew it was nothing but the glow from a half a dozen candles he had lit moments ago. When he removed the bonds and helped me over to the cedar chest at the foot of our bed I stared up at him adoringly.

"Thank you," he said, in something that had become a ritual for us. He stroked my chin with the gentlest of touches.

I smiled up at him. "You're welcome."

He wiped us both clean, then folded me into his embrace, picked me up and carried me over to the bed. Turning down the duvet, he laid me down and stood over me a moment, his gaze roving over me in a caress that left me hot. Mine moved over his achingly familiar body. The scars from his surgery were still visible, but fading, though he would always carry them as a reminder of his mortality. Something I swore I would never forget again. I was going to be everything for him. He would never want again, if I had anything to do with it.

Finally, he slid in beside me, holding me until our hearts grew calm. He petted me, smoothing his lips over the heated red flesh where his lash had touched me, letting me know how special I was. Finally, sleep claimed us both.

My Alex was well and truly back.

About the Author

PAT BROWN was born in Canada, which she is sure explains her intense dislike of all things cold and her constant striving to escape to someplace warm. Her first move took her to Los Angeles, and her fate was sealed. To this day she has a love/hate relationship with L.A, a city that was endlessly fascinating. L.A. Heat and the even darker L.A. Boneyard grew out of those dark, compelling days.

She wrote her first book at 17 – an angst ridden tome about a teenage girl hooked up with a drug user and went off the deep end. All this from a kid who hadn't done anything stronger than weed. She read her first positive gay book then too, The Lord Won't Mind, by Gordon Merrick and had her eyes open to a whole other world (which didn't exist in ultra conservative vanilla plain London, Ontario). Visit Pat on the internet at: http://www.pabrown.ca/

THE TREVOR PROJECT

The Trevor Project operates the only nationwide, around-the-clock crisis and suicide prevention helpline for lesbian, gay, bisexual, transgender and questioning youth. Every day, The Trevor Project saves lives though its free and confidential helpline, its website and its educational services. If you or a friend are feeling lost or alone call The Trevor Helpline. If you or a friend are feeling lost, alone, confused or in crisis, please call The Trevor Helpline. You'll be able to speak confidentially with a trained counselor 24/7.

The Trevor Helpline: 866-488-7386

On the Web: http://www.thetrevorproject.org/

THE GAY MEN'S DOMESTIC VIOLENCE PROJECT

Founded in 1994, The Gay Men's Domestic Violence Project is a grassroots, non-profit organization founded by a gay male survivor of domestic violence and developed through the strength, contributions and participation of the community. The Gay Men's Domestic Violence Project supports victims and survivors through education, advocacy and direct services. Understanding that the serious public health issue of domestic violence is not gender specific, we serve men in relationships with men, regardless of how they identify, and stand ready to assist them in navigating through abusive relationships.

GMDVP Helpline: 800.832.1901

On the Web: http://gmdvp.org/

THE GAY & LESBIAN ALLIANCE AGAINST DEFAMATION/GLAAD EN ESPAÑOL

The Gay & Lesbian Alliance Against Defamation (GLAAD) is dedicated to promoting and ensuring fair, accurate and inclusive representation of people and events in the media as a means of eliminating homophobia and discrimination based on gender identity and sexual orientation.

On the Web: http://www.glaad.org/

GLAAD en español:

http://www.glaad.org/espanol/bienvenido.php

Stimulate yourself.
READ.
www.manloveromance.com
THE HOTTEST M/M EROTIC AUTHORS & WEBSITES ON THE NET

Breinigsville, PA USA
08 July 2010
241370BV00001B/4/P